Daisy's Choice

by

Mike Owens

This is a work of fiction. Names, characters, places, and incidents are either the product of the author's imagination or are used fictitiously, and any resemblance to actual persons living or dead, business establishments, events, or locales, is entirely coincidental.

Daisy's Choice

Cover Art by *RJ Morris*

The Wild Rose Press, Inc.
PO Box 708
Adams Basin, NY 14410-0708
Visit us at www.thewildrosepress.com

Publishing History
First Mainstream Women's Fiction Edition, 2018
Print ISBN 978-1-5092-1997-1
Digital ISBN 978-1-5092-1998-8

Published in the United States of America

The dream still came,
but less frequently than before. It had started in the hospital, and for a long time there I didn't know what was dream and what was reality, both were equally horrible. It has come less often now, maybe a couple of times a week. Will it ever go away for good? I doubt it. I can still see it, hear it, even smell it, but worst of all I can still feel it. The pain is just as real in my dream as it was in the hospital.

I am being wheeled down to the hydrotherapy room. Even blind, I can see everything. The attendants all wear hoods that cover their faces. The corridor is almost dark, lit by candles stuck in the walls, casting wavering shadows as we pass. The floor is uneven, and the gurney bumps and lurches along. The walls are formed from cut stone, irregular, with gaps where cold damp breezes seep through. It smells of rotting flesh.

Acknowledgement

Many thanks to Lenore Hart and Lauran Strait
for assistance with this manuscript.

Chapter 1

"How on earth you're going to get along when you're married, I don't know." How many times had I heard that one? But Mom was right, and you didn't have to look far for examples. For instance, I didn't know the first thing about shopping for groceries and even less about how to turn them into a meal if I had them. Even the process where dirty clothes went into the laundry hamper and turned up washed and ironed in my closet, another mystery.

Yeah, as an eighteen-year-old girl whose mother still did her laundry, I know it looked like I was lazy or stupid or both. The sad fact was, I just couldn't figure out how to run the washing machine. All the dials, the little flashing lights meant nothing to me, even after any number of educational sessions with Mom.

My name is Daisy Sugarbush, and I live in Warrensburg, a little bump in the road—like, blink and you'll miss it—in southeastern Virginia. I've never lived anywhere else, never wanted to. I know there's a big world out there, and maybe someday I'll get around to seeing it, but for now this small town suits me just fine.

People always ask me about my plans, like, since Dad died last year maybe I should get serious about life, but I'm doing just what I want to do, thank you, very much. Of course, I'd much rather be working with my dad, but he's gone now, and I'll be damned if I'll let his little handyman business go under, not if I can help it. If the good ship Sugarbush goes down, it won't be because of lack of effort on my part.

For most of my life, it was just me, my mom and dad, but triangles as a family structure can be problematic, I've learned. For years I felt like a tug toy, pulled in two directions at once between a father and a mother. I naturally leaned in Dad's direction, because as easy and comfortable as I found Dad's world, it was just that difficult with Mom's.

None of this was lost on my mother, of course. As she pointed out over and over again, all of those domestic things that I should know about, I didn't.

She did her best, like when I stumbled into another of her little teaching sessions one Wednesday morning—washing day at the Sugarbush house. I'd just run downstairs to fetch a small Phillips screwdriver that Dad needed when Mom ambushed me by the washing machine. She started right in with her usual explanations of wash cycles, spin cycles…stuff like that. I guess she figured out quickly enough I had other things on my mind, and the finer points of washing clothes wasn't one of them.

"Daisy, you're hopeless. If you'd just pay attention, it's really easy, and you're going to have to learn someday. I'm not going to be around to wash your clothes forever."

"But why are there so many dials and buttons? It's all just soap and water, right?"

Mom rolled her eyes, like she was trying to explain algebra to a third-grader. Then there came that deep sigh, the one that made me grind my back teeth.

Finally, she pointed toward the door, and I knew I was off the hook, for now.

I'd heard "hopeless" more than a few times. On the other hand, she never called me stupid, because I could take apart the entire washing machine, dryer, too, and then put it back together in perfect working order. And she knew it. Just those damned little dials and those damned little blinking lights. Maybe it was more than coincidence that Dad had never been able operate the machine either, or so he always said.

"Thanks, Mom." I ran up the steps and out of the laundry room before she could change her mind. Dad was changing the fuel pump in the truck that day, and I didn't want to miss it.

Then, about a week later, the washing machine, with all its magical bells and whistles, conked out. Dad was away running errands, and Mom was in a rush to wash all the bedding in the house. I know it must have cost her dearly to ask me for help, but she did it.

"Please," was all she had to say.

It was a simple repair, a broken belt I replaced in about half an hour. Most of that time was spent rummaging through Dad's supply of spare belts—he had hundreds of them lined up on the wall in the garage. The belts were about the only things organized in his workshop. I swear he could have opened his own hardware store with just the stuff in the garage. There were piles of this, piles of that, and you really had to know where to look to find anything. I knew, I'd watched him sort through stuff hundreds of times, but that was part of the fun, not knowing what you'd find, or where.

"There, good as new," I said to Mom after no more

than thirty minutes of work. I did a little extra grunting and groaning, trying to make the job look more difficult than it was.

"Are you sure?" She always arched her left eyebrow when she was uncertain about something, like maybe the washing machine would burst into flames.

"Turn it on and see for yourself."

Like I said, good as new.

My last few years in high school, when the other kids were playing sports, going to parties and such, I was completely happy following my dad around, helping him with his chores. He was sort of the town handyman, and there was never a lack of jobs to be done: lawn mowers that wouldn't mow, washing machines that wouldn't wash, and car engines that wouldn't run. He tackled them all, and if it was a job he hadn't done before, he'd figure it out pretty quick. Best of all, he taught me how to do it, too.

Over those last happy years we had together, we learned to communicate on a special, non-verbal wavelength. If he needed a three-eights socket wrench, he simply stuck out his hand, and I placed the desired tool in his palm, no questions, no explanation needed. Like we were both extensions of the same brain, and, I liked to think, the same heart.

By my senior year I had a pretty good education in how most things around the house worked and what to do when they didn't, just by watching my dad. He was my mentor, and yes, I know it sounds odd for a girl to have a dad-mentor instead of a mom-mentor, but that's just the way it worked out. Things were always so easy with him. We dressed the same, walked the same, and except for a prominent set of boobs inherited from my mother, I looked like a second generation Sam Sugarbush. Everybody said so.

Right down to his hands, clever, dexterous little devices that seemed to know innately how stuff worked. Of course, the kind of work we did led to grimy, bruised knuckles and fragmented nails, hands no girl with an iota of self-respect would ever tolerate. Me, I was proud of them. I think my dad was too, even though he would never say so.

My dad was, for me, the perfect role model. If I'd been a guy, no problem. "Chip off the old block," folks could say with a wink and a nod, no harm done.

But I was a girl and my only true role model—my mom—was perfect, and I can't do perfect. Don't even want to try. I called her my Stepford mom.

Mostly she did her mom things, and, usually she let me do mine. Still, how she must have yearned for a more suitable daughter. When all the other moms she saw at church were probably talking about their daughters' plans after graduation, she had nothing to say. How could she brag about a daughter who seemed to have no more ambition than a turnip?

She tried, of course. Can't fault her for lack of effort, I never gave her much to work with.

Early August, the summer after my senior year, the last summer we'd have my dad, was the hottest anybody around Warrensburg could remember. At least, that's what everybody said. My dad seemed to wilt along with everything else, but it wasn't the heat that was driving him down. We would learn all about that later, after trying for weeks not to notice what was right under our noses.

I'd just finished mowing the lawn, the part the

summer sun hadn't burned up, and ducked into the kitchen for a glass of iced tea. I thought Mom had a church meeting that morning, and I didn't expect her to be home, but there she was, sitting on her kitchen stool by the sink peeling potatoes. And it didn't help a bit that even in the August heat her dress had nary a wrinkle. *Did she even perspire?*

Needless to say, I suffered by comparison, dirty sweaty and probably a bit pungent. A daughter to be proud of, right?

"Hot out," I said. Gulping down a cold beverage on a hot day wasn't such a good idea. I quickly got the first warning of the headache to come.

"You forgot something, Daisy."

"Huh?"

"Your bra."

"But Mom, it's so hot out, and there's nobody around but us."

"All the more reason you should take care of your appearance. It's how we look when there's no one else around that's important."

Where did she get them, all these words of wisdom she kept laying on me? Dad never seemed to care how I looked. I don't think he even noticed. But with Mom it was an argument I was bound to lose, so back to my room, put on the bra, then back to the kitchen. I even thought of ducking out the window in my bedroom, but that would have been a bit too childish, although I knew there was more to come. I could just feel it. Nothing to do now but face the music.

"You know what you're doing, don't you?" she said. "Hanging out with your father, you're just killing time. You have some decisions to make, Daisy, and the longer you put them off, the harder it's going to be."

Decisions: I never liked the sound of that word, mostly because I knew the question underneath, "Who am I?" I had no clue. I wasn't the Sugarbush son, even though I acted as if I was. It didn't help one bit that I was so different from my own mother, partly by my own choice, but mostly because looking as good as she looked was way out of reach for me, for most of the women in Warrensburg, for that matter.

At a time when most kids were already set on some path: marriage, a real job, grad school, something of the sort, I was going nowhere fast, in the company of a total stranger...me. To make matters even worse, my guiding light, my father, got knocked off the rails. That fall, 1993, a mesothelioma, a slow-growing type of lung cancer devoured him from the inside out, leaving a fragile husk that hardly resembled the man I loved more than anything in the world.

When he died I lost my anchor, my north star blinked and then went dark. I know that sounds a little over the top dramatic, but for me that's how it felt. That left just Mom and me, and that arrangement has never been exactly smooth sailing.

More than just a loss, my father's death led to a reconfiguration of the situation in our house. After dad died, Mom turned up the heat. I still tried to keep up with his round of chores, but more and more she tried to drag me into the domestic routine. And the harder she tried, the harder I resisted. I kept a pile of dad's old work clothes stashed under my bed so I could get dressed early and duck out the back window in my bedroom before she could get at me. Then it was down to Sparky's for a cup of coffee and a doughnut with my buddy Ralph, who managed the place. A near-perfect escape, and one I used often. Ralph was a third-generation owner of Sparky's, and had the good sense not to change anything about the business, which, while small, was never without an active clientele, including me. Then, after my little refueling stop, it was on with my round of handyman chores, just like my dad would have done.

The standoff lasted for almost a year, Mom insisting, me resisting, all punctuated by the occasional blowup followed by me hiding out at Sparky's again.

Sometimes Mom's not-so-subtle hints came out more like hand grenades. One of those little bombs was my former classmate Elizabeth Beeson, Lizzie to me, or Lisbeth as she preferred being called after her first year at William and Mary. *It's what all the girls call me now, just drop the E, you got it.*

I guess a truly suitable daughter would look something like Lizzie. I'm sure my mother thought so. Lizzie, Lisbeth or whatever came over to pay a courtesy call on Dad not long before his second and last admission to the hospital. I wondered whether her mom might have prodded her into the whole scene, just to show my own mother what she was missing, like, "*See what a fantastic daughter I've raised? Ever wonder where you messed up with Daisy? Just look at the poor thing.*"

Yeah, I was different. So what?

The only good thing, I was out of the house when Lizzie made her entrance, so her shining example meant nothing to me. But Mom wasn't about to let an opportunity pass by, which is why I spent as much time as possible away from home.

Put together all the fundamental differences of opinion about how I should live my life, and we had all the ingredients for a real donnybrook, one where everybody loses, just lying there, waiting for a spark. I was willing to maintain a truce, but, as usual, Mom had one more salvo to fire. She never gave up, not really, and Lizzie's visit was all the ammunition she needed.

"Your friend, Elizabeth Beeson stopped by to see your father today. I'm sorry you missed her. I haven't seen him light up like that since the day he knew he was coming home from the hospital."

Now she was talking about my dad like he wasn't even in the same room with us. "That's nice." I added a smile I didn't feel. I took refuge in a chair beside his bed and held his hand. It seemed like a pretty safe place for the time being. It would be awfully gross of her to come at me full bore when I was sitting so close to my dying father.

"Elizabeth let her hair grow out. It looks so nice. She made Dean's List this semester, you know."

"That's nice, too." Damn, why couldn't I come up with something more original than that? If I came off looking like a petulant little dork, Mom won. Of course I knew Lizzie made Dean's List. It was in the local paper. It was just one more zinger Mom had to throw in.

"She spent most of last summer in Nantucket with one of her sorority sisters. Can you imagine that?" Mom asked.

Yes, I could. I knew the rest of it by heart; she'd thrown Lizzie's accomplishments in my face so many times. Lizzie the perfect daughter, excellent grades, all the right social clubs, was now in her second year at

William & Mary. Such a pretty girl, Lizzie was a daughter any parent could be proud of.

Then there was me. Lousy grades, lousy choices, lousy all the way around, blah, blah, blah. And she'd hit the roof when she saw shop class on my senior year schedule.

"Shop? You're taking shop? Daisy, I just don't understand you."

Never mind that I'd loved the class, with its power tools and loud noises and that wonderful musty aroma that came from running a circular saw through an oak board. So what if I was the only girl in the class.

She also decided my choice of social clubs during high school and now—the local Sparky's—was "lacking." God, what a waste of time those stupid clubs had been, a bunch of girls sitting around giggling. At least Sparky's had grape slurpees. But of course, Mom didn't see it that way.

"How are you ever going to meet nice young people in those places where you hang out?"

Apparently, only not so nice people ever go to Sparky's, not even for the grape slurpees.

When arguments about general issues ensued, they always ended with Mom shaking her head and walking away defeated. God knows, she tried, but she'd been saddled with a daughter who was going nowhere fast. And yeah, I couldn't help feeling some regrets, but not enough to jump on board and try to become some sort of domestic goddess, not that I ever could.

But when the arguments got pointed and personal, like now when she compared me item by item to Lizzie Beeson, major escalation usually occurred, meaning Mom geared up for a fight. Before Dad got so sick, this kind of confrontation often lead to bouts of shouting, door slamming, or, worst of all, tears—hers, of course, not mine. What kind of cold-hearted ungrateful daughter would drive her poor mother to tears? Even when I won, I lost. So what was the point?

No way was I about to sit around here and let the discussion deteriorate further now that she'd brought the arguments back around to how wonderful Lizzie was and how much I sucked. Absolutely nothing was to be gained from it.

I managed to pry my hand out of Dad's grasp. "Bathroom break," I said.

"I want you right back in here," Mom said. "We have things to discuss."

Yeah, sure. That wasn't going to happen.

Like I'd done so many times before over the past ten years, I crawled out of my bedroom window. Whatever had set Mom off tonight, like realizing time was running out for her to remodel me into a Lizzie Beeson type, I had no intention of remaining anywhere near her. She could find some other target to lob grenades at,

My stomach clenched. No one else in the house with her but Dad and she wouldn't dare act out with him. Worry ate along the edge of my mind as I walked away from the house. At least she never had before.

So far as I knew they'd never discussed me like, "What are we going to do about Daisy?" If they ever did I expect it would be a one-sided conversation, Dad just shrugging while Mom did all the talking.

Besides, friendlier, happier faces were bound to be at Sparky's, even if they didn't measure up to Mom's standards. And what I needed now was a heaping helping of happy and friendly.

"Back already?" Ralph asked when I walked into the store.

I pulled a beer out of the cooler.

"Right to the hard stuff, I see. Trouble at home?"

"What do you think?" I can't even count the number of times I'd bent poor Ralph's ear with renditions of my Mom-battles. I reckon he would make a good bartender. He knows when to press a question and when to walk away. He walked away, and I sipped my beer. But then he came back.

"You know what you're doing, right?" Ralph said as I cowered behind the counter. He knew me too well, but sometimes his insights weren't altogether welcome.

"Okay," I said. "Let me have it."

"I think you're afraid of your mother."

"That, my friend, is ridiculous. I'm not afraid of anybody, including you."

But he was right, and I hated to admit it. I was afraid. I was afraid I couldn't measure up to her standards. The fact that she was perfect in her role made it all the more difficult. Yeah, my Stepford Mom, she always had everything under control, always did the right thing, and her badgering was getting to me, big time. When Dad was up and about, he was my role model. So long as I measured up to him, I was okay. But with him now down for the count I got a bit shaky. I wasn't quite so sure of myself anymore. Ralph's little dig about me being afraid of my mom was right on target, although I didn't want to admit it. Before long I would have to come to grips with a new role. Instead of the family son, I would become the family daughter, something entirely different.

I'd given it some thought, but like so many other troublesome issues, I simply forgot about it, swept it under the carpet. I had enough problems already. But it came slithering back.

****

"Your Mom's a real looker." Oh, man, if I had a dime for every time I heard someone say that, I'd have enough to buy several new pairs of jeans and maybe new sneakers, too.

She'd kept her looks, right into her forties. No gray hairs dared spoil the effect of that shoulder-length glossy black mane that was the envy of every woman on our block, me included.

So, around the time I got into junior high school I became aware that my own mom was different from the other moms; she was a lot better looking. Compared to her, the other moms around town looked downright frumpy. I guess they tried to keep up appearances, more makeup, new hairstyles, and such, but time and raising teenagers seemed to be taking its toll on them.

Not so with my mom. She seemed immune to the effects of passing years. Even our constant battles didn't seem to tarnish her exterior. Her hair, black and glossy as a raven's wing, was always shoulder-length, no matter what current fashion might dictate. She didn't follow fashions; she set them. However she looked was just the way things should be, and if the rest of the world was out of step, their problem.

Aside from a few smile lines at the corners of her eyes, her face weathered the years as well. She had cheekbones that could cut glass.

And don't get me started on posture. You could drop a plumb line from the back of her head to her butt, and it would fall straight and true whether she was standing, sitting, walking, or whatever. When she was sleeping? Probably.

Set all that off against a bosom that just wouldn't quit, and you had a formidable package, which, of course, caused no end of troubles for me.

So you can see my problem. Right out of the gate, I was obviously different. How could I possibly be her daughter? Instead of a rich, flowing head of hair that always remained in place, I'd inherited my father's red frizz, a hopeless situation, so I didn't even try to tame it.

Once, my seventh grade class went to Richmond for a science fair. We saw one of those Van de Graff static electricity machines, where, if you put your hands on it, your hair stood out straight. When you took your hands away, your hair fell back into place, except mine didn't. It stayed all spiky, sticking out in all directions.

That's exactly how my hair looked now, like someone had hooked electrodes to my ears and given my hair a jolt.

As horrible as it was, this was not an unfamiliar sight. I knew that any attempt to subdue this wild red bird's nest with a comb was doomed to failure, but I tried anyway. I tried so hard I broke several teeth out of the plastic comb.

In the end, I resorted to the only method that usually worked, if only temporarily. I ran a cup of water from the sink. I said to my hair, "You forced me to do this." Then I gave it a good soaking.

Game, set, and match to Daisy. Okay, it looked funny plastered down, but it was either that or go around looking as if I'd stuck my thumb in an electrical outlet. And what I couldn't control with water, I hid under a baseball cap.

As I see it, Mother Nature must have been out to lunch when she assembled the parts that would become me. She gave me boobs like Mom's and female private parts, but everything else looked like Dad. There must have been some wires crossed.

If I'd started off with a penis and a nice set of balls, life would have gone more smoothly. Take away the boobs, of course. Then I could have hung out with Dad like the son he probably wanted anyway. And, with a different set of plumbing fixtures, I wouldn't have to run off into the shrubbery to squat to pee. If I'd had a proper wanger, Dad and I could have stood side by side and irrigated whatever we wanted. We could even have little contests, like seeing who could leave watermarks the highest on the side of the garage.

And best of all, as a guy, nobody would ever compare me to my mother. Because, let's face it, stacked up against her I came up way short, even worse than the other ladies in town. So short that I avoided places she went frequently, places like church, places like shopping downtown.

The few times I ventured out with my mom, I felt like that proverbial stepchild kept locked in the basement and only let out after dark. So, yeah, you might say I was afraid, and yeah, most time we were out together I'd come up with some excuse to wait in the car. This was part of the reason that shopping for groceries, paying bills and such, all remained mysteries for me. You're bound to lose when you're up against a "looker," so why try?

Alongside Dad, no problem. But then that fucking

cancer came along and ruined everything.

I saw *Jurassic Park* three times when it came to the Rialto downtown, which is why my friends and I almost flunked eleventh grade gym class. Mr. Bennett, the gym teacher and first class dick, was pretty pissed off at us for cutting three days in a row. He gave all of us Ds. Said he would have flunked us, but he didn't want us in his class again. He was looking straight at me when he said it.

The four of us kids sat in the balcony and cheered for the raptors. And when those smaller lizards ganged up and ate the fat guy who'd turned off the power in the park, that was the best. We gave them a standing ovation.

Only one bad part, when they lowered the poor goat into the forest on a rope as bait for *Tyrannosaurus Rex*. There was all sorts of godawful screeching and growling, and when they pulled the rope back up there was nothing left but a few bloody shreds. It made me think, a lot of what happens in life depends on your position in the food chain. I mean, you might look at a goat and think about lunch, then along comes *T. Rex*, looks at you and thinks the same thing.

Yeah, I know it's way the hell too dramatic, but sometimes I felt like there was a *T. Rex* out there watching our family, and the big toothy bastard had already picked out his next meal…my dad.

****

Earlier during one of those short December afternoons Mom had to endure the ultimate punch-in-the-gut when Amy Pendergrast, another of my high school classmates, brought over her new daughter. Of course, Amy's mom would be doing back flips and handstands over her new grandchild, except that she weighed around two-fifty and would probably kill herself if she tried. I should have guessed that Amy would be the first to deliver. She came from a group of six girls, and by the time they were through I expected them to repopulate a good part of the county.

This was the first grandchild in Mom's circle of friends. I could hear the ooohhing and ahhing sounds all the way downstairs. And if I'd listened closely enough I probably could have heard Mom's heart splinter as she watched the spectacle.

Bad enough that Mrs. Pendergrast was always lording it over Mom because she'd had the good fortune to marry the local druggist, setting them a rung or two above the Sugarbush clan on the local socioeconomic ladder, now she possessed that apparently magical gift, a grandchild, while Mom's waiting arms remained empty.

Of course, I never saw the child since I hid out in the basement. I'd just got back from unplugging a toilet in one of our rental properties. The lady of the house, Mrs. Flaherty, is a redhead, just like me, and not exactly mellow, also just like me. She'd been cooped up for a couple of hours with a houseful of kids and no toilet, and I'd been up to my elbows in stuff that even my dog would find disgusting. All the while Mrs. Flaherty was close by my shoulder. "How much longer?"

I haven't punched anybody since junior high, but believe me, I was having thoughts. I think Mrs. Flaherty caught on, so she left in a huff.

When I got home, I was in no mood for entertaining mothers, new ones, old ones, any of them, but I still got a blow-by-blow account later when Mom told me all about it, about as subtle as an oncoming freight train. On and on she went, the whole time cradling her arms in front of her as if she were holding a baby, her eyes rolled back apparently beseeching the Almighty for a grandchild of her own.

"You should have seen her," Mom said when she caught up with me.

"Seen who?" I knew playing dumb wouldn't work, but I was just trying to postpone the inevitable.

"Baby Louise, such a darling." All of this with her arms still folded in front of her waiting to be filled by a bundle of joy.

Unfortunately, the whole performance was lost on me. When it came to maternal instincts, I struck out. I realized that some people had to have babies. Otherwise they would have to close the schools, and there would be a lot of teachers out of jobs. People who made diapers and baby bottles and all that other stuff that gets passed out in baby showers would have to find some other line of work. Beyond that, the idea held no great appeal for me, except for the twin girls that Ralph and his wife, Janey had brought into the world. I could get excited over those two. Mom would, too.

A bit later I slipped out the backdoor, leaving Mom to her dreams and her disappointments.

This process of procreation at which Mom hinted so shamelessly would require a substantial effort on my part, one that I had no intention of undertaking. I had no plans of becoming anybody's brood mare. I might not have a very clear idea of where I fit in the world, but for damned sure waddling around with a huge belly wasn't part of my plans. And anything that made my boobs grow bigger than they already were was out of the question.

Amy Pendergrast had made her choice, and I made mine. Instead of a baby, I chose my dog, Max, a stray of indeterminate lineage, who'd wandered up one cold December night two years ago. For sure he was one hundred percent dog, but everything else about him was questionable. Early on it required more than a little subterfuge on my part to keep him out of Mom's line of vision, but he now was an established member of the family, with full voting rights, at least where I was concerned.

Max never cried, and he never required diaper changes, and he could catch rabbits, sometimes. Show me a new baby who can match that.

Chapter 2

I don't know whether holding someone else's grandchild got Mom all stirred up, but the next day there was something in the air. I heard her singing in the kitchen early the next morning...trouble for sure. She must have decided that the slow incremental approach would never change me, so right there in December, 1994, two weeks before Christmas, she came after me full throttle.

"Daisy, Daisy, are you up yet?" I heard her right outside my door. By now I was tuned in pretty close to her voice, like, what was just a regular question, and which ones meant trouble. This one was trouble. This was the one she used when I left my dirty sneakers under the coffee table in the living room, something like that. And she never bugged me early in the morning...more trouble.

Dad had been gone for almost a year then, so she must have thought it was now or never. Her visions of grandchildren were going up in smoke, so she had to hurry. Poor Mom. She must have wondered a million times, "Where did I go wrong?" I wondered a few times myself.

I got dressed quietly and crawled out my bedroom window, a cowardly exit, but one that let me avoid any confrontation. Early morning fights are the worst, and I just wasn't up to it. Breakfast was a sausage biscuit with Ralph at Sparky's.

"I think the stress has gotten to her, and she's flipped out," I said, in between bites. My comment got an eye roll from Ralph, otherwise he remained neutral. He knew well enough about my Mom battles, enough to stay out of them.

Still, I walked right into an ambush; she was waiting for me when I got home late that afternoon. "I need you to help me with some things tomorrow," she said, more like an announcement, like it was already set in stone.

"I've got a lot to do," I said. I was already planning my next day's work, wondering how I could get everything done on time. One thing I never learned from watching Dad was how he got so much done without ever seeming to hurry. Me, I was always late, always trying to catch up. And, even though I was still trying to measure up to his standards after he was gone, I wasn't about to let things fall apart, not after he'd worked so many years putting them together. If the job took more hours, that's just how it would be.

"It will have to wait," Mom said, her tone firm, commanding. "I need you here. We have to go shopping, then we need to put up some decorations. I want this place clean, some Christmas lights, a tree. I want it looking nice for the holiday." Christmas was always a big deal at the Sugarbush house, but we'd blown off the year before because of Dad's cancer.

"Mom, Christmas is over a week away yet." It was a pretty weak attempt, but I had nothing else. Dad's death still hung in the air, and I wasn't in a holiday mood. I doubt Mom was either, but she saw the world differently, and for now she was running the show.

"No matter. We're going to be ready, and we start tomorrow." End of discussion.

The next morning I looked out my bedroom window at a clear blue sky. A cold front had crept through during the night dropping temperatures into the lower forties, so I pulled a denim jacket from my closet. Out of habit, I dressed as if for work—dirty jeans, Dad's old work shirt, also dirty—Mom thought she'd gotten rid of all of them, but I had a few stashed away—and my usual grimy sneakers. I figured the shopping trip with Mom would be a grin-and-bear-it affair, hopefully brief. The worse I looked, the less likely she would want me tagging along behind her. Then I could get on with my own chores.

Mom met me at the door, took one look at me, then pointed back where I'd had come from. The scowl on her face spoke volumes, all bad. "Go back and change into something decent. I will not have you wandering around town looking like a common laborer. You're a grown woman now."

"But, Mom...."

"Now, go, and be quick about it." Her mouth was open, as if she was going to say more, but instead she turned away, silent. This was the part I hated most, the silent treatment. I'd so much rather she scream, shout, throw things, anything but stone cold silence.

I went back to my room and rummaged through my closet. After years of disagreement with Mom, I had succeeded in making my room, my closet in particular, out of bounds. Now the clothes with which I might replace the dirty jeans and work shirt I wore lay in a pile on the floor. An outfit for a day laborer; Mom had nailed it.

I prodded the pile with my toe. Max walked over, sniffed, then hurried back into the corner.

"That bad, huh?" When your dog turns up his nose at your clothes, you have a problem. I pulled out a pair of jeans that, while far from clean, were a bit less grungy than the ones I wore. From the second drawer of my dresser I took a clean yellow pullover. The deal was, whenever I wanted something washed I put it in the hamper at the end of the hall. Mom then washed it, ironed it, whether the item needed it or not, and placed the stack of clean clothes in the chair by my door.

Mom was sitting on the sofa leafing through a magazine when I crept in again. She shook her head slowly and said, "Better, but not by much. We're going to have to add something to our shopping list—some new clothes for you."

I couldn't remember the last time I'd gone shopping with Mom. Usually I could come up with some excuse, and, after a while, she seemed to give up. But this time was obviously different. She had an agenda—me.

On the drive to downtown Warrensburg—all fifteen minutes of it—Mom seemed lost in thought, so I didn't disturb her. Traffic was already heavy, but we lucked out on a parking place right in front of Simmons's Ladies' Wear.

"Perfect," Mom said. "Couldn't have planned it any better."

Simmons's was one of the oldest family-owned businesses in town. I couldn't remember a time when it wasn't there. It was also one of few stores in town with a second floor.

"Been a long, long time since I was in here," I said.

"Don't I know it." Mom took me by the arm as if she expected me to run away. "It's way past time that we fixed you up to look like the lovely young woman that you are."

Hey, Mom, it's me, Daisy. Where'd you get that lovely young woman idea?

"It's almost Christmas. People will drop by. I want you to look nice for the holiday."

This trip wasn't just about looking nice. I could see that easily enough. It was an attempt to resurrect a Sugarbush family tradition, Christmas with all the trimmings. Mom wasn't one to give up without a fight. She could just as easily have slipped into despair over her loss and about how Christmas would never be the same without Dad, but that wasn't the way she was wired up. In her world, you took your licks and kept on keeping on. I admired that, I just wasn't so sure I wanted to be a part of the process. But this time I would look the way she wanted, dressed up and proper, even if it killed me, which seemed quite possible.

We headed up the stairs into an area that was completely new to me, Ladies' Intimate Apparel. *No way, she must be kidding.* I was not going shopping for underwear with my mother. Not going to happen. I'd rather have my fingernails pulled out.

"Mom, I don't need any underwear," I whispered.

"Daisy, I wash your clothes, so I know exactly what you wear, and you most definitely need new underwear. I'm not even sure where you buy some of that stuff you wear."

"Some advance notice would have been nice, Mom."

"If I'd given you advance notice you'd have

climbed out your bedroom window and run off."

True, but I still didn't like being tricked, especially by my own mother.

"Rhoda, it's been forever. How in the world are you?" A rotund woman with red hair almost the same shade as mine barged past me and wrapped my mother in a hug.

"Hello, Marg," Mom said, kind of wheezy, must have been a vigorous hug.

"Are you taking care of yourself?" Marg asked. The Snyders—Marg, a husband and two grown sons—attended the Warrensburg Methodist Church instead of the First Baptist where Mom went, so I guess they hadn't seen one another much.

"We're getting by," Mom said.

"Well, I haven't seen this young lady for a long time either." She patted my arm. From the look on her face she didn't exactly approve of my rumpled jeans and t-shirt combination either.

"Hi, Mrs. Snyder. How's Jimmy?" I asked. Mrs. Snyder's son, Jimmy, had been a year ahead of me at Warrensburg High.

"Still at that Air Force Base in Germany," she said.

"We're here to get Daisy outfitted for the holiday," Mom said. "We thought we'd start right with the basics."

Mrs. Snyder took me by the shoulders, looked me up and down. "You're full in the bust, just like your mom. No problem. We'll get you fixed right up."

My bust? Nobody ever called them that before. This might be even worse than I'd thought.

She led us to a long counter filled with frilly, lacy garments that didn't look like they'd hold up in a stiff breeze. Yeah, perfect for next time I had to unblock a toilet.

"I'd guess a thirty-six C, is that right?"

"I guess."

"You don't know?"

"No, I meant, that's right." And no, I didn't know for sure. I knew I had big boobs, but I had never been properly fitted out and had no intention of having it done either. This was private stuff we were talking about, right out in the open.

She gathered up four or five bras, then added another. She held it up in front of me, right there in the store with people all around. "This one's really cute. It's for when you wear something low cut, you know, a little cleavage, and, sweetheart, you've got plenty to spare."

"Oh, I like that one," Mom said. She pressed the cups up under my breasts—groped by my own mother, no less. I felt like she was getting me ready for auction.

"Those will be fine," I said.

"Oh, no," Mom said. "First you try them on, then Marg will check the fit."

"How will she do that?"

"How do you think? Honestly, Daisy, sometimes you embarrass me."

Yeah, Mrs. Snyder and me, right there in the dressing room together. I'd hung my old bra on a hook by the door.

"Where on earth do you buy your underwear?" Mrs. Snyder asked.

I couldn't remember.

"Next time, you come back here, and I'll take care of you."

I was trying on a black, lacy affair that was a lot more comfortable than I expected it to be, but about as practical as a diamond tiara at a rodeo.

"That's just darling," Mrs. Snyder said. "All the young girls are wearing these now."

Like, how would I know? I hadn't seen a girl in a bra since the locker room in high school gym class.

Four new bras later, including the one that set my boobs out like a display case, the carnage continued. Underpants. The most comfortable underpants I had was a pair of Dad's boxer shorts that I'd stolen out of the wash. But that was about to change, too.

Mom stood by a counter, elbow-deep in scanty panties. When had my mother developed this crazy taste for erotic underwear? She seemed to be having such a good time that I let her pick stuff out for me. Not like I had to wear them. I still had Dad's boxers hidden away.

I breathed a huge sigh of relief as we finally left the domain of Ladies' Intimate Apparel, and hoped I would never return.

"There, that wasn't so bad after all, was it?" Mom looked so pleased with herself that I couldn't say no.

I spotted a display of jeans in the far corner of the first floor and was ready to head in that direction when Mom tugged my arm again.

"This way," she said.

This way was skirts, blouses, and cardigans, stuff I would never have any use for. You simply cannot change your truck's broken fan belt wearing a skirt. Of course, if you're cute enough you can stand by the road looking helpless, and maybe some guy will stop and give you a hand, but who was going to stop for a frizzy-haired gnome like me? Besides, I knew more about auto repairs than most men did anyway.

Another of Mom's old friends, a Mrs. Barrow, from her church, helped us through the process of skirts and dresses. I was beginning to suspect that Mom had planted these salespeople to coax me into things she never could have talked me into alone.

One thing, though, when I checked myself out in the mirror, a plaid skirt, a little shorter than I would have chosen, and a green sweater that highlighted my assets, well, I was looking pretty good. Mom seemed pleased as punch, and I was flat out surprised, amazed, even. Who was this sharp looking chick staring back at me?

"So far, so good," Mom said. "But you don't have a single dress that you can wear anywhere special." As if I ever went anywhere special. Another tug on my arm, and we were off to another section, where, no doubt, another of her friends lay waiting in ambush, with dresses.

'Mom, I don't have any place to put all of this."

"Most of the stuff in your closet now will go straight into the trash. Then you'll have lots of room."

No great harm done among the dresses, and I was right about the saleslady-in-waiting being another of Mom's church friends. Two nice floral print dresses, cute, but about as practical as a new surfboard, but we weren't finished.

"A church dress," Mom said.

Around Warrensburg, and, I guess, in a lot of small towns, a church dress was a step up from regular every day wear. Nicer but still not frilly or fancy, and certainly not to be confused with a cocktail dress.

Cocktail parties were few and far between in Warrensburg, but church was a regular event, so a church dress was an acceptable expense, cocktail dresses, not so much.

"Got just the thing." Mabel, another of Mom's co-conspirators brought out a light blue number that shimmered even when it wasn't moving. It was cut low in front.

Mabel draped the dress over my arm and pushed me toward the fitting room.

"Wait, put this on." Mom handed me little half-bra that showed a lot more Daisy than was usually visible. And the dress had a mind of its own. It crept and clung and moved before I did. I checked out every possible angle. Wow. Hard to believe it was me. Plain old Daisy had morphed into something else entirely. Yeah, the old ugly duckling turning into the beautiful swan trick.

"Daisy, come on out so we can see you," Mom said.

So I did. I made a little pirouette in front of Mom. She clasped her hands in the prayer thing again—I wish she would stop that—and her face turned colors I hadn't seen before. "Yes, yes, yes," she said.

"That dress was made for you," Mabel said.

And it wasn't just Mom and Mable gawking. Other shoppers slowed down to take a look. Some stopped and stared outright.

"Who is she?" I heard someone whisper.

Finally, after all these years, I'd made Mom proud. And in the process I'd discovered a new Daisy. This new one was sexy as hell. Church dress, my ass. In this thing I could set off fire alarms. For sure, Mom and her friends had set me up, but I didn't care. It was worth it.

When I came out of the dressing room again, big hugs from Mom and Mabel. Mabel smelled like cinnamon.

"Daisy, honey, you're the cutest girl I've seen in a long time," Mabel said.

So, we left Simmons's, our arms loaded with packages. I bounced back and forth between exhilaration and exhaustion. Shopping was hard work.

"Almost done," Mom said.

"More?"

"Oh, yes."

We loaded our loot in the truck, and Mom led me down the street. She stopped in front of a shop with a front door outlined in pink paint.

"Alice's Beauty Salon? I'm not going in there."

"Yes, you are. You have an appointment. I phoned ahead yesterday."

Set up again. Mom had been a step ahead of me all morning. Still, a little creative foot dragging was in order here. It had been a long, long time since I'd been in a beauty salon.

Now, Billy's Barber Shop, where Dad used to get his hair cut, that was another matter. I'd been in there so many times they considered me a regular, boobs notwithstanding. I loved Billy's, the familiar old magazines, *Field & Stream*, *Popular Mechanics*, I'd leafed through all of them more than once. The conversations…ball games, crops, vehicles, all so familiar I could tune in and out without ever missing a beat. The worn leather chairs that still reeked faintly of cigar smoke, back from before Billy had to comply with a city ordinance that banned smoking. And guys came out of Billy's looking pretty much the same was when they went in, ears a little lower, but that was all.

But weird shit happened in beauty parlors. Natural colors and shapes could all be changed in a twinkle. How you looked when you walked out might be completely different from when you entered. Different magazines, completely different smells. Still, I had to admit, Mom had done okay by me so far. Besides, my frizzy mop of red hair really didn't fit my new image, and nothing I'd tried so far would make it behave. The water treatment lasted only so long as I remained wet. When my hair dried out, back came the frizz.

A robust, ruddy-cheeked woman walked up and embraced Mom. Then she turned to me. "Hi, I'm Alice. Your mom and I go way back." This was a big day for hugs. Maybe it was the holiday season effect.

Mom kinda pushed me forward. "What can you do with my daughter?"

I flinched a little as Alice ran her fingers through my hair.

"Maybe a shade darker, flatten out a bit of the frizz. Yeah," Alice said.

"And these." Mom held up my right hand, fingers splayed apart. "Aren't these about the worst looking nails you've ever seen?"

"Oh, my goodness," Alice said. "What in the world have you been doing?"

"She's been doing all the odd jobs her father used to do, and just look at what she's done to her hands."

I felt like an alien creature, something that had crawled out from beneath a woodpile. No one ever cared about my nails before.

"Well, you are going to be a challenge," Alice said. "I'll do my best."

"I'll run down to the market, finish up there while you work on my daughter." Mom smiled, patted my shoulder. "You'll hardly know yourself when Alice gets through with you." Which was exactly what I was afraid of.

But I had little time to ponder. Alice led me to a chair, draped a rubberized cape over my shoulders, then lowered the chair so my head extended over a sink. There followed a cascade of warm water, strong fingers working an aromatic lather that smelled like cotton candy into my scalp. Someone I couldn't see lifted my left hand and immersed my fingers in a warm, soapy liquid. Then she repeated the process on the right.

"That's Petra," Alice said. "She does nails."

I felt my resistance floating away in the warm lather that flowed through my hair. For the first time I could remember, I surrendered completely, I relinquished control. Now I was on the receiving end. *Okay, Mom, you win this one.*

An hour or so later—I completely lost track of time—Alice wheeled the chair around so I could see myself in the mirror.

"Holy shit."

Alice rapped me on the shoulder with a comb. "Young ladies don't talk like that."

"I'm sorry. I just can't believe the difference." Gone was the frizzy orange mop that I usually hid beneath a baseball cap. By some magical process Alice had transformed it into a wavy auburn halo. "Can I touch it?"

"Of course. It's your own hair, after all. But you'll have to take better care of it, brushing, washing and such. And I'll need to touch it up from time to time."

And I had pink fingernails to boot. Petra, a tiny, dark-skinned girl, when I finally got a look at her, said, "I did the best I could. I had to cut the nails off short, because so many of them were broken. But when they grow out they'll look nicer."

Mom's delight was obvious as soon as she entered the shop. She clasped her hands beneath her chin—the prayer pose again. "Yes," she said. "Yes, yes, yes." She embraced Alice. "You are a magician. Thank you so much."

"Not really," Alice said. "There was a beautiful girl in there all along. We just tidied things up a bit so you can see her better."

They were talking about me, using words I hadn't heard before. Beautiful? Me? I kept glancing back at the mirror. Where had the old Daisy gone? And just who was this new one? A little bit scary.

Even walking down the street alongside my mother was different from before. Guys were checking me out. Usually, if I was out with my friends, the boys zeroed in on the girl friends, not me. Now in a few short hours all that had changed.

"Stand up straight," Mom whispered.

"Oh, yeah, I forgot." But I didn't forget again.

We had one more stop to make before we headed home—the lot where the Boy Scouts were selling Christmas trees. I thought about waiting in the truck. This was Mom's idea. Let her pick one out. But she wouldn't hear of it. "Come on. I need your help."

This was another new twist, Mom asking me to help out like this. It was only a Christmas tree. How complicated could that be? But I went along with it. I owed her that much after all the trouble she'd gone through. I headed off to where the Boy Scouts, looking very sharp in their uniforms, waited. One of them, a tow-headed kid with a disarming smile trotted over.

"Hi, I'm Freddie, John's brother. Remember me?"

"Sure, hi, Freddie." I didn't bother asking about his older brother, John, who owned that same disarming smile. We'd gone out one Friday night, and the disarming smile had almost worked. *John the octopus* was how I remembered him. I still hadn't figured out how his hands could be in so many places at the same time.

I wandered among the cut fir trees, inhaling their spicy aroma. Freddie followed me closely. Soon I noticed that several other Scouts had joined in, and a little entourage of teenage boys trailed at my heels. I glanced back at Mom who was still standing beside the truck looking ever so pleased with herself. The old girl had set me up again, for sure.

Yes, things were different now. If I'd walked onto the lot in my old clothes, frizzy mop of hair under my cap, no one would have given me a second look. Probably would have thought I worked there. Instead I had half the Scout troop chasing after me.

It was just past two when we got home. Our neighbor, Mrs. West, was walking back from her mailbox by the street. One look at me and her eyes bulged. I don't think she even recognized me at first. "Oh, my, just look at you. This can't be the same girl that left here this morning."

I had blushed more in the past two hours than I had in years. I was becoming quite familiar with the warm sensation that flooded my face. "It's just me. Same old Daisy."

"Oh, no. Not even close. You're lovely, my dear."

Mom stayed behind to chat with her, and I took our packages inside. I stripped to my bra and underpants and checked myself out in the mirror above my dresser. Was it really me? I reached toward the mirror, and the hand in my reflection touched my own fingertips. Yeah, hard to believe, but it must be. I stepped back so I could get a look at myself full length. My body, to which I'd paid so little attention, had changed too. When I turned and looked at myself from the back I discovered that I had hips, and along with them, a perfectly rounded butt. *Where had that come from?*

Might as well do the whole bit, I thought. So I put on one of the bra and panty sets that we'd bought earlier. The bra just happened to be that little cut out number that really put me out there.

New hair, new underwear, new clothes, new Daisy, and now, new possibilities, lots of them. In times past my options had seemed limited. Not so now. Maybe I was about to become the daughter my mom had wanted all along. The big split in us local kids—winners and losers—had come with high school graduation. It had been pretty clear before then, the kids with good grades, advanced placement classes, all the right clubs, then there was the rest of us. Slackers, mostly, who would wind up bagging groceries or pumping gas, or, in my case, working with my dad.

"Daisy, if you would just try, even a little bit, I know you can do this work and do it well."

Same message from my teachers, my school guidance counselor, and, of course, my mom.

Sure, I could do it, but I didn't. Why? Never really sure, fear, spite, whatever. Maybe Ralph was right, I was just plain cantankerous. Whenever somebody pushed me one way, I automatically headed in the opposite direction. Then there was the thing about me being afraid of my own mother, how I could never measure up to her standards.

Now I knew different. The woman—not girl, mind you—in the mirror told me as much. And when I slipped on the blue dress I could hear doors opening onto a wide new world that didn't scare me anymore. Wait until the gang at Sparky's gets a look at me. What a difference a day makes, particularly when that day involved shopping and a trip to the beauty parlor…a complete makeover. If Lizzie Beeson could see me now. In fact, if she walked in the front door right now, I'd be the first to greet her. No more hiding out in the basement. Come on in, get an eyeful of the new Daisy. Things are going to change now, big time.

****

The call came shortly past seven o'clock. Mom and I were washing the dinner dishes together. She kept looking at me out of the corner of her eye, like she still couldn't believe how different I'd become. I was even stealing glances of myself reflected in the kitchen window…first time I've ever done that on purpose.

I answered the phone on the second ring.

"It's Don Johnson. Our furnace just quit." His voice was gruff, almost angry.

"This is Daisy. I'll come and take a look at it."

"You? You think you can fix it?"

"If I can't, I'll get somebody else who can. Is that good enough for you?" I didn't even try to keep the edge out of my voice. As a general rule, when someone pushed me I pushed back. "Make it quick. We need some heat."

"I'll be right over," I said.

"Right over where?" Mom asked. "It's freezing outside, and they're predicting sleet. I don't want you going anywhere."

"It's the Johnsons," I said. "Their furnace went out."

"Well, there's not a blessed thing we can do about it. They'll just have to call somebody else. They're two months behind in their rent as it is."

"I can handle it. I've watched Dad do it dozens of times."

Mom stood her ground, still in her most defiant posture. "No daughter of mine is going to go out tonight repairing furnaces. I don't care how many times you've watched your father do it. Let them call Virginia Power or somebody else."

I walked to my mother, stood facing her, then put my hands on her shoulders. For once I looked her straight in the eye. Yes, this was a woman to woman confrontation, and, even though I now had two new dresses hanging in my closet, I was still Daisy. For the moment the furnace was a secondary issue. There was something bigger at stake here. I was asking Mom to meet me halfway, to accept me as an adult woman who could now dress nicely, but who could also change a flat tire in a pouring rain.

Up until then it had almost been a game that I had played along with, new clothes, new nails, new hair, the whole bit, but not until that moment did I realize that Mom was asking me to make a complete break with the past. I wasn't ready; even though Dad was no longer with us, his memory hung on, and I was still daughter to both of them, father and mother, and the father's daughter had a furnace to repair. I hugged Mom and spoke softly in her ear. "Let me do this for Dad. When I get back we'll talk, just you and me. We'll get it all straightened out."

"You promise you'll be careful?"

"I promise." I kissed my mother's warm cheek and couldn't remember the last time I had done that. I held her close and couldn't remember the last time I had done that either.

"I'll be back before you know it. If it's something I can't handle, I'll call Virginia Power myself." I went into the back room just off the kitchen and grabbed dad's old tool bag, a worn leather satchel with both handles missing.

I had one more hurdle to clear. Max sat by the front door blocking my path. "Too cold out for you, boy," I said. "You stay here and take care of Mom." When I stepped around him, Max seized the cuff of my jeans and tried to pull me back into the room.

"That dog's right, you know," Mom said. "You should stay here."

I jerked out of Max's grasp, then headed out the door. On the porch, the cold made me gasp. The wind had blown the lid off a trashcan from somewhere up the street, and it bumped along the pavement as if tugged by an invisible string. Mom had been right about the sleet. I held my hand in front of my face to fend off the stinging needles of ice.

The Johnson house, one of three that Dad owned in addition to our primary residence, sat on a corner lot on Salisbury Street. I didn't find out that these properties were a sore spot between Mom and

Dad until the end of my junior year in high school. I was sitting on the back porch sipping on an iced tea. With all the windows open, their voices drifted out from the kitchen.

"Sam, you ought to sell those old houses," Mom said. They're just a big nuisance. It's bad enough that you spend half your time over there, but Daisy does, too. That's no kind of work for a girl."

"She don't seem to mind." His voice was low, like this was a conversation he didn't want to have.

"I know, I know, whatever you're doing is just fine with her."

The sentence that Mom didn't finish would have ended with her lament over a daughter who seemed beyond her reach. While I followed Dad around, she stood no chance of introducing me to adult womanhood, whatever that was.

In spite of the disagreement, no FOR SALE signs popped up on Salisbury Street that summer or the next. And when Dad got sick, confined to bed with no hope of resuming his previous activities, Mom tried a different pressure point—me.

"Daisy, can't you talk to your father about selling those rental houses? You can't manage them all by yourself, not with your dad so sick. Besides, that corner lot is worth some money. You have your own future to think about." She started up late one evening after Dad was asleep.

"Mom, if we do that now, you know what he'll think. He'll lose hope. He'll just give up." I was buying into the hope thing a lot more than I'd have expected, but we didn't have much else to hang onto.

So once again the issue slipped to the back burner,

but it continued to simmer, and sooner or later there would have to be a settlement. That settlement was Dad's death.

All three of the houses were simple, cookie-cutter types, distinguishable from each other only by the fact that Mr. Johnson had chosen to paint his a dark green. By the time I arrived, I was already having second thoughts about the trip. The roads were getting slick and sure to be worse by the time I finished up.

Tom Johnson, clad in an overcoat and reeking of beer, met me at the front door. "About time," he said. "Hurry up. We're freezing."

"Sorry about the furnace, Mr. Johnson. Things always seem to break down at the worst possible time."

Johnson took a step back. "You look different."

"Just got my hair done, for the holiday."

"You know what you're doing?" Johnson scowled at me. Clearly he doubted my ability even though I'd been doing repairs around that house for years now.

"If I can't figure it out I'll get someone in here who can."

Johnson led me through the living room where his wife and two teenage sons sat huddled in front of the fireplace. All three were wrapped in blankets. I followed Johnson down a short hallway past a bedroom. The furnace, a dilapidated, blackened metallic monster that should have been replaced years before, lurked in a small room at the back of the house. I had to shove aside several boxes to get to the side of the furnace.

"I'll be in the front room with the family," Johnson said. "Make sure you get this thing running."

"I'm on it," I said. I pulled a flashlight from my

tool bag and located the relay switch. Seems to be working okay. I pried open the small grate at the base of the furnace. Pilot light was out though. I didn't realize, until I dropped to my knees beside the hulking furnace…I was exhausted. I rested my forehead against the cold metal of the furnace door, probably creating a sooty imprint that I'd have to wash off before I went home, before Mom saw it. In less than twelve hours, my life had been turned upside down, inside out, completely changed. My father's death had been a terrible shock, worse than anything I could imagine, but at least then I was the same Daisy before and after, a little banged up, but still in the same basic packaging.

Not so now. The Daisy kneeling by a cold furnace was not the same Daisy who had followed her mother around all day, new clothes, new hair, new nails, changing from a handyman to a young woman. That's what Mom called me now, a young woman.

I guess I was still in a mild state of shock, so much change in such a short time. I'd stolen a look at myself in a mirror in the hallway as Mr. Johnson led me back to the furnace room. It couldn't possibly be me, but it was, a young woman, for real.

Yeah, my body had taken a giant leap forward, but my mind was still processing, taking baby steps. Mom seemed to take it all in stride, but for me, this transition wasn't easy. I felt drained, exhausted and elated, both at once. I seemed to be in different places at the same time, old Daisy, new Daisy, going in circles. I'd known this day was coming, but when it finally landed on me, I was completely unprepared. How do you prepare for something that grabs you by the ankles, lifts you up and spins you around so you don't know which way is up, who you are or what you are? Who was calling the shots now, old Daisy or new Daisy? Confusion and fatigue, never a good combination, maybe that's why I got stupid, why I did something my Dad had warned me never to do. I struck a match. The fireball that erupted was the last thing I would ever see.

Chapter 3

I shouldn't be here. I don't want to be here. It didn't have to be this way. Right after the blast, after they dragged out the smoking bundle of what was left of me, I heard a neighbor say, "God almighty, she's still breathing. Call an ambulance."

A wiser voice asked, "What for?"

Exactly. Better they should have left me in the rubble, but I screwed up. I breathed, and someone saw it.

"Thank God, you're alive," Mom kept saying.

You got it backward, Mom. I would thank God if I *weren't* alive. If the Big Guy had an ounce of compassion in Him, He would have taken me off the list right then and there and spared me all those months in purgatory.

Early memories of that event were vague to non-existent. I remembered bits of conversation between the EMTs during the ambulance ride. "Holy shit, I never saw anything like this."

I guessed he was talking about me.

"Best thing, give her a big slug of morphine, get it all over with."

Now you're talking. Go right ahead, the bigger the slug the better. I swear, I won't tell a soul. And when I get to the Big House, I'll put in a good word for you.

But my bad luck held, and I arrived at the hospital

alive, more or less. At about that time I realized that nothing worked. I could hear a few snatches of sound, but my arms and legs wouldn't do what I wanted, and, worst of all, I couldn't see a damned thing.

"Get a tube down her throat, quick." A masculine voice, sounded like the commander-in-chief.

Put a tube in my throat, just like they'd done to Dad when he was in the hospital, and all those other poor souls in the ICU, like so many potted plants. The ventilators all going click-wheeze, click-wheeze, click-wheeze. Still gave me nightmares. No, no, no. No tube. I lost.

Time was no longer a measurable quantity. It had no shape, no sense of moving forward or backward. So, when Mom said, "Daisy, Daisy, can you hear me?"I didn't know whether her voice came from the present or sometime in the past, or maybe I really was dead and just having one of those out-of-body experiences…I should be so lucky. No, I hurt too much to be dead.

"She can't answer you, Mrs. Sugarbush, until we get the endotracheal tube out."

"When will that be?" Mom's voice sounded far away. Maybe it really was yesterday or even the day before.

"Dr. Dawson will decide that. And don't touch her, please. Her skin is very sensitive."

Skin sensitive? What a joke. I guess the big blast was over and done with, but I was still on fire. Hell couldn't possibly be worse than this.

"It's time for your pain medication, Daisy."

The same female voice that made the crack about sensitive skin. Good, make it a big one, the bigger the better.

"She'll probably sleep for a while, Mrs. Sugarbush. Why don't you take a break? We'll call you if anything happens." A raspy voice, not exactly kind and gentle.

Blessed morphine, the best thing yet. Everything slowly fading to black. Black was good. Black didn't hurt.

I was mixing things up, but I couldn't help it. For a long time in the hospital—how long, no idea—there was nothing solid in my life, if it can be called a life. Things just happened to me for no apparent reason. Everything was upside down, like an asylum.

Someone named Linda came by. She kept blubbering, "Oh, Daisy, my poor Daisy." But who was she, and why was she blubbering all over me? She sounded upset when I asked who she was.

Then I would sink back into the void, where nothing made sense.

Eventually they took the tube out of my throat, no big announcement, like everything else, they just did it. Dr. Israel—I remembered him from his treatment of Dad—came by to do it himself. He said he usually has his staff do it, but he wanted to take care of this one personally. Then I remembered, Linda, the girl who had blubbered all over me the day before, "Oh, my poor Daisy," and all that, was his nurse. She had been so kind to all of us when Dad was in the hospital, even drove out to the house to make a home visit. I guess she'd been blasted out of my memory earlier, but then I couldn't see her either, could I?

Later, when Dr. Israel came back to check on me he listened to my chest. "Sounds pretty rough in there," he said. "You must have suffered some lung damage in the blast. Can you talk now?"

I tried. It came out as a croak, and hurt, too.

"Don't worry, tomorrow you'll be talking your head off. I hear Dr. Dawson and his group coming now, so I'll take off."

"Who's Dr. Dawson?"

"He's the chief here in the Burn Trauma Unit. He's the one who's directing your care. I'll see you later."

So, the big cheese himself was on his way to see me. Maybe now I would find out what was going on and when they would let me out of this crazy place. Better still, maybe they would decide I was just too far gone to save.

"Let's just put her out of her misery, save her and her mother a lot of grief." That's what I wanted to hear; instead, I heard several pairs of leather heels clicking on the hard floor. Along with them tramped any number of the soft-soled shoes I'd seen the nurses wear, back when I could see.

His booming voice startled me. It was so different from Dr. Israel's soft delivery, like a different language.

"And here's our miracle patient, Daisy Sugarbush." I guess he was speaking to his entourage, not me. He sounded like a public address system. "And you, Ms. Sugarbush, are a very fortunate young lady, because you're in the finest Burn Trauma Unit in the southeast."

Thanks, but I'll pass. If you're so damned good, why do I have to hurt so much?

"I see that you've been in Dr. Smithson's capable hands, so, Dr. Smithson, why don't you inform us of the extent of the patient's injuries."

"Her burns covered approximately sixty-five percent of her body, sir." The voice was halting, timid in comparison to Dawson's. Apparently this Dawson was a fearsome character.

"And how did you arrive at that measurement, Dr. Smithson?"

"By the *Rule of Nines*, sir. She gets nine points for each uninjured area. Only her upper and lower back areas and genital region escaped burn. The rest of her body, head, arms, chest, abdomen, and legs were severely burned, so each of those got nine points leaving her with only thirty percent normal tissue."

"And where would this place the likelihood of her survival, were she to have arrived at a less competent unit than ours?"

"Less than twenty percent, sir."

This little exchange of information was apparently directed at an audience, certainly not to me. If they'd offered me a choice, I would have picked the eighty percent group, make a clean break of it and have it all over and done with. I'll bet a lot of the other twenty percenters would have done the same.

"What else should we be concerned about?" Dawson, again.

"Her pulmonary and renal functions are particularly at risk, and every time we push up her pain meds her renal function heads south, so we have to be very careful with that. But her cardiac and gastrointestinal systems must be watched closely, too," Smithson said. His voice was more confident now, so he must have passed his test, most of it.

"And who will monitor these vital bodily functions every hour of every day, Dr. Smithson?"

"I will, sir."

Great, if that was meant to make me feel more confident, it flopped.

"Very good. Now, let's proceed to our next patient." The loud voice and the tramping of many feet left the room.

All of that jibber jabber, and I hadn't learned a damned thing, except all of my systems were at risk. I should be dead, like I didn't know that already. I'd had a total body meltdown. Well, Dr. Dawson with the loud voice, that's what happens when a fireball hits you right in the face, but bad news about the pain meds and my kidneys. They should give me a vote. I say pile on the morphine and screw the kidneys.

With the room quieter, one of the memory links in my brain reconnected, and I remembered something; I remembered more about Linda, who she was and what she had told me. She had a big thing going about patients' rights to choose and that sort of thing. At the time, we'd been talking about my dad, and I remembered the sad little book she'd given me by some Russian writer about a man named Ivan Ilych and his misfortune. Ivan was angry because, in the midst of his illness—cancer, like my father—everyone talked about him, but no one talked to him. Now, thanks to the almighty Dr. Dawson, I'd just had a firsthand experience of that, and I was pissed off, too.

They would not treat me like a stuffed animal. They would listen to me or I would scream until they did.

****

"Who are you?" I asked after the third time the guy had asked me if I was awake.

"I'm Larry Barton. I'm a medical student on renal medicine."

"Don't touch me," I said. "If you do I'll scream.

48

Now go away. I have to pee."

"You have a catheter in your bladder, Ms. Sugarbush. Your urine drains right into the bag beside your bed."

"Who put a catheter in my bladder? Did you do that?"

"Oh, no, not me. They put it in while you were in the Emergency Room."

Oh, great, that must have been quite a sight, me splayed out like a roasted frog while somebody poked between my legs with a catheter. No more about that. The very thought made me want to throw up.

"Why are you here?" I asked. "There's already been somebody from renal medicine asking questions."

"That was probably Dr. Bascomb. He's the senior resident on the service."

"And there was another one. He sounded older." God, there must have been a line outside the door. Maybe Mom could set up a little table and sell tickets. *Step right up and win a chance to see the new freak.*

"Dr. Gates, he's the attending physician."

"Well, go talk to them. They'll tell you everything you want to know, and you won't have to bother me."

"But they want us to take our own medical history. It's part of our training."

"Go practice on somebody else. If you keep on bugging me I'll start screaming, and I'll tell the nurse you hurt me. Believe me, you don't want that to happen."

I had only two defense mechanisms, ignore them and hope they went away, or start screaming. Not much, but it's all I could do. And it wasn't just because the student was a nuisance that I wanted him to leave.

My pain was coming back.

There existed a fundamental disconnect in the way pain medication was delivered. Nurses insisted on giving out morphine by the clock, while I begged for it when my pain began raging.

And always, someone would ask that silly question: "Where do you hurt?" Silly because the answer was always "Everywhere." A better question would be "What doesn't hurt?" but no one ever asked that.

"Please," I begged.

"You're not due for another dose until four o'clock."

"How long is that?"

"About thirty minutes."

Not very long unless your body is on fire. Then thirty minutes is an eternity.

"Can't we cheat just a little bit? Move it up thirty minutes? I swear, I won't tell a soul."

"I'll be back at four."

If only there were some way to synchronize my body with the clock on the wall, but that never happened. Really, they didn't need to talk to me at all, just look at the clock, then push in the medication. Were they treating me or the clock? No answer to that one.

Up and down, up and down, that's the way my level of consciousness went. Only it had nothing to do with any sleep cycle like normal people have, like I used to have. Mine was all about my pain medication. Consciousness up, pain up, too. Consciousness down, like comatose, no pain. I'd guess it's the same way for everybody else on this burn unit, the finest in the southeast, according to Dr. Dawson.

****

"Good morning, how are you feeling?"

Great, another one, another guy, and he snuck up on me. Must have been wearing those soft shoes that didn't make any noise.

"It's morning?" I asked. Sounded like a stupid question, but how would I know? I lived in a cocoon.

"About ten. I'm Smitty."

"Dr. Smitty? That's a funny name."

"Dr. Smithson, but everybody calls me Smitty. I'm the senior resident on Dr. Dawson's team."

"What are you going to do to me?" Usually I didn't get a chance to ask. Sometimes right in my room, sometimes they would wheel me off to another area, but always, wherever it happened, it hurt like hell.

"Nothing right now, but later a little debridement, get rid of some off the dead tissue."

I knew that word, debridement, hacking away at whatever tissue got killed in the blast but was still attached to my body. I wondered what would be left after all the hacking. But I had other more immediate concerns. "Will you give me something for the pain? That's what scares me the most."

What should scare me most, I know, would be the parts he would be cutting away. Whatever he removed was gone forever. It would never grow back.

"Definitely," he said. "And I'll have more medication standing by if you need it. Just let me know."

"Oh, I'll let you know, all right. After you've finished, could you tell me what's going on? I mean, things just happen, and I don't know why or when or who or anything."

"For sure," he said.

So Smitty, at least, had a voice and could actually engage in conversation, unlike the other robots who came in, did their thing and left. And it was a kind voice. I pictured him as having a kind face as well. Whatever, I would never see it.

It must have been the larger dose of pain medication Smitty had promised that led me down into the darkness I was beginning to know so well. When I woke again, I don't know how much later, I called out his name, but Smitty was gone.

If you ever need a way to forget your troubles, I know something that works every time…pain, guaranteed. But it has to be big time pain, not just a minor annoyance and not something that will go away quickly. Big, enduring pain, that will clear your mind right out.

In a very short time my world had constricted, coalescing around that single entity; there was nothing else that really mattered. And the monster that was pain had more than one head. There was the all-pervasive pain of burned tissue where those nerve endings that weren't killed off by the blast became hypersensitive, firing off at the lightest touch, sending pain messages all over as if the burn itself were happening all over again. The only respite was the blessed numbness of the morphine injections.

Then there was the extra jolt delivered by the host of surgeons who preyed upon my wasted body. By the second week of my stay, two of the digits on my right hand had been amputated, leaving me with a functional thumb and two fingers. My left hand fared a little better but would remain stiff and immobile, resembling a claw. Handy for hanging from tree limbs, but little else.

The plastic surgeons had begun grafting my healthy skin—of which I had little—onto sites ruined by the blast. They spent a lot of time trying to repair my face. Fortunately I would never have to look at the results of that work. My poor mother would not be spared, however. She would get a daily reminder of the calamity that had befallen her daughter, all that time spent transforming me into a *beautiful young woman*, all blasted to hell, the new hairdo I wore for less than a day. From my perspective, all of the cutting and pasting the surgeons did was just another source of pain, and about as much good as a fresh coat of paint on a jalopy.

In between grafting came the frequent debridement sessions. Smitty, God bless him, made adjustments in my medications so that his digging about produced as little discomfort as possible.

"Have to be careful with your kidney function and the pain meds," he would say.

"Screw my kidneys," I'd say, and he'd laugh.

Most painful of all were the dressing changes in the Hubbard tank. Each day my arms, legs, and torso were wrapped in dry dressings that had been soaked in something that smelled like paint thinner, and each day I was taken to a hydrotherapy tank, transferred to a gurney suspended above warm water, and dunked. After a short soak, technicians began to peel off the dressings. This was when I screamed my loudest. No amount of medication could cover the feeling of having my skin pulled off in thin strips. My pleas to stop were always ignored.

"Just a little longer, dear. It's for your own good. It

will help the healing process."

That's all I ever got in return. So now I knew what hell was like, searing pain with no end in sight, and it was for my own good.

****

During the past year or so, including Dad's cancer, I'd learned more about hospitals and illness than I ever wanted to, but that's usually the way, isn't it? You don't get to choose. I learned, too, about the extraordinary kindness that some people extended when the crap hit the fan.

My main reference point would be Dr. Israel's nurse, Linda, who not only nursed my dad, but nursed our whole family, too, both in hospital and out.

One wintry afternoon after Dad's first discharge from the hospital, when sleet or snow seemed equally likely, Linda drove out to our house. Mom seemed just as surprised to see her as I was. If we were expecting visitors she'd have spent the entire morning cleaning, even though she'd done it just the day before. No matter, we both loved Linda, Dad did, too, so anytime she came by we were happy to see her.

"I didn't know how to reach you, so I decided just to come on out." She hugged Mom.

"I'm glad you did," I said, and that got me a hug and a kiss on the cheek.

Mom helped her with her heavy parka, which seemed like appropriate apparel from the look of the sky.

"I thought I'd check on Mr. Sugarbush, see how he's doing." She pulled her stethoscope from her purse.

Wow, a house call no less, and all the way from Norfolk. But Linda, as much as I loved her now, must have a secondary agenda. So I'd just wait to see what else was on her mind.

Mom led the way into Dad's room where he lay sleeping. A little plastic collar around his neck delivered supplemental oxygen to his trach tube. When Linda touched his arm, he opened his eyes and smiled. I had the crazy thought for a moment that maybe we could adopt her.

She sat in the chair we kept beside his bed for occasions such as this. For a moment she held his hand and didn't say anything. From the big smile on Dad's face, I'd have to say he was enjoying this visit.

Linda leaned in close and whispered into his ear. Dad nodded, and his smile grew wider.

I glanced at Mom. She arched her left eyebrow the way she does when she's about to light into me. I guess no woman likes to see another female whispering into her husband's ear, particularly when he seems so pleased about it.

Then Linda slipped back into her nurse mode and placed her stethoscope on Dad's chest. As she moved it from place to place he drifted off again.

"His chest doesn't sound too bad." Her voice was a soft whisper, and we had to lean in close to hear her. I don't know whether Dad was tuned in or not. "Not good, but not too bad either. He sleeps a lot, I guess?"

"Almost all the time," Mom said.

"And you look like you could use a good night's sleep yourself." Linda took Mom's hand.

"I catch catnaps during the day. I'm fine."

"Listen to me." Linda moved in close, her face not six inches from Mom's. "Short naps are not enough. You must take better care of yourself. This round-the-clock care, this is the worst kind of fatigue, and the sneakiest, too."

Mom stood there, all meek and accepting. Either she was overwhelmed by Linda, or just too damned tired to fight back.

"You have to make a care plan, soon. You have a fine young daughter here, and neighbors who can help out. If that's not enough I'll send a nurse out nights to sit with your husband."

"Okay." The last time anybody had mentioned a nurse staying over, Mom had jumped up and down, yelling, "No strangers in the house." Now she took the recommendation without even putting up a fight. Yeah, she was whipped.

A fine young daughter, Linda had said. A fat lot of good that did. Nice going, Daisy. Real smooth. Why the hell hadn't I picked up on this? Why did someone from outside have to tell me that my own mother was exhausted? Maybe when Mom passed out on the floor, then I might notice?

So, I wasn't feeling so good at the moment. Obviously I'd had my own head so far up my own ass that I couldn't see what was going on around me, like my own problems were the only ones that counted. Sure, I would miss my Dad, but Mom would miss her husband just as much; somehow I'd overlooked that.

Linda placed both hands on Mom's shoulders. "Why don't you take a little nap now? Daisy and I will be here with your husband if he needs anything."

"But you just got here," Mom said. "I was going to make coffee."

"Daisy and I can manage that."

Mom left without another word. I doubt that she

had any idea of how tired she was. For damned sure, I hadn't.

"Now," Linda said, looking at me. "Coffee. Let's go."

Things got a bit comical in the kitchen. Apparently, Linda thought coffee came automatically from a big urn on the medical ward, while I thought it came from Mom's pot, but didn't have any real idea of how it got there.

"How can an eighteen-year-old girl not know how to make coffee?" she asked.

"The same way a nurse can't. And you think this is bad, you should see me try to peel potatoes."

"So, if you plan to attract any gentleman callers, it probably won't be because of your culinary skills," she said, laughing.

"Probably not."

"What else have you got going for you?" she asked. "Besides the obvious." She looked at my boobs and grinned.

"For your information, I can do automotive repair, engine, transmissions and such. Light construction projects, plumbing, electrical. Mind you, I'm not licensed in plumbing or electrical work, but I can usually get the job done."

"Good heavens, where did you learn to do stuff like that? I don't know many men who can do all that." She looked doubtful, like she thought I was stretching things a bit.

"Working with my dad. He can...he could do almost anything."

"Okay." She put her arm around my shoulders. "I think I'm beginning to get the picture."

"When you do, maybe you'll explain it to me." As if I didn't already know. I'd been playing that game, Dad's little helper, for years now, pretending that it was a long-term solution, knowing all along that it wasn't.

We kept the door to Dad's room open wide and our voices low in case he needed attention.

"I think our coffee is ready," I said. "Wonder how it's going to taste. If it's really bad we have lots of cream and sugar."

"Whatever, it's bound to be better than hospital coffee." She looked at me, all serious like. "You're going to have a tough time with your mom."

News flash, I've been having a tough time with Mom for years now.

"I've seen this so many times before, she'll keep on until she collapses," Linda said.

"I feel pretty crappy about it. I haven't been much help to her." In fact, I felt like the stuff you wipe off the bottoms of your shoes after you've walked through a barnyard.

"Don't beat yourself up. It happens, that's all. Besides, you have your own grief to deal with."

Oh, yeah, grief, that other black cloud that follows you around at times like this. If it was just the extra work, my own and now Dad's, I think I could manage. Same for Mom. When it came to hard work she wouldn't bat an eye. But grief seemed to make everything twice as hard. Just knowing that, in the end, all of your efforts would come up short, it drained the spirit right out of you. Grief sucks, and it's a sneaky bastard, to boot.

While we sipped our coffee, Linda suggested we draw up a schedule for Dad's care, split between Mom and me. "It's a start," she said. "I doubt that your mom will stick to it, but at least it will show her you're serious about helping out."

"Worth a try," I said. "Are you hungry? We've got cookies, cakes, pies galore. As soon as Dad got back home the neighbors brought stuff over again. No way we can eat all of it."

"No, thanks, I had a big lunch. Um, what kind of pie?"

"Apple or pecan. Mrs. West, our neighbor next door, makes a killer pecan pie, and she brought one over yesterday."

"Maybe a little slice, then."

Between the two of us we made a sizeable dent in Mrs. West's pie. I expected Linda to leave then, after all, she had a full-time job. But she lingered, as if there was something else she wanted to say, but wasn't sure she should.

"I'm going to check on your dad," Linda said. "You stay. I'll only be a minute."

"Sleeping soundly," she said when she returned. She pushed the remaining crumbs around on her pie plate. "Have you ever talked with your dad about dying? I mean, would he have any special requests? I don't mean just the Advance Directive part but anything in particular he might want."

"Like what? I mean, if he had a choice he would go right on living, but that's not going to happen." And the Advance Directive bit had come up in the hospital before. It seemed like a pretty good idea to me, but Mom threw a fit, so that idea went straight into the toilet, flushed and done with.

"What I meant was that some patients prefer dying

at home with friends and family. Much more quiet and peaceful that way. Others might want the full court press, hospitalization, resuscitation, everything."

"I'm sure he never wants to go back to the hospital, but that's not up to me to decide."

"I know, I'm sorry. I'm putting you in an impossible situation."

"If Mom ever found out I talked with Dad about anything of the sort she would totally freak. And she would probably throw me out of the house. According to Mom, whatever happens is God's will, and you don't mess with God."

God difficult? How about impossible? How can you have a meaningful conversation about anything when somebody invokes the "God's will" clause? Mom didn't use it that often, but when she did it was her way of putting a lid on the discussion. Nothing more to be said.

"That's a tough one," Linda said. "I don't mean that it's wrong, just that it makes discussion really difficult. Can we move to the sofa? It looks a lot more comfortable than these chairs."

In the living room, Linda pulled a small pillow from the corner of the sofa and wrapped her arms around it, like a child might cling to a stuffed animal. Yeah, something was up, for sure. My friend had a bee in her bonnet, and my role, as I saw it, was to sit and listen.

"You remember when we went for a walk around the ICU, and you said those patients on ventilators really got to you, like, would they want to live like that if they really had a choice?"

"Yeah." I didn't want to remember, but it was hard

to forget. Maybe my comparison to the victims in *Coma* was a little extreme, but it still stuck with me. Linda had turned a little pale when I suggested it.

"Well, they get to me, too, have for years. I see them lying there day after day, clueless about anything that goes on around them, while we keep hearts and lungs going with machines. I watch their families and loved ones come and go, how they sit there for a few minutes, say 'I love you,' then get away as fast as they can.

"Because it's a terrible thing when a couple of machines are all that keeps you alive. And the time when that could have been avoided seems long past. It's like the only control is in the hospital, the people who run the machines, and they won't stop. It's not their job to stop. Their job is to treat. I include myself in this, of course."

By now tears had formed in the corners of Linda's eyes, then, right on schedule, they tumbled down her cheeks. But if she even noticed, she paid them no mind. I slipped in close beside her and put my arm around her shoulders.

I didn't know if maybe she would push me away. I mean, officially I was still a kid, eighteen, and she was a real adult, twenty-six with a real job. And if you cry with someone, I mean really let go like you're going to throw up but somehow don't, there has to be an element of trust there, if not before, afterward for sure. And an obligation, too.

It would make sense if it were the other way around, me blubbering and Linda comforting, but somehow things had gotten mixed up.

I had no idea what kind of bombshell she might

drop on me next, something to do with that freedom to choose kick she was on, most likely. But I wasn't sure I was ready for that. Not like Planet Sugarbush was floating in a smooth orbit just now.

Linda took a deep breath, and I thought whatever she was trying to convince me of was about to be pushed into my face. I tensed, waiting for her outburst of unclear origin to occur. Instead she stared straight ahead as if collecting her thoughts.

"No," she said. "This is wrong. I shouldn't be dumping my problems on you."

"What problems?"

"This morning at the hospital I had a sizeable chunk of my backside bitten off. I was just talking to a patient, a young woman with metastatic breast cancer, about her options, how the final decisions were up to her. Must have been a family member who overheard me, then she told the charge nurse, the charge nurse told the attending physician. Next thing I knew I was standing in the nursing supervisor's office, and she was asking me for one good reason why she shouldn't fire me on the spot."

"But she didn't, I mean, you're still working for Dr. Israel, right?"

"So far as I know. Dr. Israel went to bat for me with the nursing supervisor, but it cost him. If the other attending physicians get pissed off at him because of me, he's in just as much trouble as I am."

I went back into hugging mode. What else could I do? Offer her another slice of pecan pie? Anyway, the very idea that doctors and nurses got into fights just like everyone else shocked me. I'd always pictured them as far above all the petty bickering that everybody else got into, but from what Linda had just told me that medical pedestal wasn't so puncture-proof as I'd thought. And to think, not too long ago, I used to wonder if nurses even had to go to the bathroom like regular people. "This will all blow over before you know it, and things will be back to the way they were," I said.

"I don't think so. This wasn't the first time I've been caught. Same thing happened last year. I got off with a warning then. This time, I don't know," she said.

"It will work out, you'll see."

"I'm sorry for dumping all of this on you. I had to get out of the hospital and find a friendly face, and I do consider you a friend."

"You got that right," I said. She'd come to me for companionship like I'd gone to Ralph at Sparky's. Only I had no weed or beer to offer her, and I really think it would have helped.

"I brought you something." She fumbled in her purse.

Outstanding. I loved getting presents. Instead of baked goods, some of the neighbors had brought candy, just fine by me. Mom wouldn't eat it, neither would Dad. Max would eat anything, but he couldn't have chocolate. So that left me to show the family's appreciation by eating all of it. I always did my best.

"Here it is." She handed me a book, a thin one but still a book. A book with death in the title, *The Death of Ivan Ilych*. What fun. If this was supposed to cheer me up, she'd missed the mark by a mile.

"Oh, wow, thanks." I hope I sounded more enthusiastic than I felt.

"It's my own copy, so it's all marked up. It's about a guy with terminal cancer, and how his family and friends isolate him by talking over him, around him, but never telling him the truth. But he knows exactly what's going on."

She thumbed through several pages until she reached a section highlighted in yellow marker.

"Here, even if you don't read anything else, read this part. Then maybe I won't sound so crazy."

"I never thought you were crazy," I said. "I just never felt as strongly about this choice thing as you do."

"Please, read the section I showed you. Who knows, you might change your mind about a few things," she said.

At that moment Mom staggered out of her bedroom looking a bit wild. Her hair stood out in all directions, and this was a woman who wouldn't even walk out to the mailbox without a quick brush job. "What happened?" she asked, eyes wide.

"Your husband is as fine as could be expected of anyone suffering from terminal lung cancer," Linda said not unkindly, but still, she'd used the dreaded C-word right out in the open, something I was still afraid to do. "We've been watching him. I hope you had a good nap. You needed one."

Mom still looked a bit bewildered, but apparently some of the lights in her brain were going back on. She hurried into Dad's room and emerged a few minutes later. "He looks good," she said. "What have you two been up to?"

"Mostly Mrs. West's pecan pie," I said. "And some girl talk."

"I should be getting back to the hospital." Linda went to the closet for her coat.

"You come back any time," Mom said. "We love seeing you."

I followed Linda to the door. "Good luck."

"I'll need it. Hospitals are small communities, and if you get labeled a troublemaker in one, it spreads all around quickly. Then I'll be looking for a new job, far, far away."

"Dr. Israel won't let that happen. I doubt he could get along without you. We can't either."

"I should try to follow the advice a friend gave me after my first fiasco. 'Keep your head down and your mouth shut,' " she said.

"But you didn't."

"No, I didn't, and I'll bet you won't either."

****

That night the wind picked up, thrashing the branches of the oak beside the house against the window. Dad had talked about taking that tree down before it crashed into the living room, but somehow we'd never gotten around to it. Now he never would. Another nasty trick that terminal illness played, all of your plans turned into wet tissue paper, unreadable and worthless.

I sat beside a lamp in the corner where I could keep one eye on my father and one eye on Linda's book. I kept it hidden in an old copy of *Popular Mechanics*, so Mom couldn't see it. If she saw anything about death in the title she would explode for sure.

Honestly, I didn't get too far into the book before I started nodding off. It just didn't hold my attention. Poor old Ivan Ilych couldn't catch a break, and while I felt bad for him, enough dying was already going on in our house. I didn't need to read about it, too.

I sat on the book and leafed through the pages of my magazine. Dad had kept up a subscription for as long as I could remember, and when his copy arrived in the mail he was not to be disturbed for the next hour or so. Now thumbing through one of his old copies, one that he would have gone through so carefully, made me feel closer to him, much more so than reading about poor Ivan Ilych ever could.

After I got torched I had lots of time to think, since I couldn't do anything else, and I thought back on those rather curious times with Linda when I emerged from my morphine coma. My own situation seemed so different from how Dad's had been. As he lay there struggling for every breath, did he want things over and done with? I would never know. For myself, however, things became more clear every day. Living the way I was wasn't living at all.

Chapter 4

Mom didn't visit me in the hospital every day. Just as well, since my days were so full of cutting, soaking and skin grafting that I hardly had time to entertain guests. Even when she showed up things were awkward at best. Lots of tears—hers. Neither of us knew exactly what to say. If I heard, "Oh, my poor Daisy," one more time my head would explode.

But I guess those little encounters were just as difficult for her as they were for me, maybe even tougher, because she could see me, see the roasted carcass of her daughter. I could only guess what a god-awful sight I must be, but I would never know for sure. Maybe this was God's idea of an act of kindness, blinding me to spare me looking at my own gruesome face.

And the saddest part, we had come so close, hadn't we, Mom, to transforming me into a suitable daughter? New clothes for me, new hair, new nails. Finally, after all those years, a daughter you could go shopping with, walk down the streets of Warrensburg arm-in-arm with. A daughter the neighbors would admire and tell you how great your kid looked, or maybe, as you said, what a lovely young woman I'd become. And the calls from guys, not just to fix their lawnmower, but for real dress up and go out dates. Wow, imagine that. And maybe, somewhere in the future, I might deliver up a little bundle of joy for you to cuddle and spoil. Sorry, Mom, I blew it again.

I'll bet you even held onto hope that I might accompany you to church. Of course, that would require a new church dress, not that clingy blue number that would make Preacher Daugherty's jaw drop. Something more frilly that made the swishing noise yours made when you walked. Maybe even a bit of that lavender scent you wear to top it off.

Mother and daughter arriving together, taking their seats side by side. I could have done that for you. God knows, I have done little else to give you pleasure. Yes, things could have been so different, except they weren't, and now never would be. All blown to hell in the time it takes to strike a match.

Even those days when Mom didn't come into my hospital room, she came and stood by the door, watching me. I could hear her weeping, the most heartbreaking sound in the world, a mother trying to hide her tears.

"Your mom is the saddest looking woman I've ever seen," raspy-voiced nurse said. "I know you got it tough, but it ain't easy for her either."

It's easy to think of my own pain as something confined to me, to my own body and nothing else, but that's not the way it works. Pain ripples out so those close to you, friends and family, get a taste, too. Mom got more than a taste. She got the full course. As I see it, better for her if I'd never been born.

When I thought about it, I started messing things up for her before I had even arrived. I wouldn't have ever known about the Julliard thing if my ninth grade homeroom teacher, Mr. Gleason, who also taught science and civics, hadn't mentioned it. He also directed the Warrensburg High School Glee Club.

"Why don't you join our glee club, Daisy?" he asked one afternoon.

"Are you kidding? I'm about as musical as a fence post."

"I find that hard to believe, considering your mother's talent."

"Yeah, she plays the piano sometimes. Not very often, though." The family piano, an old upright, sat alone in the front room, which would have been called a parlor if houses still had parlors. It was there because we had no other place to put it. The only other possibility was the basement, but it would have been impossible to get it down the narrow staircase.

Anyway, Mr. Gleason gave me that look, with his eyebrows raised like I'd just tracked mud across the classroom floor.

"Your mother was once considered a major talent. She had a full scholarship to the Julliard. If she had taken it she might very well be performing in concert halls now."

Whoa, were we talking about the same person? I knew Mom played the piano for church services, but only as a substitute when the regular lady was out. And what was this Julliard he was talking about? Never heard of it.

That afternoon I found our neighbor, Mrs. West out weeding her garden. Having her knees wedged into fresh dirt didn't seem to bother her one bit, one of many things I liked about her.

"If I could grow tomatoes as well as I grow weeds I could go into business," she said. "And bugs, too. I've never seen such a bad year for beetles. They don't bother the tomatoes so much, but they've ruined my bean crop."

"Mrs. West, when you taught at Warrensburg, Mom was one of your students, wasn't she?"

"Indeed, she was. An excellent student. I only wish there had been more like her. Maybe I wouldn't have taken early retirement."

"How about music?"

"A shining star. We had a baby grand piano in the music room back then, but the fire destroyed it along with every instrument we had."

"I didn't know about the fire."

"Some students—not your mother—used to smoke in the small room where we stored the band instruments. We think that's how the fire got started. Lost everything, including that beautiful piano.

"But you were asking about your mother. She never got what you could call first rate instruction. Old Ms. Foreman—she died just last year—taught her all she could, but that was just the basics. The rest of it your mother picked up on her own. And, let me tell you, she was something. She was winning state competitions by her freshman year, and just kept getting better and better."

"Mr. Gleason said something about a Julliard."

"Oh yes, that was big news around here. The Julliard is a famous school for performing arts in New York, very competitive." She said the word slowly like she was talking in capital letters.

"If you're lucky enough to get there, your ticket is punched. You might wind up almost anywhere. When your mother was offered a full scholarship, it made all the papers. Nothing that big had ever happened around here."

"But she didn't go. Why not?"

"Life has little twists and turns, and sometimes our plans change."

"I don't understand. Why did she pass up the scholarship?"

Mrs. West suddenly got very interested in the beetles on a tomato plant. "You came along."

Yeah, Daisy, the daughter from hell. There must have been something in my life that I didn't screw up, but I couldn't think of one. Now I could add Mom's Julliard scholarship to the list. The hits just keep on coming.

It didn't take a rocket scientist to see that the solution to Mom's pain and mine, too, would be solved if I wasn't around any longer. I couldn't very well go back and fix all that I had already messed up, but if I had died in the blast neither of us would have to go through the horror that our lives had become, because of me. It was a little late in the game now, but if you can solve a problem by removing one piece, like taking a rotten apple out of a barrel, why not do it?

Maybe things were rough for Linda to handle, too. I know she had come by that first day, and even after all the time we'd spent together during Dad's illness, I didn't even recognize her then. I didn't know anybody then.

"Sorry it's been so long." The nurse had just taken my lunch tray away. They had to feed me, spoonful by spoonful. "Things have been crazy busy."

"No problem. I'm glad you're here."

Linda sighed, a deep gulping sound like she'd

swallowed something that got stuck halfway down.

"That was a damned lie," she said. "I could have made time if you were just another patient, but you're not. You're my friend. I've been to your home. And, God forgive me, I just couldn't handle seeing you like this."

She must have given up trying to hold back, because it came out a gusher. I could feel her tears as they dropped on the dressing covering my arm. At this rate I figured she might throw up on me, too, but she didn't.

"That first day when I saw you, I went home and drank all the wine in the apartment. I swore, I cursed God and everybody else I could think of. It didn't help you at all, and it gave me a bitch of a hangover.

"So, when the shit hit the fan, I let you down. I deserted you. Some friend…."

"You are my friend," I said. "No, wait, don't hug me. My skin is unbelievably sensitive. I can't bear to be touched."

"That sucks," Linda said.

"Yeah, for the time being, I'm living in a bubble."

"Have they given you any idea of when things should start to improve?

"I don't know much about anything. It's my own fault for not asking more questions, but nobody has time for me, nobody but Smitty."

"Who's Smitty?"

"He's one of the surgeons working under Dr. Dawson. He's the only one who takes time to explain things. Trouble is, while he's explaining, he's usually cutting away parts of me. Dead tissue, he says, and I must have a hell of a lot of it from the time he spends."

"And all of these procedures, do they ask your permission before they do them?"

"No way. They just do it. Smitty says Dr. Dawson talks to my mom, so I guess she gives him the go ahead."

"Still, they ought to include you in the discussion. It's your body. You remember, we talked about this before when your dad was in the ICU."

I don't think I'd ever heard of Advance Directives before Dr. Israel brought it up the first time Dad was admitted to the hospital. Of course, Linda gave me an earful during the next couple of weeks. What I understood, thanks to Linda, was that an Advance Directive was a document, nothing more,and like all documents, it could be ignored.

"One more thing," he'd said to mom during Dad's first admission. "Does your husband have an Advance Directive?"

Mom was still a bit out of it then, so a new communication path had been activated—Dr. Israel to Mom, then Mom to me, then me back to Dr. Israel. "I'm pretty sure he doesn't, unless you know about one, Mom?"

She shook her head, and obviously Dr. Israel had some explaining to do.

"It's a document that spells out which treatments Mr. Sugarbush would want us to use if things don't go well, and, just as importantly, what he wouldn't want. The Advance Directive helps us honor his wishes, that's about it. We advise everyone to complete one."

"Do you have one?" I asked. I guess that sounded a bit impertinent, but I wanted to know if he was just blowing smoke.

"Oh, yes. So does my entire family."

"But you're healthy," I said.

"And that's the best time to make decisions like this, something else for you to think about.

We didn't discuss it any further until Dad was readmitted. I wasn't sure whether Mom might have simply forgotten about it, so I brought it up myself during one of Linda's visits to his room.

"Linda, when we were here before, Dr. Israel mentioned an Advance Directive. He seemed to think it was important," I said.

"Daisy." Mom snapped at me. "What on earth are you talking about? Your father is sick, but he isn't dying, and I don't want to hear another word about any directives. What happens here is God's will, and it doesn't have anything to do with directives."

"I agree that this is not the time for such discussions," Linda said. "I'll bring the forms by for you, and you can talk it over when you get home."

"Don't bother," Mom said. "We aren't interested."

Linda patted my hand, then left. I think she rolled her eyes just a bit, like she'd heard this one before.

So Mom hadn't forgotten after all. She'd thought about it, for damned sure, and made sure that it wasn't up for further discussion. Not much I could do, though, since I was only a junior partner. Maybe Mom and Dad had agreed that this conspiracy of silence was the best way to proceed. Not my first choice, but I wasn't calling the shots.

The closest Dad and I ever came to a conversation about the inevitable end was one afternoon when he said, "You take care of your mother."

"Sure, Dad, I will." I held his hand and waited for

him to continue, but that was all he said.

During Dad's illness death was sort of like a silent partner. It hung in the rooms of our house like a black mist, but was never mentioned, let alone discussed.

But Linda, God bless her, wasn't going to let go so easily. I had just returned from a stroll around the ICU, and I guess I looked a little green around the gills.

"Are you feeling all right?" she asked me.

"It's this ICU. I've never seen people so sick. I didn't know someone could look that sick and still be alive. My own father, as bad off as he is, isn't the worst, not by a long shot. This is a terrible place."

"Yeah, sometimes it seems that way to me, too. You know, a few years back, my situation was a lot like yours. My first year in nursing school I lost my dad. He had lung cancer, only his was one of the fast growing types. Only three weeks."

"Ouch. You didn't have much time at all," I said.

"No, and even worse, he never knew what was going on. My mother was very clear about that, under no circumstances was I to tell him anything about his illness. Things got pretty heated back then. Mom threatened to disown me if I said anything. She made it clear that the rest of the family would have nothing to do with me.

"And keeping things quiet seemed to be hospital policy, too. Somewhere during one of those conversations, I don't know yet who might have said it, there was a hint that I might get thrown out of nursing school if I didn't keep my mouth shut."

"They can do that?" I asked.

"Maybe, I don't know for sure. But if it happened I'd be out on the street without a friend in the world."

"Wouldn't be worth it," I said. "Losing your job, your family, that's too much to risk."

"Yeah, but I've regretted it ever since, because I've seen it happen over and over again. You remember what Dr. Israel said before about how people have a legal right to choose what therapies they're comfortable with and which ones they don't want to have anything to do with? But first they should know they have options and what those options are, and that's the problem."

Linda's pager buzzed, and she pulled it out of her pocket. "Oh, crap, it's Dr. Israel. I'd better run, but I want to talk to you some more about this." She patted my shoulder and was gone.

I loved this girl dearly, but I was relieved when she left the room. Linda clearly had a bug up her butt about this choices thing, but her enthusiasm was something I did not share. Let sleeping dogs lie, that's the motto I got from my dad, and I saw no reason to change it. Besides, Mom would jump right down my throat if I even tried.

As I strolled back to Dad's room I looked in again on the poor folks and their respirators. Whatever you want to call it, this didn't look like living to me. As a girl who spent her time doing odd jobs with her father, it was all way over my head anyway. So, as Dad taught me, best let those sleeping dogs lie, not much else they could do anyway.

I had never given dying much thought, and all of a sudden it was getting more complicated than I'd ever imagined. It happens, I guess, when something like cancer comes in and plops its big fat ass right in the middle of your family. One thing, though, for damned sure, when my time came, no way was I going to be hooked up to one of those bloody machines.

But now my time had come, right? Courtesy of the Johnson's furnace. One lit match and I was blasted, not really into eternity, but close enough. I could no longer dismiss the idea of choices, not unless I was ready to place my present and my future in the hands of others, which I definitely was not. This wasn't about mucking around with my dad's life or his choices, and it didn't have a damned thing to do with God's will, no matter what my mother said. This was about me and my decisions. Okay, Daisy, how do you want this to play out? Time to step up, girl.

I'd just spent another awkward visit with my mom. She brought along our neighbor this time. There was that little gasp when Mrs. West walked into the room, but I'm used to that now. Few people have seen anything quite like me, and it's a bit of a shock at first. But Mrs. West was good people. She had a ton of good will built up over the years, so she could gasp if she had to. No problem. It was nice to know that Mom had friends like her to lean on. God knows she needed them.

Soon after they left, Linda dropped by.

"I ran into your mom in the hallway," she said. "She's looking a little frayed around the edges."

"I'm not surprised. She's had her butt kicked all over the place for the past couple of years. She could use a break."

"Poor woman, I don't know how she keeps it all together."

I could think of one way to lighten her load. If she didn't have to look forward to waiting on me hand and foot, things would be better for sure, and not having to look at my hideous face day after day. She deserved better, and for all I knew, she was thinking the same thing.

"Daisy, are you all right? You drifted away there."

"Just thinking," I said. "The surgeons can graft and debride and amputate until hell freezes over, and they're not going to make me any better than I am. They can't fix me."

"It's a tough situation for sure," Linda said.

From the way she spoke it sounded like she was just saying something to fill in the space, before I said something she didn't want to hear.

"So, the best I can hope for is being blind, crippled and ugly as sin. What's the point?"

Some deep sighs coming from Linda's direction. How I wish I could see her face, her reaction.

"Daisy, I know where you're going with this, and all I can say is please, don't. Let's at least talk about it."

"Am I wrong? I should have a choice. You said so yourself."

This time the quick exiting footsteps were Linda's. It was a crappy thing I'd just done, throwing her own words back at her like that. But I'd suspected all along, talking about things was different from putting them into practice. Filling in the blanks on an Advance Directive was one thing, making it happen was very different. That was one of the things I loved about working with Dad, he never talked much about things he was going to do, he just did them.

Talk didn't accomplish much, but I would owe Linda a huge apology. I didn't have many friends as it was, and if I crapped all over the few I had, I wouldn't have any left at all.

****

Dialysis. I learned a new word, and I didn't like it one bit. Not long after Linda left, another medical team came into my room. I now divided people into familiar or unfamiliar based on whether I recognized their footsteps. I didn't recognize these, not until they introduced themselves.

"Good afternoon, Ms. Sugarbush. I'm Dr. Gates, renal medicine. Dr. Dawson has asked us to follow your course in the hospital. It appears you sustained some damage to your kidneys as a result of your burns, and it's getting worse."

I vaguely remembered Dr. Gates from an earlier visit, but I guess he thought I was too out of it to remember meeting him.

"My kidneys got burned?" I asked. That seemed a little far-fetched, but he was the expert. Nobody had really told me much about the kidney damage except that it limited how far they could push the pain medications. The pain meds made my blood pressure drop, which made my kidneys unhappy, like I really cared. I wasn't having kidney pain; I was having total body pain. Let the damned kidneys fend for themselves.

"No, nothing like that. In severe burns like yours a lot of cellular debris winds up in the bloodstream, and some of it winds up in your kidneys. Your kidney function was impaired soon after you got into the hospital, and it's worse now than then. So much worse, in fact, that we should so something about it."

What next? I had no idea what was coming. Chalk up another part of me that was now damaged goods. I doubt I could sell my entire body for ten bucks.

"What I'm proposing is a short-term course of

dialysis to take over the function of your kidneys while they have a chance to heal. We'll do the dialysis right here in your room with a machine that we bring right to your bedside. We purify your blood just like your own kidneys would by running it through the machine where it is filtered, then returned to you. The procedure takes about two hours. Do you have any questions?"

"Does my mom know about this?"

"Dr. Dawson and I discussed it, and I believe he has discussed it with your mother. We'll bring the dialysis machine to your room tomorrow morning, and we should be through by lunchtime. We'll repeat it two to three times a week, until we get a better idea of how your kidneys will respond."

Would it make me beautiful again? I almost asked that, you know, like a joke, but I didn't. This kidney business must be serious stuff. But Mom should have told me about it. It's my body, after all. Yeah, it should be my choice, or so I thought. For certain, Linda would have agreed with me, but I'm thinking that, if she tried to stand up to the big medical machine it would grind her into hamburger, sort of like it was doing to me.

Still, I wondered, what if we did nothing, just let the kidneys work it out for themselves, and if they weren't up to the job just let nature take its course. Maybe that's one way of thinking about God's will, but I doubt Mom would agree.

The dialysis group came in and set up shop the next morning. I'd expected a lot of banging and clanging, a lot more drama, but the dialysis process seemed sort of low key. Best of all, it didn't hurt. They used my existing IV lines, so I didn't even have to get stuck again. My job? Just lie back and let it happen.

The dialysis technicians seemed nice enough, Lucy and Carla, I think their names were. Except for a few people like Linda and Smitty, I didn't try to remember names any more, because they changed so frequently. As soon as you got to know Jane, she would be replaced by Alice, and so on. Of course, nametags didn't help at all. I couldn't see them.

I didn't even know Mom was in the room until she said, "Can I talk to my daughter?"

"Oh, sure," Lucy or Carla, whichever.

I was still a little pissed, because she'd let loose the dialysis team on me with no warning. So I gave her the silent treatment. Nothing major, just a few moments so she'd know I wasn't happy. But I caved in when she spoke in a voice that sounded so fatigued that it was heartbreaking. Meanwhile the dialysis folks carried on undeterred.

"You sound tired, Mom. Are you getting any rest at all?" It was a stupid question. I knew well enough she'd keep right on going until she dropped, just like when she was caring for Dad.

A whirring noise at the bedside. "We're starting up now," one of the dialysis techs said. "You won't feel a thing." A little buzzing from the machine, a little chit chat from the technicians, and that was about all.

I finally talked Mom into going back home. "And stay home until you've rested, you hear me?"

I've never heard her sound so tired before. Her speech slurred, and she seemed to fumble for words, like a drunk, but Mom never drank. Even as she left the room, she dragged her feet, something she would never have done before. I could picture her slumped over like an old lady. Something had to give, or what little remained of the Sugarbush family would fly off the hinges. Mom couldn't do it, so I would have to step up. How and what, I had no idea. No, that wasn't true, I knew exactly what to do. And sooner or later I'd figure out how.

****

Christmas Carols. They woke me up, and left me disoriented. I'd lost track of things like holidays and such. From what I'd learned so far, if you stayed in hospital long enough you could lose track of time completely, maybe permanently. One day ran into the next, all the same.

"Administrators." It was raspy-voiced nurse again. "They do this every year, and, between you and me, they never get any better. They could use some practice, but since they only do it once a year that probably won't happen. I guess it's the thought that counts."

Yeah, the thought would count. And my thought was to go right back to sleep.

But it was a short nap.

"Good morning, Daisy. Merry Christmas." It was Smitty's voice, much more cheerful than usual. "I brought you a present. I didn't wrap it because I figured you would never get the wrapping off."

"It feels fuzzy. What is it?"

"It's a little black dog. I ran him through the sterilization unit before I brought him up, so he's noninfectious."

"You zapped him? He needs a name, I suppose. Maybe I'll call him Dr. Dawson."

"Oh, ho, be careful with that. Don't want to get on the boss's wrong side."

"It's just a little joke, and if he can't take a joke then too bad for him."

'Is your mom coming up today?"

"I told her to stay home. She's really stressed out. Some rest will do her good."

"Anything else you want for Christmas?"

"Oh, yeah, lots of things. I want my hair back, a new face, some new fingers, new eyes, things like that. And I want my own bottle of morphine, a big pint bottle that I can use whenever I want it."

"Good luck with that."

"You must have a box of spare parts somewhere, you know, old fingers that nobody wants, maybe a nose. I really would like a new nose."

"I gotta go," he said. "I'll check around the department, see if there are any spare parts lying around. But don't get your hopes up."

"Wait, I have one more question. All these treatments, has anybody ever stopped them, just let nature take its course?"

"I don't know what you're asking," he said.

Of course, Smitty knew exactly what I meant. No doubt he'd heard the same request from other patients. But quitting was not part of the equation around here. The Burn Trauma bunch apparently didn't know the meaning of the word. Once the train left the station it would not stop, and the patients on the unit, including me, were just along for the ride.

****

After spending all of my eighteen Christmas holidays at our home in Warrensburg, I had come to expect that they would always be the same, all the sights, sounds, smells, tastes, everything. All of these sensory impressions rolled into one spelled Christmas. All gone now. All replaced with new sensations. The usual smell now was that given off by a topical disinfectant called betadine, not so pungent as Clorox, but so pervasive that it didn't have to be.

Of course, the dominant aroma was that of burned flesh, which smelled not unlike bacon. Living in it, as I now did, I hardly noticed it. Only when I left the unit for my hydrotherapy sessions where the chlorine smell in the Hubbard tank was a bit like our neighborhood swimming pool, did I notice the change when they brought me back. Yep, bacon. Max might love it, me, not so much. Part of that burned flesh was my own.

December twenty-fifth, day ten on Burn Trauma. I asked one of the nurses about the average stay there.

"Oh, weeks, months sometimes."

"Months? Oh, my God. How about for somebody like me? Have you ever had anybody as bad as me?"

"A few," she said.

"What happened to them?"

"A couple of them didn't make it. You have to remember that people burned as bad as you, most don't survive. Dr. Dawson has made a big difference in the survival statistics. You're lucky, you know."

If only I'd been a little bit luckier I wouldn't be here at all.

"The survivors, what happens to them?" I asked.

"I only know for sure about one. A girl, a few years younger than you. Her parents had to put her in a skilled nursing facility. They couldn't manage her at home."

Home, now there's something that really didn't fit into my plans. Going home would amount to your basic lose-lose situation. I'd be of no use at all to Mom, just something else she'd have to feed and water and clean up after. At least Max could go outside to do his business, and he could drink out of his water dish whenever he wanted. I couldn't even do that. Just another stone around her neck, that's all I would be.

And it wouldn't be much better for me. What, parties, dates, driving around town with my friends? Like hell. No, I knew the answer. What I lacked was the method. And the person I could always go to for advice about almost anything—Dad—wouldn't be there to help with this one. Stuff that was beyond repair we always carted out to the county dump, but there's probably some law against disposing of burned bodies that way.

The arrival of lunch trays wafted in from the hallway. No matter what might be listed on the menu, which someone had to read to me, it always smelled the same. Meal time wasn't exactly a bright spot for me, because, in addition to the unappealing grub, I still needed help feeding myself.

Mom to the rescue; might as well get used to it. "I thought you were going to stay home today, get some rest," I said.

"I couldn't very well let you spend Christmas Day by yourself. I didn't get to do much shopping for presents this year," she said.

"Guess I won't be getting that new bicycle, huh?"

"No, no bicycle," she said. At least that got a little chuckle.

"I asked one of the surgeons for a new nose, and he said he would look around."

"A new nose? Are you serious?"

"No, Mom, that was a joke. Things get a little weird in here."

"Ah, lunch, I got here just in time," she said. "Looks pretty good."

"Help yourself."

"No, you have to eat, Daisy. Keep your strength up. Now, open wide."

"Tell me what it is first."

"It's some kind of meat. I'm not sure…"

We hadn't shared a laugh in many days. Thank God for small favors. But the laughing triggered the coughing which triggered the pain. Some days you can't catch a break.

Chapter 5

We charged into 1994, full speed ahead, dialyzing, a little more skin grafting, and, of course, dunking me in the Hubbard tank, and I still screamed, and they still ignored me, but maybe, just maybe the pain was a little less than before. Not so much with the debrideing now. I guess Smitty had run out of dead tissue to trim off, or maybe he'd just written it off as so much wasted effort. How much of me remained? I didn't want to know. Still, he came by for little visits. It was clear he wasn't about to give away any trade secrets about how long this madness might continue. The end was not in sight. Maybe there wasn't an end at all.

Dr. Israel came to see me, and I must say I enjoyed his visits most. Linda was with him, but she didn't say much. I guess the things she and I had to discuss were best kept between us.

"No doubt, there was inhalation lung damage at the time of the blast," he said in his soft voice.

"You mean, if I'd kept my mouth shut my lungs might be okay?"

"You had no control over that. I'm sure there's a lot of scarring of your lungs. Eventually, when your acute care period is over I can do some pulmonary function tests to see what kind of residual you have."

Years before we got the Ford F-150 truck we still have, Dad drove an old clunker that Mom always referred to as "that piece of junk." On those occasions when she needed transportation—to church on rainy days or to the grocery store—her complaints grew even more vigorous. "The shame of it all," she'd say. "Like we can't afford anything better."

Thing was, Dad loved that old truck. Its frequent breakdowns seemed to make him love it all the more. Popping up the hood and tinkering with the engine was his idea of a good day, a feeling I shared with him. As a concession to Mom he offered to paint it, any color she chose.

"Paint all you want, it's still a piece of junk," she said.

That sums up all of the things they were doing to me now. They could put on as many fresh coats of paint as they wanted, but my body would still be a piece of junk, not something you'd want to be seen with in public.

In spite of what seemed to me to be a futile attempt, Dr Israel was doing the best job he could, and I appreciated his efforts. I only wish I could have given him more to work with. You can't do much with a piece of junk.

The dialysis team apparently decided they'd given it their best shot, so, around the end of January, they thought they'd let my kidneys fly solo for a while. Dr. Gates came by to give me an update. From the bustling noises that followed him in there were others in attendance, but I didn't know who they might be. Some of them just curiosity seekers, wanting to get a look at the burned freak. When the attending physicians came around with their entire group, they spoke as if they were giving a lecture. They'd make out like they were talking to me, but I was just the body in the bed, could have been anyone.

"When the body sustains great trauma, as yours has, there's a lot of cell breakdown product that eventually makes its way to the kidneys," Dr. Gates said. "This is a crude way of putting it, but the kidneys become sort of a toxic waste dump. Once the debris is settled in there is no way to get it out, and the damage is done.

"The course of dialysis helped somewhat, but not as much as we'd hoped, so your renal function will always be precarious. You'll need to be very careful with your fluid intake and avoid dehydration. I'll share all this information with Dr. Dawson and his team."

So, bad lungs, bad kidneys, ruined body, what else? If I still thought of myself as a truck, Dad would say my engine was shot, and my transmission was on its last legs. And the body? Hopeless. Time for a new model. Or, at least, time to get rid of the old one.

****

Late February, two days after Presidents' Day, brought snowfall to our area. Four to six inches of wet, heavy snow that left Mom high and dry in Warrensburg for three days. Even with the inconvenience, snow was an event. The Burn Trauma staff seemed excited, running from window to window to watch the flakes drifting down. The entire affair turned into a slushy nuisance by the second day. Nurses complained about having their kids home from school during the day. I couldn't quite figure that out, because, on the few snow days I remember, we kids went inside for meals, but little else. There were snowballs to throw and snow forts to build, and Max loved playing in the snow. He was an absolute champ at catching tossed snowballs, but I doubt that his arthritic hips would tolerate much of that now. No problem, I guess my snowball tossing days are over.

Mom was finally out and about by Thursday, but only because my pal, Ralph from Sparky's came over and shoveled the driveway. Yeah, the same Ralph who got into my pants back in the storeroom the week before I got burned.

I'd gotten into a funk thinking about Dad and how much I missed him, and none of my usual remedies made it any better. Of course, I had more options before I got burned and chained to a bed. Back when I was up and about my best bet was staying busy. There's something to be said for keeping busy, or trying. Routine activity was best because I didn't have to think, just do whatever I was doing it the same way I always did it.

Thinking invariably led back to that bad place. Once there, I was boxed in again, I could either sit down and bawl, or curse God for taking a sweet, gentle man like my father and beating the crap out of him, finally taking him away from us forever. What had he ever done to deserve such treatment? For that matter, what had *we*?

Neither of those two alternatives, crying or cursing, accomplished very much. Busy, busy, busy, that was the only way to get through the day, but that escape route, like many others, was closed to me now.

Before my big burn, when I could come and go much as I pleased, there was an even better alternative. Several times a week, late afternoon, when the crowd at Sparky's had cleared out, I used to drop by for a chat with Ralph, the manager and one of my best friends. What I liked most about Ralph was, he was never judgmental. Life was a little bumpy at the Sugarbush house back then, wondering whether every breath my dad drew would be his last. Poor Mom was trying so hard to keep the family ship afloat, and I needed a friendly ear, without a lot of recommendations about things we might do different.

"How's it going?" Ralph leaned across the counter. "You hungry?"

"No, thanks. Mom gets all bent out of shape if I eat anything before dinner. Says it's disrespectful when she's working so hard cooking."

"I got cold beer back in the storeroom. Interested?" he asked.

"You read my mind." I followed him into the storeroom.

The oversized closet where he kept all of the goodies was closed up most of the time, and smelled that way. Ralph didn't stock a lot of any particular item, but he had stores of many, many different things. Canned goods, dry goods, frozen foods, gadgets of all sort, he had them. He told me once that, since he got restocked weekly, there was no need to accumulate a big inventory of any one item. That gave the storeroom a blended aroma, mostly fresh.

"You need a couple of windows in here," I said.

"I'll be sure to pass your suggestions along to corporate headquarters." He laughed and plucked a couple of cold ones from a picnic cooler. There was no corporate headquarters; Sparky's was as local as you can get.

"Maybe a few chairs, too. These boxes are hard on

my butt."

"For your information, this is not a lounge."

"What are you doing in here then, drinking beer?" I asked.

"I'm taking a break. I am entitled by contract to three breaks a day, which, if you had a regular job, you'd know all about." Since Ralph wrote his own contract, if he had one at all, he could take as many breaks as he wanted, and we both knew it.

"That was a low blow. You take it back or I'll throw something at you." The beer was tasting better and better. Ralph seemed to be enjoying his as well. In fact, he'd dribbled a bit on his shirt, but I decided not to tell him. Let him explain it to Janey when he got home. Serve him right for that crack about me not having a regular job.

"Dang, you get more cantankerous every year," he said. "You must be hell to live with."

"I'm sure my mom would agree with you."

"Well, I got something that might help you mellow out." He pulled a hand-rolled smoke from his shirt pocket.

"Is that one of those weird cigarettes I hear about?"

"As if you didn't know."

"I get a little crazy when I smoke that stuff."

"I remember," he said. "That's why we're in a closed room. You can't get into much trouble in here, and even if you do, nobody's going to see it, not like last time."

Yeah, last time, a memory that should have made me blush, but didn't. It was still sort of funny, to me at least. An unseasonably warm New Year's Eve, my junior year. All the cool kids were rocking the night away at their supervised parties, while us delinquents were making do however we could, and having a lot more fun.

Four of us, three guys and me, were splashing around in the fountain in front of the courthouse while others cheered us on. In a short time we were drenched, laughing like crazy. I don't know who brought the marijuana, and, shared among a dozen kids, nobody could have got more than a couple of puffs. But for me, that was plenty. Since I'd been drinking beer all evening, you probably could have waved the weed under my nose, and that would have put me in orbit.

Anyway, the guys jumped out of the fountain, leaving me as the star attraction. They started up a chant, "Take it off, take it off." What the hell? With my shirt plastered on like a second skin and my nipples threatening to poke right through the fabric, there wasn't much left to see that couldn't be seen already. And anyway, they were my friends, right?

A soaked shirt presented a major problem. The buttons were impossible, so I pulled it up as far as I could. And cold, wet bra fasteners? No way, not with cold, clumsy fingers.

I got one of them undone, then I was hoisted up in two burly arms. "That's enough," Ralph said. "You're going home."

"But I want to stay for the fireworks."

"You'll get enough fireworks from your mom when you get home."

And that was all that happened. No full frontal nudity, no fucking in the fountain, not the way everybody said. And Ralph was right about the fireworks at home. Yeah, my reputation was shot to hell, but I never cared about that anyway. Dad didn't have much to say, but for Mom, though, it was apocalyptic.

"What will the neighbors think? How can I ever hold my head up in this town? And the church, people will laugh at me, I just know it."

No big deal for me, but the First Baptist Church of Warrensburg was an anchor for Mom. She never missed a service. Volunteered for every committee, even the ones that were still in the planning stage. Anything that made church life difficult for her was a big deal, especially a daughter who made a spectacle of herself in a public fountain right in the middle of town. Yeah, 1992 was off to a rocky start. I took care of that.

We survived, though. It would take more than a bump in the road to derail the Sugarbush family, but all too soon we got that bump, staring us right in the face, and its name was cancer.

Illness moved into our house and knocked everything upside down. Each passing day brought us closer and closer to that day when Dad wouldn't be there any longer. Illness, I began to realize, was like that, driving away hope and happiness. It was like a gluttonous, uninvited guest showing up at a party. The pig ate all the food, drank all the booze, then passed out on the couch, and there was nothing left.

Even though he'd been gone for over a year and a half, right now, at this very moment, I needed a warm, safe place, and drinking beer and smoking pot in the storeroom with Ralph did the trick for me, even if my butt was sore from sitting on a case of canned goods.

"You probably feel like you're the only person anywhere like this, your dad being gone, I mean,"

Ralph said.

"No, I saw plenty of sick people in the hospital. But I didn't know any of them. It was different with Dad. When it's the people who brought you into the world, even if you don't get along all the time, it's a big deal."

"As big as they get," Ralph said.

"Anyone close to you died, family, friends?"

"Yeah, the people who come in here, you'd be surprised how many of them have a sad tale to tell. And you go out and talk to people, you'll be hard pressed to find somebody who hadn't been touched by the cold, damp finger of death."

"Cold, damp finger of death? You've been reading too many ghost stories, Ralph." That said, I started to giggle. Best thing I could wish for, a good giggle.

"What's funny?" Ralph asked.

"Nothing, nothing at all." So I kept right on giggling at nothing. Then, right on schedule, I got hungry, and the solution sat right on the top shelf. "Crackerjacks," I yelled.

"I thought you quit."

"Never, once you're hooked on Crackerjacks, you're hooked for life."

A whole case of that earthly delight sat just out of my reach. I stood on another case, and steadied myself against Ralph. The case was heavier than I expected, and it slipped through my fingers and onto Ralph's head. He let out a howl, and I was sure I'd injured him, maybe severely.

But he wasn't howling in pain; he was laughing, that big goofy grin of his spread ear to ear. Then things happened. My underwear along with my shirt and jeans were lying on the floor beside Ralph's pants and the yellow apron he wore behind the counter.

He pushed two cases of Dole Pineapple and one case of Campbell's Tomato Soup end to end and laid me across them. Maybe if he'd put the Campbell's case in the middle the edges wouldn't have ground into me, but it was too late for moving furniture. Maybe this wouldn't last too long.

But it lasted a long time, and Ralph was heavy, and I felt as if I might get dismembered if I didn't move soon. Poor Ralph, his penis wouldn't cooperate. That meant poor me, too.

"It's the pot we smoked," I said. "I can help you out, if you want."

Ralph climbed off of me, and I began checking for missing body parts. Next came putting my clothes back on, which went smoothly as long as I didn't have to bend at the waist.

Ralph was still sitting on the floor, his head between his knees. I knelt beside him and put my arm around his shoulders. "It's okay, Ralph. I read somewhere that pot will do that. Don't worry about it."

"This never happened," he said.

"That's what I just said."

"No, it really never happened. If Janey ever found out that would be the end of our marriage." He looked up at me, and his goofy grin had inverted. His was one sad face.

"Put it out of your mind, pal. We drank some beer, smoked some pot, and that's all. Now, stand up and put on your pants."

I slipped his apron over his head and kept my arms around his neck. "Look, Ralph, you're my best friend ever, and I want it to stay just like it's always been."

"Yeah, you bet." He gave me hug, painful because he'd given my breasts a real workout while he was trying to jump-start his uncooperative penis. "See you tomorrow," he said.

"Can I still have some Crackerjacks?"

****

I didn't go straight home after I left Sparky's. The beer and pot were wearing off, and my mind began to slip right back into the same stinking muddle.

I drove downtown, which could be covered end-to-end in about three blocks. A few late shoppers scurried about, but only a few. Warrensburg would never progress into an after-hours commercial hub, and that was okay with me. I liked the sameness, the way the same sad string of Christmas lights reappeared above the streets each year, always a few more bulbs missing than the year before. If I could, I would stop everything right there, just as it was. And Dad would be fine, and Mom would still get on my case about being a more suitable daughter, and this would be perfect.

Except that it wasn't, and wouldn't ever be again.

I drove around a little longer, across Cherry Street then back down the main drag. I stopped at what everyone called the town center, just a green patch with a statue of a soldier wearing a funny hat and carrying a rifle in the middle. Dad told me he was a local boy who'd died in World War I. Now he was just a convenient roost for pigeons, and every Halloween we draped him in toilet paper. The next day an article always appeared in the Warrensburg Gazette about hoodlums running wild in the streets. Could be worse.

I gave the soldier statue a little salute, and I meant

it. Things hadn't worked out according to plan for him either. It made my own problems seem small for a minute, and they slunk back into their hole. But soon enough, they would crawl out again, tying my eighteen-year-old gut into knots.

As I sat on the curb by the monument, a patrol car pulled into the space beside my truck. "Everything okay here?" the officer inside called out.

I couldn't see his face, but I knew the voice. "Hey, Sheriff Tate. Yeah, everything is fine."

"Daisy? That you?"

"Yes, sir."

He came over and sat beside me on the curb. "What in the world are you doing sitting out here? It's almost dark."

"Right, I was just fixing to leave."

"Sorry about your dad." Sheriff Tate and my father had crossed paths in the navy many years before. They'd shared a six-month deployment together on the same destroyer, but I never could remember the name of the ship. Even so, one of my favorite things was to listen to them swap war stories, another thing I would miss.

I shook my head, not much of an answer to the sheriff, but the best I could do. "Anything I can do, you let me know." He put a meaty hand on my shoulder. "I thought the world of your father."

Now the waterworks kicked in again. Lately it was as if they turned on and off on their own, without waiting to hear from me.

"I'm sorry, Daisy. Maybe I shouldn't have said anything. You want me to drive you home?"

"No, sir. Thanks. I think I'll just sit here for a few

minutes. I'll be all right."

He gave me one last squeeze then stood up. "Not too late now, you hear?" he said. "And go easy on the beer. It won't help."

"Tell Daisy hello for me," Ralph had said, according to Mom, a day later when she stopped by Sparky's for milk. She said he looked kind of sheepish when he said it, like, was there something going on between the two of us? No way, not with a happily married man, particularly since that married man was my best friend, and I wouldn't hurt him for anything in the world.

The fact that he'd seen my bare ass once upon a time, something Mom didn't know, wasn't such a big deal, maybe back then but not any more. Most of the staff on Burn Trauma had seen it, along with an army of consultants. In fact, my bare butt on a billboard probably wouldn't slow traffic in the hallway.

"Dr. Dawson says you're done with dialysis. I know you're glad that's finished," Mom said.

"He told you? When?"

"I went by his office earlier."

"You did what? I can't get him to give me the time of day, and you go to his office?"

"Daisy, there's no need to shout. You're just getting all upset for nothing. Dr. Dawson wants to keep me informed, because he's afraid you're too sick to really understand the situation yet."

If it was possible for a human being to explode, I would have done so at that moment. The very thought of my mother cozying up to Dr. Dawson, plotting out what they would do to me next hurt worse than a hydrotherapy treatment. And all because they thought I was too goddam stupid to understand what was going on.

"You had no right to do that," I said.

"It was for your own good," she said. "We just want the best for you."

"Did you ever consider what I might want? Oh, I forgot, I'm too dumb to know what I want."

"Stop talking like that. You're just making things worse."

She was dead right about making things worse. The more I thought about it, the madder I got. Dr. Dawson had been the focal point of my anger up until now. I had him pegged as some autocratic bastard who thought the sun wouldn't rise without his prior approval. Now I find that my own mother has been party to the process of deciding what was best for poor dumb Daisy.

"Would it have killed you, or Dawson or somebody to spend five minutes talking to me about what's going on? Like, how long will I be here, a week, a month, forever?" Right now that's all I wanted. I'd thought this through pretty thoroughly and knew what I wanted. What I lacked was somebody who would listen to me without calling me crazy or stupid or just running out of the room.

Before she could answer my cough kicked in big time. One of the nurses had to apply an oxygen mask. "I'm going to give Dr. Israel a call," said the nurse holding the mask. "See if he has any suggestions. Your cough is getting worse."

My coughing jag had settled down by the time Dr. Israel arrived. Mom had apparently slipped away while I was barking my head off.

"She can't stand to see you like this," the nurse

said.

Understandable, I thought. Maybe she went back to Dr. Dawson's office for coffee and another discussion of my case. After all, it was for my own good, right?

Dr. Israel brought along several inhalers for me to try. "They won't improve the underlying problem, just the symptoms."

Symptoms sounded good enough to me. The only problem was finding one of the gadgets that I could operate with my mangled hands. Linda helped me try them out one by one, until we found one I was comfortable with.

"I'll bring along a couple of spares," she said. "Sometimes things disappear around here. How are you doing otherwise?"

"Same old same old," I said. "One day is pretty much like the rest of them."

I thought of telling her about the little spat I'd just had with Mom, about how some things never seem to change, about how I didn't have much say in what happened to me.

But what could she do about it? She was already walking on eggshells for trying to help another patient make some decisions. Jumping into my situation would probably get her fired.

****

Around the middle of March, the Burn Trauma Unit had an unwelcome visitor, Pseudomonas. Pseudomonas, a nasty species of bacteria, was the scourge of units like the one where I was kept hostage. I got this information from Smitty, not the hostage part, just the bacterial bit. Two patients had infected burn wounds, and they even got a positive culture from somewhere in the Hubbard tank area.

Finding the source of the Pseudomonas and the extent to which it had spread brought out not only the Infectious Disease consultants, but an administrative group called Infection Control. Entry of the Control group made it an official inquiry, which was kind of exciting.

The big search brought all elective surgical procedures to a halt. Best of all, hydrotherapy sessions were put on hold, so between the two opposing sides, I was pulling for Pseudomonas. I didn't want any other patients harmed, but anything that might temporarily derail the torture treatments got my vote.

But the good times were not to last. It seemed hardly any time had passed before a familiar voice said, "Time to go for your hydrotherapy treatment."

"But I heard the treatment room was infected," I said.

"That's all taken care of now. No more bacteria."

"How can you be so sure? No need to rush back into things. I don't want to risk an infection." Most of all I didn't want another hydrotherapy session.

"There's no risk. Infection Control has given us the all-clear."

Lousy Pseudomonas. You'd think it could have put up a better fight.

****

Mom blew a gasket the first time I told her I wanted to stop all the treatments, everything.

"Daisy, no, you can't say things like that." Her voice had a panicky edge to it.

"I just said it, Mom. I've been thinking about this for weeks now, and it's time. I've had enough."

"You don't know what you're saying. You can't think straight. It's all the medication you're taking. Dr. Dawson told me."

"Mom, sooner or later you're going to have to talk to me, not just Dr. Dawson. And I know exactly what I'm saying."

"This won't do," she said. "You have to stay strong, and talking like this doesn't help one bit. I'm going to ask the Reverend Daughtery to come and talk with you."

"Please, don't do that. I don't need a sermon. All I need is someone to listen to me." Linda's book about Ivan Ilych was beginning to make more and more sense.

And that's exactly what I got, a professional listener. She said she was a psychologist, and Dr. Dawson had sent her. Sounded like she was typing her notes into her computer.

"I'm going to ask you a few simple questions. Who is the President?"

"The president of what?"

"The President of the United States."

"Why?" I asked.

"To assess your mental status."

Of course, perfect. Now we'd find out that poor Daisy wasn't just stupid, she was crazy as well, and nobody has to pay any mind to what a crazy person says.

"Go fuck yourself."

"What did you say?" A little gasp in her voice. I loved it.

"Go fuck yourself." I don't know where the first one came from, nor the second, for that matter. It just popped out of my mouth.

"I hardly think that's appropriate," she said.

"Go fuck fuck fuck fuck FUCK yourself." What great fun. I could just see her notes about the interview, "patient hostile, uncooperative, belligerent." Yep, that's me, hostile Daisy. Get put through the wringer like I have and you'd be hostile and then some.

The computer lid slammed shut, and rapid footsteps indicated her hasty exit. Good riddance. The psychologist's brief visit proved to be the high point of my day. I hoped she would come back. If not, maybe they would send another one. I could use another good laugh. Of course, after the laugh, came the cough, but it was worth it.

The next day I got promoted to the Rehab Unit. It seemed I didn't need the level of care on the acute ward, so they moved me out. They were probably glad to get rid of me. It was quieter on Rehab, and the nurses were not so tight-assed about pain medications. I still got dunked in the Hubbard tank, but the areas of my body covered by the dressings became smaller, so the ordeal was shorter.

Smitty dropped by to see me before I got moved out.

"Just wanted to wish you luck," he said. He could hold my hand now. It didn't hurt.

"Does this mean you won't come to see me any more?"

"Maybe I'll drop by, check up on you."

"You can still debride if you want to. I'm not picky about what you want to trim away."

"No more debrideing." He laughed. "You've had more than your share."

"I hope you'll come. You know what I'm going to ask next, don't you?" I guessed it was now mid-April, my fifth month in the hospital.

"Yeah, I know. I still don't have an exact date from Dr. Dawson. I'd guess maybe a month or so."

"If I work hard in Rehab will you let me out sooner?"

"It can't hurt."

So, I did, work hard. And when the flexing and bending hurt, which it always did, I'd remind myself about how I'd already endured far worse.

I got much better at feeding myself. Of course, I was far less successful with some foods than others. I could handle meals that were relatively dry and cubed, but no way when it came to things like soup or spaghetti.

The strengthening exercises were a joke at first. I couldn't do anything. The rubber band games, pushing and pulling, left me wasted, and coughing like crazy.

"Be patient," the therapist kept telling me. "You've been on bed rest for a long time. You'll get stronger, but it takes time."

After about a week they tried standing me up. I passed out.

"Orthostatic hypotension," the therapist said. "Your blood pressure drops when you stand up. It happens to everybody a little, but it can be extreme when you've been lying in bed for a long time. That will improve. Patience, remember."

I began taking a few puffs on my inhaler before my exercise sessions, which helped my breathing, but the cough, not so much. I had another reason for wanting to speed things along; I hadn't seen my dog, Max in almost five months now, and would never see him again, not visually, but at least I could touch him. I missed him like crazy, but would he even recognize me? I could only hope he and Mom had gotten along. Max was never her idea of the ideal house pet. When he got excited, he ran around in circles, and whatever happened to be in his way usually got knocked over. I'm guessing Mom would be happier with goldfish.

I had my nineteenth birthday right here in this hospital, April 23, 1994. I prayed it would be the last of them. In my grand plan, step one was get out of the hospital; step two was just get out…period.

Linda came to see me the second week I was in Rehab. "Moving up in the world, I see."

"If you can call it that. I'm glad you came."

"How is your cough? I know Dr. Israel will ask me."

"It comes and goes. The inhaler helps sometimes, but when I have a bad episode it's scary."

"I can imagine. Pain?"

"Still around, but not as bad as before. The surgeons are pretty much done with me, so this is as good as I'm going to look. All downhill from here."

"Don't say that. The therapists tell me you're getting stronger every day. Do you know when you'll be going home?"

"Nothing definite, but it's been almost five months. That's enough, don't you think?"

"Patience, patience."

"That's what everybody keeps telling me."

I could hear her settle into the chair beside my bed. After knowing someone for awhile, you can sort of tell by the length of the gaps in your conversation when something special is about to come in, so when my friend remained quiet for just a few seconds longer than usual, I knew something was up. "When we talked a while back you said you'd figure out some way to end things, to take your own life. Do you still feel that way?" She said this in a voice so soft it was almost a whisper.

"Yes." Lying to her was not even a consideration. For now, she was my sounding board, the one who would provide some desperately needed feedback, even though my mind was made up.

Now the quiet time again, and this time it was my turn to take the next step. What to say next? At least she was listening.

"I know I can't get them to stop treatments here in the hospital, but when I'm home, things will be different."

"Have you talked with your mother about it?"

"When I asked her to try to get everything stopped she went ballistic. They sent a psychologist to see me. I guess they think nobody in their right mind would ask something like that."

"But you haven't really talked to anybody about your decision, about why you want it to be over."

"Don't need to." Linda was the only person who would listen to me without bouncing off the walls, so I could say things to her, things I knew she didn't want to hear. "I've had a long time to think about it, and like you told me before, I have the right to choose. Of course, that doesn't count in the hospital. As I see it, all the rights in the world don't count for anything unless you have the power to enforce them. Here the hospital and the doctors have all the power. When I'm home things will be different."

"I don't question your right to choose. After all, it was sort of my idea in the first place. I just want to be sure that you've looked at it from all the angles, really thought it through. I mean, if you had a terminal disease, that's different, but you don't," she said.

"I know where you're going with this," I said. "Just do this, put yourself in my position, blind, crippled and ugly as sin. For the rest of my life I'll be totally dependent on someone else to take care of me. I can't be left alone for more than a couple of hours, and I'll be a terrible burden on my mother. Now, you tell me, what kind of life is this? What would you do if you were me?"

"That's not fair, Daisy."

"It's perfectly fair, and you know it. And it's the right question. Nothing else matters."

"What about the people you'll hurt if you go through with it?"

"I worry about Mom the most. She's really getting a raw deal, losing Dad and me both. Yeah, I know it will hurt a lot at first, but with me gone she won't be saddled with taking care of me all the time. As long as I'm around she'll never have any time for herself."

I couldn't help but think about the Julliard fellowship she'd had to give up because of me. If taking care of a new baby Daisy wasn't tough enough, taking care of a deformed, blind, crippled adult version would be even tougher. Why not give the poor woman a break?

"So, you're just a burden for her."

"Pretty much."

"What do you think she'd say if you told her about

your plans?"

"When I brought it up she went through the roof, but she's a mom, and that's what moms do. That's exactly why I'm not going to tell her any more. Believe me, she'll be better off without me."

More quiet time, but it didn't bother me now. Complete silence, that's where I was headed, so I might as well get used to it.

"Can I hold your hand?" she asked.

"Sure, if you can stand the sight of it."

She took my hand, held it gently, rotated it side to side. "Can you move your fingers?"

"Just a little. I'm getting better at feeding myself."

"So, you're not completely helpless."

"Close enough," I said.

"I wanted you to know that there are other people who care about you, and are very sad about your plans."

"Thanks" I said. "That means a lot." I gave her hand a little squeeze, which was all I could manage. "When Dad was still alive, sometimes I'd sit and hold his hand. I never realized until now just how good that felt."

"Just remember, no matter what, you're still Daisy, and you're still loved."

Chapter 6

I would be lying if I said the thought of death didn't scare me. I mean, once you're there, if you don't like it, tough, because there's no going back.

As I saw it, death and dying were two different things. Dying was more of a process, and I think that was what scared most people, like, would it hurt? But how much worse could it be than what I'd already been through? After those sessions in the hydrotherapy tank I figured I'd earned a merit badge in pain.

Death was like a destination. It was a matter of not being any more. How could I be unhappy if I didn't exist? How could I have any feelings at all? Of course, if Mom was right, and hell fire and damnation awaited people who did what I planned to do, I was screwed. But that was a chance I'd take. For that matter, hell fire really didn't scare me much any more. After the Hubbard tank, how much worse could hell be?

And who knew, really? Whatever lay out there in the great beyond was revealed to very few, or so it seemed. Once when I was sitting with Dad—he was barely hanging on then—he opened his eyes and stared past me. Was he looking at something I couldn't see? I asked Mom one day, had she seen him do the same thing?

"Oh, yes," she said. "Many times."

"What's he looking at?"

She wrapped her arms around me and held me close. "Eternity," she whispered.

"Come on, Mom, nobody can see eternity."

"You can't, and I can't, but he can. Count on it."

Then Dad stopped staring over my shoulder and turned his gaze on me.

"I love you," I said.

No sooner were the words out of my mouth than he smiled, one of those little half-smiles that had been a beacon for me all of my eighteen years. That smile meant everything was okay, even when it wasn't.

So I was making my big decision on incomplete information, but that's how it would have to be. Dad didn't seem particularly upset by the eternity thing, or whatever he saw, so maybe it wouldn't be so terrible after all. And the doctors had already given me the means to pull it off. Every time Dr. Gates and his renal team came by he warned me about my fluid intake.

"This is critical, Daisy. You must monitor your fluid intake very carefully. Eight glasses of liquid every day. I'd advise you to keep some sort of record, so you know you've taken enough. I'll talk with your mother about how important this is."

"No, that's okay. I'll talk with her. We'll work out a plan, just the two of us."

Thanks, Dr. Gates. Thanks big time. You've told me exactly what I needed to know. I'd never get away with it here in the hospital. Around here they measure exactly what you take in and exactly what you pee out, but home would be a different story.

****

April moved with all the speed of sludge. By the month of May, the sludge thickened, barely moving at all. Spring might well be bursting forth outside, but inside, which was my world, nothing changed. Why was I still here?

"We want to give the skin grafts plenty of time to heal. These things take time," some surgeon said.

Oh, yeah, time. I knew well enough, no matter what the calendar or the clock on the wall might say, time could speed up or slow down, all on its own. Like those school days leading up to summer vacation, they seemed to never end, while those around the end of those same summer retreats went by in a flash.

When you're stuck inside the same room, the same bed, time hardly moves at all. I'm certain that, if an hourglass were placed at my bedside, the grains of sand would fall in slow motion. Sometimes they would halt altogether and hang there in mid-air.

The brief burst of enthusiasm I'd felt a couple of months back when I moved to Rehab had run its course, and now was replaced by a feeling of hopelessness. Working hard in Rehab didn't seem to move things along, even a little bit. Was this going to last forever? It seemed possible that it would. I've always been kind of a here and now person; the past is over and done with, can't be changed, and the future, well, I'll know when I get there. Now I lived in a fugue state, whatever movement occurred was circular, repetitive, and always left me right where I started. Looking around for exit signs didn't help; there were none to be seen.

Having no other option as I saw it, I withdrew. I went deep inside myself and formed an invisible shield between me and a situation over which I had no control. There was probably a fancy psychological term for such a process, but that was for someone else to worry about, not me. I only allowed a select few inside my cocoon—Linda, Smitty, and sometimes Mom. Most of the time it was just me in there, a sort of practice for things to come.

I slammed the door on all the rehab people, the physical therapists, occupational therapists, all of them. They could twist and fold me all they wanted, but they might as well be manipulating a ragdoll; I was giving them nothing. They were not very happy with me.

"You're just going to lie there and rot, are you?" one of them asked.

Why, yes, I am. Surprised it took you so long to catch on.

Then, finally it happened. Smitty brought me the news—one more night in the asylum, then home tomorrow. Outstanding.

****

I couldn't seem to get on the right page. Here it was, my big day, the day when I would be released from the cell where I'd been locked up for six months. But it was all wrong. I couldn't move. If one of the staff members rolled me right up to the door and said, "You're free to go," I couldn't. I couldn't cross the threshold, because I was scared. I was scared right down to my toenails.

I thought I had everything wrapped into a neat little package, and all I needed was the opportunity to set it in motion. Now I wasn't sure about anything. What if I couldn't do it? I'd be condemned to life as a freak, free only to make everybody around me miserable.

I felt stronger so long as I had something to be really pissed off about, and I had that and more in the Burn Trauma Unit, people treating me like a bag of spoiled vegetables, never listening to me. Anger sustained me. Now that support was going away, and all that was left was fear. Yeah, I'd made plans. I knew what I had to do, and how to do it, but now that the opportunity was coming into focus, I was scared half to death.

But scared or not, it was going to happen. For patients who made it through the long ordeal beginning in the Burn Trauma Unit, eventually ending up in Rehab after surviving everything in between, including multiple plastic surgery procedures, the Rehab staff made the discharge day an event, or so I was told. In my case, feelings of most of the staff members were probably mixed, a blend of celebration and relief. They could congratulate themselves on a job well done, and get rid of their least favorite patient at the same time.

Like most health care workers, I was sure they liked to feel that their efforts and expertise were appreciated, but they got no such feedback from me. I was still burrowed deep into my cocoon where little got out, or in. I was like one of those little black holes in space where stuff that got sucked in never came out again.

Mom got to the hospital early, and I guess she tried to spread the good will and gratitude that I didn't, or couldn't. She blessed, she thanked, she hugged everyone in sight. "Oh, Daisy, I wish you could see all they've done for your discharge. There are colored streamers and even a chocolate cake with your name inscribed in white frosting. Oh, thank all of you so much for the wonderful job you've done all these months."

Pour it on, Mom, just don't expect me to pitch in.

Linda came by to say goodbye. "Bet you're excited about going home," she said.

"Not particularly."

"Don't worry about it," she said.

But now I realized why I was being such a prick on what was supposed to be my big day.

"Linda, please, stay with me."

"Okay, but what's wrong?"

"I'm scared. I'm scared to death."

"Talk to me, Daisy."

"I'm scared of leaving. I know I've bitched and moaned the whole time I've been here, but the thought of going back out again terrifies me."

"I halfway expected something like this. I know you've got concerns of your very own, but the person you are now is not the same one who came in here. You're somebody else now. Look, we'll get you out of here, then into your car, and you're gone. Once you're back in your own home I'll guarantee you'll feel different. I'll get out to see you later this week."

By the time Smitty came by to see me, I was beginning to feel better. Maybe I could do this after all. "Do you two know each other?" I asked both Linda and Smitty.

Turns out they were acquainted, had been for some time.

I still clutched the little stuffed dog that Smitty had given to me when I was still on Burn Trauma. "Is this little guy going home with you?" Linda asked.

"My dog? Yeah, he's coming with me."

"We've had a whole change of seasons since you got here. Winter's gone. Getting warmer out," Smitty said.

One of the staff approached and said "We have to get you ready to go outdoors. You'll be chilled after being inside so long."

They wrapped me in an oversized hospital gown that covered everything but my face and hands. The staff also gave me a baseball cap and dark glasses, but the glasses kept slipping down because the bridge of my reconstructed nose was too small to support them.

Linda, at my request and over the objections of the Rehab staff, took command of my wheelchair. "Please," I said. "I can't go through this without you."

"You got it, babe," Linda said. "Anybody messes with you, I'll smack the shit out of them."

"Damned balloons," she said.

"What balloons?"

"They've decorated your wheelchair in balloons. Oh, God, I wish you could get a look at Dr. Dawson out by the car with your mother. There's a photographer getting some touching shots of them together, and she's looking up at his face like he's God Almighty. Just wait, it'll be in tomorrow's paper, A Grateful Mother Thanks Doctor for Saving Daughter's Life. I always figured him for somebody who'd enjoy being in front of a camera."

"But I'm not, definitely. For God's sakes, don't let them take pictures of me."

"Don't worry. I don't think they'll try, but if they do I'll give them a smack."

"You're almost violent today," I said. "Didn't sleep well last night?"

"We'll talk more when you get home, but I'll just say I was scared for you, too. This move is huge. I mean, I love you to death, but will that be enough? Be strong for me, okay?"

Footsteps on the walkway approaching my wheelchair. Must have been the photographer, because Linda warned him off. "No pictures of the patient," she said.

I guess he got a good look at me and decided I wasn't good photo material. Even if he got his shots nobody would believe them. I would look a lot worse than most of the photos in the obituary section.

A reporter from the Warrensburg Chronicle somehow got past my watchdog, Linda.

"Daisy, can you tell us what it's like going home after all these months in the hospital?"

I gave her no answer. Let her make something up. She was supposed to be a writer.

Linda to the rescue. I felt her protective hand on my shoulder. "She's still a little overcome, you know, all that time inside." With that she wheeled me right past the reporter. I wouldn't have been surprised if she'd run over the reporter's toes.

During all of that, Dr. Dawson never once approached me, never said a word of farewell, nothing. But that wasn't so bad. If I never heard his voice again that would be soon enough.

"Mrs. West will drive us home," Mom said. "I don't know what we'd do without her."

Mrs. West gave me a tentative hug, including the gasp when she got a look at me even though she'd seen me before. The hospital staff were so used to me that they hardly noticed, but outside would be different. Nobody had seen anything like me, ever. I would have to get used to that sharp intake of air, to that unsaid "Oh, my God."

They helped me into the back seat of Mrs. West's Roadmaster, spacious and comfortable and smelling slightly of cooking spices. Mom said an aide helped them load my wheelchair into the back, after they'd released the balloons. A neat thought, drifting up through the spring sky, toward the clouds, then vanishing altogether. I could go for the balloon thing.

"I'll bet you're glad to say goodbye to that hospital," Mrs. West said.

"Yes, ma'am, I am. And thank you for coming to get me."

"It was nice of them to go to all that trouble, the nurses and all," Mom said.

That was about it for conversation for a while. Mom and Mrs. West chatted away like the old friends they were, while the eight-hundred-pound gorilla— me—sat quietly in the back seat. The ride home revived me a little, just the sensation of being somewhere other than a hospital bed was refreshing.

So, there it was, the end of a phase in which my life was changed forever. The fear still lingered, but was replaced by an emptiness, which, I guessed, would be my constant companion from here on out.

At least I had choices now, some control over my own life. All I had to do was stick to my plan. I'd done all my homework. All I needed was the courage to carry it out.

"Fluid intake will be the most important thing," one of the nephrologists had said again on my last day. From his accent, I thought perhaps he was from India. He seemed kind and gentle, and I liked him, particularly since he'd reminded me of the key to controlling my own destiny. All I had to do was stop drinking.

And the process itself seemed manageable, at least from what I was told. Back in February, when they'd told me about my ailing kidneys, I asked Linda, "What is it like, dying from renal failure?"

"It can take some time, weeks, maybe, depending on how bad your kidneys are to start with. But it's rather peaceful, no pain. That's what I've heard anyway. Why do you ask?"

"Just wondering." Peaceful and painless. If only they'd left me alone like I wanted, all this horrible mess would be over now.

"You're not planning something crazy , are you?" Linda asked.

"What good would it do? I don't have any say about what happens to me here. If I did, we wouldn't be having this conversation."

Simple enough, not difficult at all.

So now I was riding along in the backseat of Mrs. West's car, in command of my own destiny at last. Some time passed before Mom spoke again. "There's a nice little Rehab facility, just opened up next to the Drug Emporium. I checked it out. It looks nice, and I think you'll really like the staff there, a sweet bunch of girls."

"Forget it," I said. "No more rehab." Rehab was pointless, a waste of time and resources. I had my own plans now, and they didn't include rehab.

"They'll even send someone out to the house, work with you right in your own room if you want. It costs a little more, but if that would be better for you I'll set it up."

"No."

"We'll talk later, when you're all settled in."

"Don't bother, Mom. I won't do it." God, it felt good to be able to refuse, to be able to say no. I don't know what Mrs. West must have thought, me mouthing off at Mom like I did, but I couldn't help it.

Of course, I'd refused stuff in the hospital for months, but hospitals were tricky places. You could say no until your head fell off, and they would still find a way to get you to do what they wanted. Won't eat? They stick a tube down your nose into your stomach. Won't drink? They stick a needle into your arm and get the job done intravenously. Won't do the rehab thing? They twist you and bend you, two of them at a time if necessary, however they liked.

Now I had only my mother to contend with, and she couldn't force me to eat, couldn't force me to drink, and definitely could not force me into rehab. This time *I* would win.

But there was unfinished business, too, things I had to deal with before I pulled the plug on my own life, such as a few goodbyes and a final farewell to my father. Who knew? Maybe I'd see him again before too long. And Max...how do you tell your dog you're leaving him forever? Crap...being simple enough didn't necessarily mean it would be easy.

Eventually the drive that seemed to have begun hours, maybe days ago, ended as we pulled into the driveway. "Sit tight for a second while I get the wheelchair out of the back," Mom said.

"I can walk if you'll help me."

"Tell you the truth, I'm not feeling very steady myself. Let me get the chair," Mom said.

The bark was so familiar, as were the thudding feet

of a heavy dog hurdling across the lawn. "Hey, Max," Mom said. "Look who's come home."

I swung my feet out of the door and clapped my scarred palms together. "Max, oh, Max, come here, boy."

Would he even know me? I didn't even resemble the person he'd known before, even smelled different. Still, with some special dog sense he recognized me. Almost immediately I was pinned back into my seat as Max climbed on top of me, sniffing, licking, loving. I wrapped my arms tightly around him, and, if I'd still possessed functioning tear ducts, they would have been gushing.

"Enough, Max. She's not strong enough to play with you yet." Mom pulled him away.

"Who took care of him while I was gone?"

"I did, of course. We've become real pals, right Max? Honestly, there were days I couldn't have made it without him."

"You took care of my dog. Thank you for that." I know this required some very big compromises on her part, and it meant a lot that she had made room for him.

"No problem," Mom said. "He's part of the family too. Here, let's get you into this chair." But Mom struggled to push me to the front door.

"It's these little narrow wheels. They might do fine indoors, but they were definitely not designed to maneuver on soft lawns."

"Could we stop for a minute?" I asked. For the first time in months I sat in a place without walls, with no ceiling. Even the tight cocoon I'd woven around myself became more porous. A gentle gust of wind swept across the lawn, and it seemed to flow right through me.

An event of which I would have taken no notice before now seemed a gift from heaven.

"You must be cold, just that flimsy robe," Mom said.

"Not a bit." Cold was good. Cold was different.

Wheelchairs didn't climb front porch stairs any more easily than they crossed lawns, so Mom had me sit on the porch while she pulled the chair up, panting with the effort.

She left me parked in the living room while she said goodbye to Mrs. West. When she came back she was sniffling. "God bless Althea. The woman has been a real angel."

"Althea?"

"Mrs. West, Althea is her first name."

"I never knew that."

"The hospice nurse was a big help with your father's medical care, but there are some things you can only share with a good friend, and Althea is the best, the very best."

She wheeled me into my bedroom and helped me into bed.

"I guess you're all tired out," she said. "Are you hungry?"

"Not hungry, but I could use a nap."

"I bought new pajamas for you, if you want to change."

"Yeah, that would be great. These clothes smell like the hospital. You'll have to help me get dressed, and, Mom, you might want to close your eyes."

I don't think she had ever seen my burned body, not all of it anyway. Of course, I hadn't seen it myself, and didn't want to.

She helped me pull the top of the scrub suit over my head. She gasped. "Oh, Daisy, my poor girl. I never realized…."

"Hurry up with the pajamas, Mom. I'm cold."

She had much the same reaction when I changed into the pajama bottoms. If it was going to be this way every time I'd better learn to dress myself, and fast. *Sorry, Mom, this is as good as it gets.*

"Are you having much pain?" she asked.

"Yeah, I could use one of my pain pills."

"I've got all of your medication here in a bag. One of your nurses went over the schedule with me yesterday until I memorized it." Mom tried to make out all casual about the morphine tablets, but I knew better. I could pick out the slight tremor in her voice when she tried to talk about my pain pills as if she were leaving a couple of aspirins on my nightstand. For sure, the nurses at the hospital had grilled her about the horror of me turning into a dope fiend, even worse than looking like something that crawled out of a damp basement…a dope fiend, God forbid.

"Never more than two tablets every six hours, Mrs. Sugarbush. Morphine is a dangerous drug." How many times would they have laid that mantra on her? Now my poor mother, after she'd so carefully dispensed my "dangerous drug," would go back into the kitchen, back to the little notebook I'm sure she kept hidden away, even though I couldn't see it if she'd left it in the middle of the kitchen table, to write down the time of each and every dose.

"And make sure she swallows them. Don't let her stash them away, try to take a lot of them all at once. Patients do some crazy things with morphine." Yeah, she would have heard that one as well. What they didn't say, so far as I knew, was if I died of an overdose, it would be her fault. Nice trick to play on a grieving mother.

Anyway, I have my own game plan for getting rid of myself, one that doesn't involve overdosing, and one that won't cause any more harm than necessary to the few people I'll leave behind. Just a quick clean break; I'll be gone, and we'll all be better off.

Sound depressed, do I? To that I say, big fucking deal. It's my depression, MINE! So, to every well-intentioned visiting therapist with degrees and citations hanging from their walls, who might show up with ideas about improving my mental and physical well-being, I say leave me the fuck alone. Just don't bother.

Max jumped into bed with me. "Better get down, boy," I said.

"New house rules," Mom said. "Max sleeps wherever he wants to. Most nights he and I slept on the sofa together. I think I'd have gone crazy without him."

I couldn't quite get my head around this one, my mother sleeping on the sofa with a dog. But then, I knew what a comfort his warm, fuzzy body could be, even if it was a bit pungent. And as crappy as things had been in the hospital, I guess they hadn't been so great at home either.

I reached out my arms. She must have knelt beside the bed. I'll bet we made quite a sight, Mom, me and Max all wrapped up together.

My pain medication kicked in, and I drifted away into my deep narcotic slumber. Quieter this time, no bad hospital dreams, no screaming, no begging, no Hubbard tank. Much better.

When I woke the house was quiet. Maybe Mom was finally getting some rest. Max was still wedged against me. "You're due for a bath, my friend."

I could probably use one myself.

Mom came in a bit later. I could tell she was trying to be quiet. "I'm awake," I said.

"You must be starving. How about some soup?"

"I can't do soup, Mom. I spill it all over myself."

"I'll help you. Next time I'll fix something solid. I have your wheelchair right by the bed."

"I want to try to walk, if you'll help."

"Wonderful, we'll go nice and slow."

And slow it was. The short trip that I'd always completed in a flash now seemed to take forever. By the time I reached my chair by the kitchen table I was exhausted.

Cream of tomato soup. I've consumed gallons of it over the years. Now each spoonful was a special event, even though Mom had to feed me. She topped it off with a glass of milk, which I could manage myself.

"I should have fixed you something more substantial," she said.

"That was perfect."

"Can you sit on the sofa with me for a while?" she asked.

"I can manage that, sure."

"If you're cold, I bought a new robe for you."

In a moment she had me wrapped in a cozy fleece robe.

"It's light blue. It looks good on you," she said.

"You don't have to say that, Mom. We both know that nothing will look good on me, ever again."

"Don't say that, Daisy. It isn't true. Now, I want

you to try on these new slippers. They'll keep your feet warm, but I'm afraid they won't be much good for walking. I'll have to find something a little more sturdy for when you go out."

"Mom, I can't go out, unless you put a bag over my head."

"Daisy, stop it. That kind of talk is hurtful, for both of us."

I leaned my head back against the sofa. "It seems so strange being here now. I remember the room perfectly, even though I can't see it."

The sofa creaked as she sat down beside me. "Can I hold you?" she asked. "I've wanted to for so long, but they kept you all bandaged up in the hospital."

"Sure, why not?" It didn't feel half-bad. In fact, it felt good. For a while there we were mother and daughter again. Not like old times, of course, but good anyway.

Obviously, things were not going as planned. For someone with plans to starve herself to death I was off to a lousy start. It was Mom's fault, as usual. This was a lot easier when I could make her out as the villain, in cahoots with Dr. Dawson, both of them conspiring to keep me imprisoned and in pain, all for my own good, of course.

It would be tougher than I'd thought. So long as I had anger to fuel my intentions, I could be sure of success. But now, with Mom's arm around me, back to the mother daughter thing, my anger was fizzling like a campfire doused with water.

No matter. I was going to do this as much for her as for myself. When she saw what a total pain in the ass I'd become, she'd feel differently. She'd be glad to see me gone. It would take some time, I knew, but eventually she'd see it my way.

****

"Daisy, I'll only be gone for an hour, maybe less. Are you sure there's nothing special you want from the market? Ice cream, maybe?"

"No, Mom. I'll be fine."

"If the phone rings, just ignore it. We have an answering machine now. I'm still learning how to operate it."

She was hovering right beside my bed, trying so hard to make things normal again. God bless her for trying, but she faced an impossible task.

"Your pain medication is right here in this little cup. I only left a couple of pills, because I'll be back before you need any more. Let's see, inhaler is right here, water glass, too. Can you think of anything else?"

"You've thought of everything. Take your time shopping. I'll be okay."

I did worry about her, but she had such a great circle of friends that I thought she'd be okay when it happened. Then she could get on with her life, and I'd be rid of mine.

Sometimes I missed the bustle of the hospital, even though some of what happened left me screaming my head off. I was nineteen years old, and, even though I had a clear plan, it was hard to turn my brain off. It was hard to turn my heart off, too. What I really needed was something to keep me pissed off. When I was angry it was like facing a green wall, there was no light coming through from either side, just the wall. It worked, but sometimes I forgot.

It just isn't natural or effective to flush out

emotions and hope that they don't come back. But then, I'm not natural either. It would have been better if I hadn't lost my sight. Then, every time I looked in a mirror, I could see the freakish thing I'd become. That should be all the motivation I'd need.

But I'd have to stay alert. Warm, fuzzy feeling…that was the enemy. That's what I had to extinguish. So I had to rebuild my wall, my big green wall, and I had to start right away.

Another coughing jag, a short time after Mom left. By the time I got my inhaler lined up it was too late to help much. I wondered for a while whether my burned lungs might do me in before my kidneys failed. Of the two, I'd certainly prefer the kidney route. Gasping for breath in between coughs was no fun at all. I'd watched my poor father go through that all too often.

Predictably pain followed the cough, and I wolfed down my pills. Do you cough when you're dead? Probably not, and no pain either. That's the way I had it figured.

One little setback this afternoon—ice cream for lunch. This definitely did not fit in with my plans, but after the fit of coughing earlier I deserved a treat. I couldn't very well turn down a bowl of rum raisin. It had been Dad's favorite; and therefore, mine. Mom remembered for sure.

She had me sit at the table with her. "Here's your spoon, and here's your ice cream dish."

"I'll make a big mess of this myself."

"Go right ahead. Nobody here but us. Max will clean up anything you drop on the floor, and I'll take care of the rest."

I never liked hypocrites, people who said one thing

then did something else, like talking about starvation, then tearing into a bowl of rum raisin ice cream. I would kick my own ass if I could, but my legs won't bend well enough to do that. Thinking about it didn't slow me down, though, because it was more than just ice cream. It was about having someone who remembered your favorite, then took the trouble to get it for you. It was about family, something I'd forgotten about.

"You did really well with that," Mom said. "Not much of a mess at all. Poor Max looks disappointed. Here, why don't you give him one of these."

"What is it?" She put something into my hand that felt like a thick cookie.

"It's one of his peanut butter treats. He loves them."

I lowered my hand and felt his moist nose in my palm as he took his treat. Wonder of wonders, my mother buying doggy treats. What next?

"Hamburgers okay for dinner?" she asked.

"Sure, great."

Back in the day, back when we were a complete and healthy family, hamburgers would not have been on the menu. I used to call Mom the food Nazi because of her insistence on nutritious meals, now, hamburgers.

Okay, a little setback with the ice cream, but only temporary. Nobody said it had to be this week. There's always tomorrow. Still, the longer I put it off, the harder it was going to be, or so I kept telling myself. And going slowly, like sticking my toe into a swimming pool to test the water, then slipping in gradually, wasn't working. I began having serious doubts about my ability to pull it off, dying, that is.

Because departing wouldn't come like a bolt out of the blue, like an airplane crash. It was an event I would have to bring about by myself. And I had no cheering section rooting for me. Talk about lonely. Wonder if there's a support group that helps people kill themselves.

Chapter 7

We didn't have many visitors during the days and weeks that followed my return home. A few of Mom's closer friends came by, but I expect even she was getting fed up with gasps, unbelieving stares and forced small talk, followed by a hurried departure. Soon the doorbell stopped ringing altogether.

Mom had left me parked in the living room, my usual place when she was out, and was headed out to the dry cleaners' when I heard her stop at the front door.

"Why, Carolyn and Louise, what a surprise. You've come to visit Daisy. How nice. I'm going to run off to pick up the dry cleaning, so you girls can have a nice chat."

Carolyn and Louise, the Turlington twins, were one year behind me in school. We'd never been close friends. They were cute girls, but they fit into that group about which Dad said "Can't trust them." So I didn't trust them, didn't even like them. What the hell were they up to now?

"My God, you know what she looks like?" Carolyn spoke with a slight lisp, so I knew it was her. "E.T., that thing in the movie, from outer space."

"Yeah," Louise said. "E.T." Somehow she'd gotten alongside my wheelchair without me hearing her.

"Nice cap," Louise said. "Didn't know you were a

Red Sox fan." She dropped the cap into my lap.

Two soft clicks, then giggles.

"Take one more," Louise said. Then cackles, rapid footsteps followed by the front door slamming.

A camera. The sorry little bitches had taken photos, pictures of a freak, something to show their friends.

Yeah, a freak. A goddam freak. That's all I was, and all I ever would be, in case I needed reminding. Sure, I wished it was all different, but it wasn't, and it wasn't going to change. Time to stop fooling around and get down to business. Sorry, Mom, but this is the way it has to be, my choice, now.

When Mom got back in I was in my bed.

"Are you all right?" She put her hand on my forehead, the universal mom method of checking for fever.

"Just tired."

"Did you have a nice visit with your friends?"

"Oh, yeah, great." Maybe they'd done me a favor. They reminded me of what I am, and what I have to do.

Mom sounded disappointed when I asked to eat in my room. "But I thought we could talk a bit."

"I don't feel up to it," I said. Somehow I would have to stay out of the kitchen, too much temptation in there, and Mom would be watching me too closely.

Some foods flush easily enough. For those that don't, burgers and fries, for instance, a dog with a big appetite is the next best thing. And the can of Coke, which I really, really wanted…right down the drain. It was a start, at least. Fluid intake, that was the thing, and with luck it wouldn't take too long.

My stomach went into full revolt, growling and snarling like a hungry beast. If that wasn't enough it started cramping the next day. This hunger strike was going to be harder that I thought, but it had to be done. It was the only way out. I guess I could concentrate on just the liquid stuff, but it seemed better to make a clean break of it. If I ate, I'd want to drink, and I'd be right back where I started.

By the third day the cramping alternated with a dull ache, not so bad as my hospital pain, but bad enough. Mom kept on fixing meals, and I kept on flushing them.

"Daisy, talk to me, please. What's wrong?" She sat on the edge of my bed with her hand resting on my back. I spent a lot of time rolled into the fetal position, because that made the cramps a little more bearable.

"I'm fine, Mom, really."

"You most certainly are not. If you tried to stand up now you'd fall flat on your face. Is it something I'm doing, or not doing?"

"No, you're not doing anything wrong."

"Then why aren't you eating?"

"I eat. I'm just not very hungry."

"Daisy, there are green beans in the toilet."

"I threw up."

"No, those beans have never been chewed, not even a little. Are you deliberately trying to starve yourself?"

"No."

"Then please, don't do this. If not for me, then have pity on poor Max. You've got him all upset, and God knows the poor dog has been through enough with your father, then taking care of me. This isn't fair to him."

I almost caved in when she said that. Max takes his role as comforter-in-chief for this family very seriously.

I saw—back when I could see—how he attached himself to Dad in those last days, and, from what Mom says, he took care of her as well. Now he has me to worry about. How much can the poor dog give before he crashes, too?

"Can I give him a treat?" I asked.

"Sure, I'll get one."

A peanut butter cookie seemed a small reward for all the time and emotional effort Max had put in, but for now it was the best I could do.

Mom left quietly. I knew she was hurting. We'd talked in circles without saying anything, but she knew what was going on. Look at it this way, the world could do with one less freak. There, I could say it even if she couldn't.

At the end of the week Linda showed up. Mom might have called her, I didn't know. I could hear the two of them talking in low tones in the kitchen.

Linda came in and sat on the edge of my bed. At this point I was too weak to get up and greet her properly.

"I hear you've been a bad girl," she said.

"No, I'm just doing what I have to do."

'How do you feel?"

"Fine."

"Liar. I'll bet you can't stand without assistance."

"All part of the process," I said.

'Look, I know you've thought this through, and I'm not here to try to change your mind. I just want you to do one thing for me."

"Shoot."

"I want to send out a therapist to see you. He's a special friend of mine. Will you do it as a favor to me, just one visit?"

"It won't change anything."

"Just one visit, for me?"

"Just one, then. What's her name?"

"It's a guy, and his name is Arthur."

"Just Arthur?" I asked.

"Just Arthur. He'll be here tomorrow. I've already cleared it with your mother."

"But tomorrow is Saturday. He works weekends?"

She gave my hand a squeeze. "From the looks of you, the sooner the better."

No big deal, I thought. I'd chased off half of the therapists in the county. One more wouldn't be a problem.

Mom was up early Saturday morning. I heard her working in the kitchen. When she came to my room a little later, the aroma of one of her favorite treats followed her in.

"Cinnamon buns, Mom? You're making cinnamon buns?"

"Your new therapist, he might be hungry."

What a dirty trick. Her cinnamon buns pushed all my buttons, and she knew it. In no time flat, my stomach started a tap dance.

"I hear the doorbell," she said. "He's early."

Max jumped off the bed to follow her.

Their voices were audible through my open door, beginning with Mom's "Oh, my goodness." Her voice a mixture of alarm and surprise.

"Morning, Ms. Sugarbush. I'm Arthur. Got caught in the rain here." Then a laugh, more of a sonic boom, actually. Window panes, the china in the kitchen cabinets, all vibrated, or so it seemed. I did too, a little.

"Not quite what you expected, right?" Another sonic boom.

Mom sounded clueless, but Max was yelping away, his happy bark saying come on in, glad to see you.

"I'll get a towel," Mom said, still sounding unsure of the situation.

Max was undeterred. He formed opinions quickly, and usually correctly, and Arthur got a passing grade before he ever stepped through the door.

"Who is this handsome fellow?" Arthur's deep voice.

"This is Max, our dog. He's friendly. I'll get that towel." From the sound of Arthur's voice it had better be a very large towel.

While our guest blotted away the rain that had apparently soaked him through, Mom said, "Daisy's still asleep. Maybe we should talk in the kitchen."

The floor creaked and groaned under his heavy tread. Was Arthur a giant?

Mom must have held her breath when he sat in one of her spindly kitchen chairs. She'd inherited the set from her mother, but they were not built for extra, extra large people.

"I'll tell you a bit about Daisy," she said. My door was open, and she wasn't making any attempt at concealing her voice. Not that it would make much difference, Arthur generated enough volume for both of them.

Oh, great, another conversation about me that didn't include me. If I weren't so damned weak I'd march right in and tell him myself. And then chase him off.

"Coffee?" Mom asked him. "And how about a

cinnamon bun. I just baked them this morning."

"Outstanding," he said.

Damn, it just wasn't fair. I could almost see him bite through the sweet, creamy icing, through the crunchy sugar frosting, into the warm bun where the cinnamon lay in swirls. I could taste it. Right about now I would kill for one of Mom's cinnamon buns, and she was feeding them to a total stranger.

Low voices that I couldn't make out, until Mom said, "Please, have another one. I can't possibly eat all of them, and Daisy isn't eating hardly anything now."

Just one damned minute, if you please. This hunger strike was never intended to include cinnamon buns. Fat lot of good it did. They ate, I listened. Not fair.

Eventually they made time for me. "Daisy, are you awake?" Mom asked.

Like anybody could sleep with that eating orgy going on in the next room.

"This is Arthur, Linda's friend. Can you talk to him?"

"We'll be okay, Ms. Sugarbush. Just take a little time to get acquainted."

"Okay, I'll leave you two. And please, call me Rhoda."

The floor creaked, the chair creaked, and he laughed. Of course, he could laugh. He'd probably wolfed down the whole plate of cinnamon buns. But he was getting nothing from me. He could talk to the walls for all I cared.

Nothing. Then he started humming, a low rumbling sound like a big truck climbing the hill out on the four-lane. Well, you can rumble 'til your head falls off, big guy, you're getting nothing from me.

"Max, you like your ears scratched, don't you? Maybe next time I'll bring a tennis ball, and we can play in the back yard."

"You leave my dog alone," I said.

"Well, Miss Daisy is awake after all."

"I want you to leave."

"Yeah, I hear you."

"Go away." I yelled for Mom.

She must have been lurking by the door. She was there in an instant. "What is it, sweetheart? What's wrong?"

"I want him to go away."

More rumbling laughter. God, I was getting tired of this. What the hell was so funny anyway?

"Always starts out like this, Rhoda," he said. "Just takes a little time, is all."

"If you're sure," she said.

"We'll do just fine."

That was it. I was tuning out. And next time I saw Linda I'd let her have it for sending some big fat idiot out here.

"Miss Daisy, she don't talk much, does she Max?"

Silence.

"No problem. I get paid by the hour. She talks, okay. She don't talk, that's okay too. Let's see, I got thirty-eight minutes left."

I got it now, just ignore him. He'll never last that thirty-eight minutes, not even half of that. I'd blown away a half dozen therapists in the hospital with this technique; he would be no problem.

"You're a puny little thing, ain't you?" he said.

"What? Puny? You called me puny? Is that one of your fancy clinical diagnoses? Someone trained you to figure that out? If they did, they wasted their time."

"Yeah, puny. A breeze would blow you right over."

Bastard.

"Twenty-nine minutes. Slow day, huh Max?"

"I'm going to take a nap."

"Guess it's just you and me, Max. What do you think about Miss Daisy? Seems like she's trying to shut the whole world out, don't it?"

"Talk all you want, just don't talk about me like I'm not here." I'd had enough of that already.

"I thought you were going to take a nap."

"How can anybody sleep with you yapping?"

He laughed like an idiot, a very large idiot. Maybe he really was stupid.

"Dang, if you ain't just about the maddest thing I've seen lately. And I've seen some angry women, oh yeah."

Yeah, he was getting to me now. If I needed something or somebody to really piss me off, it had walked right through the front door less than an hour ago. "You haven't seen anything yet. If you keep talking like that I will show you mad and then some."

"Okay, I'll just sit here and scratch old Max. Say, Miss Daisy, you hurt anywhere?"

"If you're talking to me, my name just plain Daisy, and no, I don't hurt."

"That's good, so when we start to work I don't have to worry about causing you any pain."

"You don't have to worry at all, because we aren't going to start anything, nothing, you hear me?" I yelled at him, a mixture of fear and anger and some other stuff I didn't understand yet. Pissed off, you bet, but scared, too.

This time it was the laughter, full bore. On the same wavelength as all the glassware, everything rattled. Max was dancing around the floor, yipping his happy dog talk the way he used to greet me when I came home from school.

"They told me you would be a tough case. Guess they got that right." More laughter.

Dammit, this had to stop. How long before I would be prancing on the floor like Max, dancing to that crazy laugh? I yelled as loud as I could. "Go away and stay away."

"Is everything all right?" Mom again. She could have chased him off, but she didn't.

"Oh, sure," he said. "We're just getting acquainted."

And so it went, more taunts, more laughter. By the time he got up to leave I was exhausted.

"See you Monday," he said.

"Don't bother."

"Bye, Max."

****

"Is that what I think it is?" I asked after Mom placed a plate on my bedside table. The aroma of cinnamon buns was unmistakable, so the question was unnecessary.

"Yes, but if you don't want them, I'll take them away. Just don't give them to Max. He's getting fat."

She sat on the bed beside me. "Arthur is undoubtedly the biggest man I've ever seen. If I met him on the street I'd probably run the other way. I mean, he's got an eye patch and three long scars down the left side of his face. What did you think of him?"

"I think he's crazy. I can't believe Max likes him."

"Well, he sure likes my cinnamon buns. He'll be back on Monday, so he says."

"Don't let him in. I don't want to see him."

"What were you yelling about before?"

"He kept bugging me. He scares me." He really did. It started off as anger, but sort of transformed into fear. He was full of tricks, this one.

"I can't believe I just let him in the house like that. But Max seemed to think he's okay, and he's usually right, and Linda said really good things about him. I think we should give him a chance. Don't you?"

"I hope he doesn't come back." But he would, I knew that much. Ignoring him, yelling at him, none of that made any difference. He would be trouble.

The cinnamon buns, both of them, went down way too fast and came right back up again.

"I shouldn't have given you two of them," Mom said. She was holding my head over the toilet. She cleaned me up with a washcloth, then put me back to bed. "You know, we really should come to some agreement about whether you're going to eat or not. No sense in me fixing stuff that you're just going to flush down the toilet, but I don't want you going hungry either. So you think about it, and tell me what you want to do."

So much for my grand subterfuge. My secret plan was as plain as day. But Mom was exactly right; this on again, off again bit was just creating misery for both of us. Trouble was, my resolutions were like tissue paper. No sooner did I get started than I'd fall off the wagon, if not cinnamon buns, something else would come along.

Now Arthur. If I wasn't careful he would wreck everything, then I'd be right back at square one, a helpless little freak.

****

Monday morning there he was again, Mom and Max both happy to see him. Mom took him into the kitchen for coffee. I know she was concerned about all the shouting before. I edged closer to the door, trying to pick up on their conversation.

"You brought flowers," she said.

"Yeah, they're for Daisy. I picked them in front of my apartment this morning."

"She hasn't changed much," Mom said. "Still doesn't talk, except to complain about you."

"Perfect," Arthur said. "It takes a little time, you know. For now we'll just let her focus all that anger on me."

"You *want* her mad at you?"

"It's all a part of the process. Sounds a little crazy though, huh?"

"If you say so. Mostly it seems the only person she's mad at is me."

"Daisy is mad at the world right now, and I don't blame her. But that's hard to work with, somebody mad at everything and everybody. Maybe if I can get her to center it on me we can work with it."

"Good luck."

I heard every word. So that was his game, get me pissed off, then get inside my head. Well, do your best, big guy. I don't plan to make it easy for you.

At least he could never sneak up on me. Every step he took made the floor creak.

"Hey, girl," he said.

"Name's Daisy, in case you forgot."

"I didn't forget. I brought you some flowers, cheer you up a little."

"Nice try, but what do I care? I can't see them."

"Maybe you're not looking hard enough."

"Real cute," I said. "Don't start that mumbo-jumbo with me. There's no point in you hanging around. I'm not doing anything today."

"No problem," he said. "Like I told you before, I get paid by the hour. I brought a book, just in case." He pulled a chair across the floor to my bedside.

"You're just gonna sit there on your fat ass and read? They pay you to do that?" How did he get to me so fast? He hadn't been in the room for five minutes, and already I was foaming at the mouth.

"By the hour," he said. "And how do you know my ass is fat?"

"I know you're a big man. I hear the floor creaking when you walk on it. I just guessed about the fat ass part."

"Pretty good book, *Great Expectations*, Charles Dickens. You ever heard of him?"

"I did go to school, you know."

"This lady in the book got burned real bad. Some coincidence, huh?"

"Coincidence my ass. I know what you're up to."

"Okay, you caught me. Since you don't want to talk, I'll just sit here and read."

But that wasn't all he was doing. He started that damned humming again.

"Can't you do that someplace else?"

"I have to be in the room. Otherwise I don't get paid, and I got bills, like everybody else."

The fat bastard was laughing again, and that was worse than the humming.

"Just stop it, will you? Get the hell out of my room."

"Paid by the hour, remember?"

"Damn you. I want you to leave." I moved to the edge of the bed, my feet dangling just above the floor.

"You're pissed off, aren't you? Really, really pissed off."

"Of course I am, you idiot."

"Show me," he said.

"What?" I heard him move closer to the bed.

"Show me you're pissed off."

"I could kill you." I stood, supporting myself with one hand on the bed. Then I took a weak swing at him with my free hand, a blow that bounced off his shoulder with no effect at all.

"No, you can't kill anybody. Can't even throw a decent punch." He gave me a little shove, and I toppled back onto the bed. "All you can do is lie around and complain."

"You son of a bitch," I yelled.

"That the best you got?" Arthur said. "Not much. Not much at all."

Max began to growl at him. "It's all right, Max, we just playing."

The right word from me, and Max wouldn't be playing any longer; he would be biting. So tempting, see how the big man likes a dog bite.

The chair creaked under his weight. I guess he was through tormenting me for the moment.

"I'm going to tell you a story," he said. "Happened to me just this morning."

"Keep it. I don't want to hear it."

"I'm going to tell you anyway, because you need to hear it, and I need to tell it. I figure you stay cooped up in here so nobody can see you, because you think you're ugly. Well, I know a little about ugly.

"A couple of blocks from my apartment there's a bridge over the river. I like to walk out there in the morning, especially on beautiful days like this. When I get to the middle of the bridge I can see all the way down the river, all the azaleas blooming on the banks."

"If you're trying to make me feel shitty because I'll never see any of that, you're doing a good job." I did not need reminding that I'd seen my last azalea in bloom, and all I would have is memories.

"I'm sorry. I didn't mean it that way. What I wanted you to hear was , while I was standing in the middle of the bridge, admiring the view, a young lady was jogging up from the other side. She had her head down so she didn't see me until she was about ten feet from me. When she looked up, I've seen that same shocked expression hundreds of times. Even your mother looked at me like that the first time, eyes wide, face all pale.

"Anyway, this girl ran over to the other side of the road without even checking for traffic. Kept looking back over her shoulder to see if I was coming after her." He laughed that rumbling sound, but not so happy this time.

"Big ugly black dude standing in the middle of the bridge, must have scared her half to death."

"So, what's your point?"

"I'm not even sure myself. But if you're a freak, I'm a freak, too. Maybe we're all freaks. I don't know.

But we can all hurt, I know that."

I could hear him breathing, otherwise, nothing. Maybe it was all bullshit, what he'd just said, and maybe it wasn't. As I saw it, he and I had nothing in common, but he'd just told me otherwise. I didn't understand it, not completely, but I wouldn't forget it.

"What are you doing now?" I asked.

"Book," he said.

"Read it out loud so I can hear."

"You want me to read to you?"

"Yes."

"You got it, girl."

****

The roar of the vacuum cleaner pulled me out of my deep snooze. It woke Max, because he began licking my toes, his signal to go out. Whether he had to pee or just wanted to get away from the vacuum, which he hated, made little difference. I would have no peace until he got his way. I turned on the baby monitor mom had set up beside my bed.

"Mom, Max needs to go out."

She must have been right outside the door. "Good, you're awake. Come on, Max." She was back at my bedside shortly. "What would you like for breakfast?"

"Not very hungry," I said. "Maybe just coffee."

"Why don't you come into the kitchen? Then I can do a quick vacuum in your room. It's been over a week."

All a part of the plan, I knew. Like, *for every action there's an equal and opposite reaction.* Feed Daisy in the kitchen where she can't dump her plate down the toilet.

In the two weeks since I'd come home, I wasn't

any closer to my goal than when I'd started. Of course, fasting was virtually impossible with the aroma of cinnamon buns floating around, and when I got to the kitchen I discovered another trap waiting for me—sugar cookies. Mom was baking sugar cookies.

You can't trust mothers. They remember too much. I had forgotten that, for a plate of her sugar cookies, I would do back flips and blow bubbles out my nose, but she remembered. This was war.

Mom followed me in and pulled out a chair for me. "Sure I can't fix you something?" she asked. "Toast, maybe?"

"Sure, toast would be good."

"And maybe some strawberry jam?"

"Okay, jam." What the hell, today would be a total loss. Maybe I could start tomorrow. "You're baking again," I said.

"Sugar cookies. I guess you forgot that Linda is coming for a visit today."

"I guess so." But I didn't forget, because this was the first I'd heard of it. This was beginning to stink of conspiracy—not stink, exactly. Sugar cookies don't stink. If the aroma of sugar cookies in the oven could be infused into the atmosphere, the world would be a better place. I'm sure of it.

But this conspiracy, which I'd just realized, was serious business. Mom, Arthur, and Linda uniting to thwart my plans. Mom with her cinnamon buns and sugar cookies, Arthur the trickster, and Linda the organizer.

In the hospital I had no choice. They forced me to do terrible things, always "for my own good." Never mind that what they considered best for me was completely different from my own wishes, they won, always. They were never subtle in the hospital. They didn't have to be.

Same game, different rules now, and I seem to be on the losing end once again, so much for my new freedom to choose. Of course, no one forced me to eat cinnamon buns, and no one forced me to talk to Arthur. I could have cut him off cold, but I hadn't. And Linda had rights and privileges because she was my friend. My few friends were special to me, because I probably wouldn't be making any more of them.

It was no coincidence that the same three people I designated as co-conspirators were also the only three with whom I had any regular contact. The customary elements of a social transaction, the essential give and take, lay beyond my ability. I could take, but I couldn't give. A smile from a face so ghastly that it caused little children to hide behind their mother's skirts wasn't really much of a smile. And a hug from arms that looked like pieces of withered fruit didn't cut it either. I was like a radio receiver that could take in signals, but could transmit nothing.

"Your real friends won't care," Mom always said about my freakish appearance. But that was just Mom talk. Mothers, I think, cannot fail to love something to which they've given birth. Even if, like me, it didn't look particularly human, they'd still love it. Not to belittle maternal love, the strongest of all social bonds, but it's automatic. You didn't have to earn it. You didn't even have to deserve it.

So, I'd messed up over these first few days, but that didn't mean I'd failed. Nobody said this had to go smoothly from beginning to end. The trick was, I guess, to keep the goal in sight, because there was no other way.

"We're out of milk," Mom said. "I'm going to run over to Sparky's. Any messages for Ralph?"

"Just say 'hi' for me."

I managed to get my breakfast plate into the sink without breaking it. Mom had let Max back in before she left, and he was circling around, hungry. "Sorry, boy, I can't feed you. Mom will be back in a minute."

If I tried to feed him there would be dog food strewn all over the kitchen floor that Mom had just cleaned, and I didn't need another reminder of how helpless I'd become. Besides, almost any movement outside my usual limping around brought on pain, and my tolerance to discomfort was wearing thin, very thin.

Some people have gimpy joints, knees, or hips that stiffen up, so they have to work them a bit, loosen them up before heading out for the day. With me it was my skin. When I stayed in one position for very long, it seemed to shrink and moving around hurt like hell.

My father used to tell a story—he always had a story—about how the Apache Indians, when they captured a cowboy, would tie a wet rawhide noose around his neck. Not so bad at first, but as the noose dried in the sun it gradually choked him to death. It had sounded pretty scary at the time, but not anymore. The unfortunate cowboy's agony might have lasted for an hour or so. Mine has gone on months. In the end, the cowboy got to die; I am condemned to life, for now.

I didn't have long for ruminations. Mom's trip to Sparky's only took a couple of minutes.

"They all asked about you," she said. "Ralph sent you a grape slurpee. He wouldn't take any money for it, said it was a present. Do you want me to bring it in?"

"No." But I couldn't resist a grape slurpee any more than I could refuse sugar cookies. "Yes."

"Good girl."

A grape slurpee, pure heaven. For probably the last five years I had never gone longer than a week without one. Now it had been six months, and this was the best one ever. *God bless you*, Ralph. I'd have to add Ralph's name to my friends list, bringing my grand total to four.

"Mom, make sure to thank Ralph for me."

"Why don't you do it yourself? He said he'd really like to see you. Said he'd fix you a chili dog just the way you like them, on the house."

"I don't want him to see me like this."

"Look, he knows about your burns, but he said he'd love to see you anyway. Your real friends won't care, Daisy, remember that. Now, I've got to check those cookies."

More Mom-speak, "Your real friends won't care, why, they probably won't even notice." Yeah, right.

Linda arrived just after one o'clock. Mom was all primed and ready to fix lunch, but Linda said she'd already eaten. Mom didn't give up so easy. She brought in a platter with milk and cookies.

"Milk and cookies," Linda said. "I haven't had milk and cookies for years. What a treat."

In spite of feeling bloated with my slurpee, I wolfed down a couple of cookies.

"Too good to resist," Linda said. "These are delicious."

"Mom will give you some to take home. She always does." Another Mom rule, visitors never left the house empty-handed.

"You know what, we should go outside. It's a beautiful day."

"I don't go out."

"Just a few minutes. We can come back in whenever you want."

Another one of my new rules just melted away, but how could I say no to Linda? Now, what to wear? I wanted something that would cover me head to toe if possible. I didn't think the outside world was quite ready for me. Maybe a sheet draped over my head, wouldn't even have to cut out holes for the eyes, since I didn't have any.

After a lot of deliberation, I wound up wearing my ball cap, dark glasses, and a robe that covered my arms and most of my legs. The short trip still seemed questionable, I mean, what good was a spring day if you couldn't see anything? Big deal. But I went, because it was what Linda wanted.

Even swathed as I was, almost head to toe, sightless, the joy of a spring afternoon still caught up with me. It enveloped me as soon as the front door closed behind me. I gulped in the fresh air like a fish plucked from a pond.

"Guess you haven't been outside for a while," Linda said.

"Not since I got home."

"Good heavens, that will not do, not at all. I'm going to have a talk with your mom."

"It's not her fault," I said. "I've been kind of hard on her." Bitchy would have been more accurate, but I didn't like the sound of that.

"Still, you ought to get out while this weather lasts. Before you know it, it will be hot as blazes. You want to take a little ride, just down to the corner?"

"This is great, right here." And it was great. I'd expected nothing, inside, outside, no difference. But it was so very different. I would never see another spring day, not the way other people see them, but I could remember. I could remember new leaves rustling in a light breeze, the smell of newly mown grass. In summers past I'd been the designated lawn mower at our house, and those first few cuttings in the spring, before the summer heat dried out the grass, were like nectar.

I'd heard and smelled all those things around me before, but now was like the very first time. I wanted to hold onto each sensation, capture it in a jar where I could let it out in secret whenever I wanted. Times past I would have kicked off my shoes and raced Max across the lawn. Well, things were different now, different but no less special.

"How are things going with Arthur?" Linda asked.

"Oh, yeah, Arthur. He's driving me crazy."

She laughed. "That's Arthur, all right."

I listened closely to Linda's laugh. So different from Arthur's, yet similar. The volume, the pitch was all different, but it was genuine, like Arthur's. I had heard enough forced laughter during the past few months to last me forever. How refreshing to hear someone laugh because they were happy. I wondered about that happy place from which such laughter arose. Would I ever again laugh like that?

"Tell me about him," I said.

Linda didn't respond at first. "Suppose I let him tell you about himself."

"Oh, come on," I said. "Give me something, at

least. I need to know what I'm getting into here."

"Let me push you over to that chair by the tree. I need to sit down."

"Wait. Let me see if I can drive this thing by myself." I struggled for a moment, but couldn't get the wheelchair started. Dammit.

"It's the grass. These things are hard to move in grass. Let's both push together." The wooden lawn chair beneath our maple tree creaked as Linda settled into it. From down the street tires screeched, a horn blared, but there were no sounds of a collision. Behind us, probably in the same red maple that I had helped Dad plant years before, a blue jay began to fuss.

"So, talk to me," I said.

"I'll tell you how I met Arthur," she said. Her voice dropped to just above a whisper, and a deep sadness crept in.

"Wait, you don't have to tell me stuff if you don't want to. I mean, your private life is your own business."

"No, it might do me good to talk about it. I haven't told anybody else, so this is just between us, okay? I was married before, too young to know what I was doing. I won't go into details, but it got bad, really bad. I tried to make it work, alcohol, mostly. You can guess how that turned out."

She went quiet. I heard her breathing deeply, almost gasping. Should I stop her? No. Whatever was festering inside my friend had to come out, and all I could do was listen, bear witness.

"Sometimes I drank at work. I kept a bottle of mouthwash in my locker. But people knew. That's the kind of thing you can only hide for so long. I was right on the edge. You know, when you talked about wanting out, just wanting it all to be over and done with? I've been there.

"Then one day, right out of the blue, there was Arthur. I mean, he was just there. I don't know if somebody sent him, but there he was. At first I wanted nothing to do with him, but you know Arthur. He's hard to stop."

I detected yet another change in Linda's voice. Despair had given way to hope, the possibility of something better. Then soft laughter, memory of a happier time, like crawling out of the depths and seeing the sun shine for the first time in a long while.

"I thought he was worse than anything I'd gone through before." Now the very happy laughter bubbled out. "I hated him. I screamed, yelled, threw things at him. But he wouldn't quit. To make a long story short, he saved my ass, when I didn't really want to be saved. He's why I'm still around today. And that's all I'm going to say about that."

I reached out my hand, and she took it. So we sat, no need for more words. This much I know, whether you can see the hurt places immediately, like mine, or whether they're hidden away inside, like Linda's, they all hurt.

I hadn't learned the specifics about how he'd helped her turn her life around, but I knew all I was going to know, all I needed to know. That encounter, Linda and Arthur, had been intense and personal, much like my own. I had to decide, do I really want someone digging around in my head the way Arthur was doing? Do I want him to save my ass?

A school bus passed by filling the air with noise and diesel fumes. I heard the chair creak as Linda stood.

"If I'm going to beat the tunnel traffic I'd better get a move on."

Back inside I asked Mom to leave me sitting on the sofa.

"Good," she said. "That will give me a chance to tidy your room up a bit. How about a few more cookies, maybe a glass of milk?"

"Yes, please." My resistance had sunk to a new low. I was like Max when he was offered a treat. He took it without a second thought. Now I was doing the same.

And I paid a price. A little later, "Mom, I'm going to be sick."

We made it to the half-bath just off the front hallway where I disgorged most of a grape slurpee, several sugar cookies and almost two glasses of milk, all of which had found their way into a stomach that had been in near-starvation mode for almost a week.

"Oh, I should have been more careful," mom said as she swabbed my face with a damp washcloth. "That was way too much for you, all at once. I was just so happy to see you eating again."

She helped me back to bed, then bundled me into a light blanket. "So sorry," she said over and over.

I drifted off to sleep, then woke sometime later with a ravenous thirst. I ran my hand across my nightstand to locate the glass and water pitcher that Mom always left there for me. I drank in small sips. One episode of vomiting was quite enough for the day.

Chapter 8

"Are you sure you'll be all right? I'll only be gone for an hour or so." Sunday morning and Mom was all gussied up for church. I didn't need to see her to know almost exactly how she looked, not lavish, but everything from her perfectly groomed hair down to her low-heeled shoes all properly done up with care and attention to detail. And always there was that faint scent of lavender, and the rustle of fabric from one of Mom's Sunday dresses, the click of her heels on the hardwood floor.

Mom wore a dress every day, never the same one two days in a row, each day a freshly washed and ironed garment. Not that she had a closet full of them, because she did not. I knew this. More like, this was who she was, a statement of her identity. I had never seen her wearing slacks, and jeans, out of the question.

On Sunday she wore a pearl necklace and earrings, and, if you got close, within three feet or so, you would catch that same faint aroma of lavender. To me this scent always brought back childhood memories, when she came in to tuck me into bed and leaned down to kiss me good night.

For a few brief hours, I had come so close to that world, playing dress up, learning how to walk all over again, learning how to sit and cross my legs just so. For most of my life I had emulated my father's postures.

That meant leaning back with my legs splayed out, feet wide apart. Since my clothes usually consisted of jeans and one of Dad's cast-off work shirts, how I chose to sit made no difference.

But Mom saw things differently. "Young ladies do *not* sit like that. Sit up straight and keep your knees together, always." If she had admonished me once, she had done so a thousand times, to no avail. Now, as before, it made no difference how I sat. Freaks could sit any way they wanted. Who cared?

I rolled my wheelchair over by the open window next to my bed. The mockingbird that had taken up residence in the maple tree out back was singing nonstop. Before, when my vision was intact and my waking/sleeping cycles were more regular, that same bird had made a damned nuisance of itself, often starting up just before sunrise, hours before I was ready to face the day. Sometimes I would chunk stones into the tree trying to scare it off, but it always returned. Like so much of my life now, I could do nothing about the bird, so I sat and listened.

"Change what you can, and the rest, just live with it." Words of wisdom from my father.

****

"Mom, can we visit Dad's grave?" I asked on Monday morning. This thought had come to me in the middle of the night; I had to go and pay my respects to the man who had been such a huge part of my life. Some people lose their parents in faraway places, wars and such, but my own father lay less than a mile away from our house.

"Of course. I went there yesterday after church and put out some fresh flowers. We can certainly go over this morning, before it gets too hot outside. Tell me, any special reason you wanted to go today?"

"I want to say goodbye." Before I was burned I made many visits to his grave, sometimes to chat, more often just to sit quietly the way we'd done so often when he was alive. But I hadn't been there since I'd returned from the hospital. I had to go, and I had to go today.

I'd left my father's funeral feeling incomplete, unable to let go. There was no sense of finality even with it staring me right in the face. Wishful thinking, maybe, I don't know, hoping this wasn't the end when I knew it was.

The number of people who'd come during the memorial service, there were so many of them. The line at Drummond's Funeral Home seemed endless. I had no idea that Dad had so many friends, and about half of them were in tears, even the men. Damndest thing I'd ever seen.

And the food, it filled up our kitchen, our little dining room, and still it kept coming. In a small town that's what you did, someone died, you brought food.

And through it all, Mom was a rock. How she held it together I'll never know. Just another way I could never hope to measure up to her. I thought at first that she'd become numb, like I was, and stuff just rolled off because she didn't feel anything. But that wasn't the case, not by a long shot.

What gave her away was her eyes, even a glance and it was like you were peering into the pool that all of human misery drained into. How someone could look so together yet hurt so bad, something else I would have to learn on my own.

All through that bad time, Mom and I did our grieving apart. For me, there was more than a little denial, like, don't talk about it, and maybe it never happened. Kid stuff, I know, but when it takes all you've got just to stay afloat, you do whatever works. But I knew that sooner or later we would have to share that burden, lest it overwhelm us separately. Now, it seemed, that time had come.

"What would you like to wear?" Mom asked. "Remember, it's going to be warm out, so that fleece robe won't do at all."

"I have to cover up." Anyone who saw me for the first time in all my charred glory might think I was some specter rising up from the grave.

"Do you think I look like a zombie?"

"Daisy, stop it. I will not have you talking like that."

"It was only a joke, Mom."

"Not a very funny one. Now, let's have no more of that. I washed the scrub suit and gown that you wore home from the hospital. That might work."

So that's how I dressed, like a hospital escapee, complete with my baseball cap, dark glasses and grubby sneakers.

"I'll park the truck as close as I can, but we'll still have a short walk. I'm sure we won't be able to push your wheelchair over the ground. We'll just have to take it slow."

No sooner did we get me dressed than Max started whining.

"You don't suppose he knows where we're going?" I asked.

"Wouldn't surprise me. Max, if we take you along

you're going to have to behave. Do you understand me?"

That Mom would ever consider taking Max along was a big surprise for me. She would have her hands full, getting me there and back, let alone a dog.

"If he starts running all over the place we'll just have to let him go," she said.

Our strange little trio made it out to the truck. Mom was right, it was uncomfortably warm, and we hadn't even reached the noon hour yet.

"Last week of June," Mom said. "The real hot weather hasn't even started."

A short time later we pulled off the pavement and onto a gravel path. "Looks like we've got the place to ourselves," Mom said.

Not really, I thought. You can't ever be alone in a cemetery; they might not talk to you, but they're there just the same. And one of them is my father.

The cemetery in back of First Baptist is big, like a couple of football fields joined by a road running down its center. It ends on two sides where county road number twelve wraps around, so all the expansion has been eastward.

A number of Warrensburg's older families could point out several generations of ancestors, usually lying in small groups. Now it's so crowded that I hear you're lucky to get two adjoining plots.

When I was a kid that cemetery was a big playground. Our games never had official names, we'd just run around like crazy until we got tired out, then we'd head home.

I got my first real kiss in that cemetery. Larry Elliott and I were hiding behind a tombstone when he planted one on me, right on the lips. I thought he wanted to wrestle, so I shoved him, and he cracked his head on the granite. I didn't get another kiss until junior high.

One night someone suggested tipping over a few tombstones, so we did, about a dozen or so. The next afternoon when I got home from school, Sheriff Tate's car was in our driveway, and he, Mom, and Dad were all sitting on the sofa waiting for me.

My parents didn't say a word. They just watched me with the most painful expressions you can imagine, like I'd drowned a bunch of puppies. But Sheriff Tate had a lot to say, all about how, even though the folks in the cemetery were dead and gone, they were still important to those they'd left behind. He went on and on, but that's what I remember most.

He ended up by suggesting that my friends and I— he knew all of our names—spend a few weekends cleaning up the graveyard, picking up trash, clearing out weeds and such. I felt like such a weasel, sitting there with tears pouring down my face, hearing about all the pain I'd caused by being so disrespectful. A good old-fashioned ass whipping couldn't have made me feel any worse. Live and learn, I guess.

"I forgot," Mom said. "There is a path that runs down the middle. It looks firm enough that I can probably push your wheelchair part of the way."

"Max, come back here." Mom's voice had just a touch of panic, like maybe this three-ring circus was more than she could handle.

"Max." I yelled, and shortly I felt his heavy body pressing against my leg.

A click. "Okay, that's the dog's leash attached.

Now if I can get your wheelchair out of the back."

"I can walk, Mom, if you help me."

Nobody ever said a mother's job would be easy, but with a puny, crippled daughter on one arm and a vigorous, lunging dog on the other, we set off. We didn't get far. By three steps I was wobbly. Four steps and I was on my knees. How did I ever get so weak?

"I was afraid of this," Mom said. "Except for a few steps inside the house, you haven't been on your feet for over six months. We'll have to use your chair."

She helped me back to the truck, and from the amount of scraping and banging she was having quite a time wrestling the chair out.

"Where's Max?" I asked.

"He's wandering around sniffing everything. If he doesn't behave he's going right back into the truck, and I think he knows it."

Yeah, I guess for an animal that explores the world with his nose, a graveyard would be a fascinating place to investigate.

Our second start was more successful. I held Max's leash, while Mom pushed the chair. The temperature seemed to have risen ten degrees since we'd arrived, and I really felt sorry for Mom. The path was firm enough, but full of bumps, so it must have felt like she was always pushing uphill.

"Maybe this wasn't such a great idea," I said.

"We're here, and we're going to do what we came to do. It's important, for both of us."

Mom was beginning to sound like one of those polar expedition leaders who just kept going on and on and wouldn't quit no matter how tough the trip became. By the time we finally stopped she was panting like

Max.

"This is your father's row. Now we'll have to figure out how to get you there. This ground is way too soft to push your chair."

"Can you pull it instead?"

"Why didn't I think of that?" she said.

After a few moments of tugging me backward, Mom stopped. "Time for a short break," she said.

"Are we there yet?"

"No, we're right beside Mr. Darcy's grave. He lived just down the street, the little white colonial with the rose garden off to the side, remember? Sometimes I think that rose garden was what kept him going so long. He was ninety when he died."

"I remember the Halloween when someone threw toilet paper in the tree in his front yard. He always blamed me for that."

"Well, he was right, wasn't he?"

"I'm not gonna say, especially not sitting right beside his grave."

A little farther down Mom stopped again. "This is it."

I pushed myself out of the chair and leaned forward so I could grasp the headstone. Then I knelt down and ran my fingertips over the lettering: *Samuel G. Sugarbush, Beloved Husband and Father, 1941-1993.* I knew it by heart from my previous visits. He wanted to keep it simple. No poems or sonnets, just the basics.

"What was his middle name?" I asked.

"George, after his father."

I scooted over, still on my knees, to where the low earth mound began. It had settled back into place and now was almost level with the level ground. I placed my palms in the center and leaned over it. "Bye, Dad. Hope you're happy up there. I miss you, and I love you." I felt my mother kneel at my side and knew that she was praying. A good daughter, a regular daughter would, without hesitation, have joined her mother in prayer, but I was none of these.

I knelt there by the ruins of the Sugarbush family: father/husband dead in the ground, daughter a deformed freakish thing with neither present nor future, mother grieving for all of us. It might have been better if I'd had a sibling, a backup child to carry on our name, but that was not to be. This was all of it, right here. Prayer seemed like a lot of wasted effort.

Years before, watching the evening news with Dad, I'd seen film clips where entire families had been destroyed by some catastrophe, fire, floods, maybe gunned down by a deranged relative. After something like that, what was there left to pray for? It seemed silly to pray to be delivered from evil when that evil had already come and kicked your ass all over the county.

And all that crap about God's mercy? Where was God when they were ripping my skin off in that hospital? If God had even an iota of mercy, He would have ended my miserable existence then and there. But no, I was still up and about, scaring children, being led around by a dog. Sometimes I thought maybe Dad got off easy.

Mom shifted at my side, her arm slipped around my shoulder. Something was coming, I could feel it, something that had probably been brewing for a long time.

"I'm sorry," she said.

"Not your fault. He was so sick."

"That's not what I mean. I'm talking about the hospital. I'm asking you to forgive me."

"Mom?"

"In the hospital, when you begged us to stop treatment, just let you go. There's not a day goes by I don't feel sick over what I did, making you go through those horrible procedures."

I pushed myself up. I felt woozy and put my hand on her shoulder for support. As soon as I felt steady enough, I took a few steps away. "And you want me to say it's all okay now?"

"No, I know that's too much to ask."

"Mom, I hated you for that, for what all of you did to me."

"I hated myself. Every day I'd come home from the hospital, read my Bible, pray. Try to make it out like I was doing God's will. Finally I had to admit to myself it had nothing to do with God's will. It was all about me, what I wanted. I'd just lost Sam. I couldn't bear to lose you, too."

"It's over now, Mom. I don't want to talk about it any more."

"Daisy, I'm sorry, but I have to. Can't you put yourself in my position, even a little?"

"Mom, just let it go."

She was at my side, holding on to me. It wasn't a hug, more like a desperate clinging, like if she let go she'd drown. "Please," she said.

"How about, did you ever put yourself in my position? Did you ever do that? Do you know what it was like every day, every night, for months?" For me, the horror was always there close by. All I had to do was open that door just a crack, and it all came cascading back in, the pain, my screams, while, as best I could tell, nobody listened.

Sure, I'd love to let her off the hook, forgive and forget, but I could no more forget than I could fly. Even as I listened to her sobbing, I could not relent. "It's not okay, Mom. It's not okay to do that to somebody when they're begging you to stop."

"I'm sorry. I'm so sorry."

I could hardly breathe. I gasped for air like I sometimes did at the end of one of my coughing jags. Then it softened. For the moment, at least, it was over. "Let it go, Mom. I do forgive you, absolutely. I love you. But it's still not okay."

"What can I do to make it right? I don't know how to fix it between us."

We sat on the ground, arms wrapped around each other. Somehow Max managed to wedge his head between us. Healing would take a long, long time. I guess my dog knew as much and wanted to be part of the process, but if things went according to plan, I wouldn't have a long time, so whatever fence-mending took place would have to happen sooner rather than later.

"It's not just between us," I said. "It's the whole lousy hospital system. Yeah, I know they do a fantastic job, saving lives and all, but I'm as sure as anything that right now on that same Burn Trauma Unit there are people in just as much pain as I was, screaming just as loud as I did. People have rights, and if they're able, they should be allowed to choose. It has to be that way, but I don't know how to fix it." And now I never would; that part of my life was over. Someone else would have to fight that battle, maybe Linda. Just getting through the day was all I could manage now.

"We should go," Mom said. "I think it might rain."

We got home just before an afternoon thunderstorm erupted. Mom ran around the house checking for open windows, then she went to her bedroom, and I went to mine. Some grief you share, some you don't. I'd thought that this little trip would help us shoulder the burden together, but I'd just uncovered more open wounds. I'm sure Mom felt the same way.

I stayed in my room for the rest of the day stewing over things I knew I couldn't change, but stewing all the same. And sleep? Nothing doing. Besides not being able to sleep I had another clue that I'd messed up…Max. My dog always slept at the foot of my bed, but tonight he'd found somewhere else to snooze. Bad news for me. When your dog can't stand your company, you've got a big problem. And I didn't have very far to look, did I?

Daisy Sugarbush, first class dickhead, that's your problem.

But hold on, I've got every right to be pissed off, my life was ruined, I've suffered a great injustice.

Well, big fucking deal, like you're the only one who ever got the short end of the stick. And to make matters worse you dumped all over your poor mother today. She might have said it was all about her, keeping you alive so she wouldn't have to be alone, but that was a crock. Whatever she did she did because she loves you. So there, how do you feel now? Proud of yourself?

Oh, shit.

You can do better than that. Go tell your mother you're sorry, and do it right now. By tomorrow you'll have figured a way to weasel out of it.

Okay, just stop yelling at me.

Mom's bedroom door was open, I guess so she could listen out for me at night.

"Mom?" I whispered, half hoping that she wouldn't hear.

"Daisy, what's the matter?"

"I know it's late, but can we talk for a minute?"

"Of course, sweetheart. Come over and sit on the bed."

She sat beside me, her arm wrapped around my shoulders. "What is it?"

"I'm sorry I was such a little creep today, all that stuff I said about hating you for not stopping those treatments. You were just doing what you thought was best for me."

She sighed, like the deepest of all sighs. "But I was still wrong in doing it. I made a decision for you that really wasn't mine to make," she said.

She was shaking a little now, or maybe it was me or maybe both of us. But my own choice, back during those awful days would have been to stop everything, just let me go, let those bombed out kidneys of mine peter out and take me with them. My choice would have put me in the ground alongside my dad, or maybe just cremation, since I was halfway there already.

"I can't take back what I did, Daisy, and I can't promise you that, if I had it to do all over again that I wouldn't do the same thing."

Another deep sigh, this time I joined her, and to the sigh I added a shudder, because her last statement chilled me to the bone. I thought our emotional exchange at the cemetery had paved over some of those issues about who should make choices about my life, but I was wrong. From what she just said, if the blast happened tomorrow instead of nine months ago, and if my mom—the same mom who earlier in the day had begged forgiveness for putting me through treatments too painful to imagine, who kept me alive when all I wanted, *all I wanted*, was to die—if she were calling the shots, I would probably be right back on that conveyer belt to hell.

She could have lied or said nothing at all, and I would have been none the wiser, but I guess she wanted me to know that whatever drove her before was still in play. Maybe she wasn't so sure herself, maybe it was love, maybe it was fear of being alone, or maybe the "God's will" thing was needling her, but something very powerful was pushing her buttons.

And where did that leave me? In a very uncertain place, that's where. I'd thought when I got home from the hospital that I would be in charge of my own life, and, up to a point, I was. Of course, my starvation diet plan hadn't proved very convincing; shove a platter of freshly baked cinnamon buns under my nose, and my resolve folded like a house of cards in a breeze.

It was small comfort knowing that I'd already been hurt so badly that nothing could ever really hurt me any worse. If the guys from our local chapter of the Spanish Inquisition came for me, I could laugh in their faces. "Just what do you bastards think you can do to me that hasn't been done already? Burn me at the stake? Been there, done that, so fuck off and go scare somebody else."

Yeah, there's something to be said for having nothing left to lose. But the fact of having limited options still doesn't answer the question of who gets to choose, who gets to make the big decisions. For my mother it seems to be a case of the end justifying the means. I'm still alive, so whatever it took to keep me breathing was okay. I disagree.

It's a maze, this choices thing, full of dead ends and trap doors. Even my friend Linda, to whom patient autonomy, as she calls it, is like the holy grail, has been undercut a number of times.

So it all seems perfectly clear in principle when it's written out on paper: the patient, so long as he/she is capable of making decisions, has the absolute right to decide about his/her treatment. But when you bring the discussion right down to the bedside it becomes a muddle, because at that level it involves people and beliefs and emotion and God-only-knows what else, so you might as well fold your sheet of principles into a paper airplane and sail it out the window.

****

I really wasn't up to an Arthur visit Tuesday morning. After the heart-to-heart Mom and I had had the day before, I felt drained. Lack of sleep didn't help. But then, there he was, big booming laugh at the front door like he'd just walked into a fun house.

"Hi, Rhoda, hey Max." More stupid laughter. Mom joined in, Max barked, I sulked.

Yeah, Mom was still Mom, or Rhoda, Max was still Max, and I was still Miss Daisy, *Miss,* like I was some sort of idiot that might forget who I was or where I lived. I rolled into a ball facing the wall. Maybe he would take the hint and go away. Fat chance.

"Hey, there, Miss Daisy," he said. Then he sat in the same chair as before.

I heard paper rattling, then the aroma. If I were put to sleep for ten years, I would still know that aroma right off. My salivary glands kicked into overdrive. Sometimes I felt as if drooling was the only thing I could still do right, and I was doing it now.

There is, on the western edge of town, which is only a mile and a half from the eastern edge, our edge, a hole-in-the-wall burger joint named Leroy's. Nothing else, just Leroy's. But you could say the word to anyone in Warrensburg, and they would know exactly what you meant.

To enter this magical kingdom you opened a weathered, flimsy door with a handle that sometimes turned one way, sometimes, the other. I've seen more impressive doors on public toilets. Then you stepped inside, and immediately that special aroma lifted you a couple of inches off the floor. I'd bet there aren't ten people in Warrensburg, outside of Leroy himself, who could tell you what the inside of Leroy's looked like, because nobody ever bothered to look.

We all knew about the four booths, always empty. Your elbows stuck to the tabletops, and your feet stuck to the floor, which could have been why nobody ever sat down in Leroy's.

The cook at Leroy's served up only two items, cheeseburgers and fries. You want a hot dog? Go someplace else. Leroy's famous cheeseburgers always draped over the sides of the bun, so you had to lick your entire hand, not just your fingertips, to make sure you'd got it all. But the thing that drew the crowds was Leroy's special sauce. Sure, it tasted great, but that tangy aroma was what drove us all wild. Was it better than sugar cookies in the oven? I'm afraid so, but don't tell Mom. Rumor had it that Leroy made it up every day in a back room and wouldn't let anybody in until he was finished.

And now Arthur had brought that heavenly aroma into my bedroom.

"What's that you've got?" I asked, as if I didn't know.

"My lunch. Big old juicy cheeseburger, oh, yeah, and fries. Hey, would you look at that. Max likes fries." More happy laughter. God, didn't he ever stop?

Max was a noisy eater. The sound of the dog gulping down French fries caused my stomach to rumble even more. And the aroma was driving me crazy.

"Can I have some?" I asked.

"Hmm, what do you think, Max? We got enough for Miss Daisy?"

"Just one bite, one lousy bite."

"Okay, but there's a catch."

"Dammit, I knew it was a trick," I said. If it smells too good to be true, it probably is.

Big laugh. "There's always a catch. You know that by now. Here's the deal. I feed you, then you work with me."

"What do you mean?"

"Just some regular physical therapy stuff, flexibility, strengthening stuff. But be warned, when I say work, I mean work. None of that half-assed business."

"Have you been talking to my mother?"

"No, I'm just tired of looking at you being so puny."

"Okay, whatever." Ordinarily I would really let

him have it for talking like that, but he was holding the trump card, and he knew it.

"We got a deal then. Just so happens I got an extra cheeseburger in here, a little carton of fries, plus a coke. Got it at Leroy's. You ever heard of the place?"

"No, never." That glorious aroma was making my head spin.

"I'm gonna put it all on your little table here. Don't worry about Max. I'll feed him."

I took a deep breath, inhaling as much as I could, then, a bite. Pure heaven on a toasted bun, that first bite. Nothing, absolutely nothing could have given me as much pleasure as sinking my teeth into an authentic Leroy's cheeseburger.

"Slow down," Arthur said. "Don't eat so fast. Make yourself sick."

I could hardly control myself, but I did finish slowly like he said, then licked my fingers, then my entire hand. If I hadn't enjoyed the burger so much I would have been mad as hell at him right now, tricking me like that, the same way you'd train a dog to sit—give them a command, then the treat, except he'd done it in reverse.

"Okay, I'm ready. Do your worst."

"Not quite yet," he said. "You need to rest a bit after you eat."

"So, what, you're just going to sit there?"

"Nope, the book, remember, *Great Expectations*. I'm going to read some more to you. Then we'll get to work."

Sometime later I lay on my back pushing against Arthur's massive hands, all the while he was coaching me. "Push, girl, push."

"That's all I can do." I gasped for breath. My arms and legs lay limp like overdone pasta strands on the bed.

"We got a lot of work to do."

"Why? What difference does it make? I can't walk. Even if I could, I can't see where I'm going."

"It's all part of the process, Daisy. You're gonna surprise yourself, you'll see." Then, of course, he laughed, that knowing, rumbling laugh that was really getting on my nerves.

"I wish you'd tell me what you think is so damned funny."

"You'll find out soon enough. See you Thursday."

****

It seemed now that my whole life revolved around Arthur, and every visit brought something new. On Thursday it sounded as if he was bringing in a large pile of scrap metal. I heard Mom offer to help, but Arthur refused. "I got it," he said. "And there's a few more pieces out in the car. I had to break it down to get it all to fit inside."

He was panting by the time he brought in the last load. He asked my mother to stay and watch while he set things up. "Daisy needs to work on this every day, so when I'm not around you'll be in charge, make sure she does like she's supposed to."

"I'm right here," I said. "Don't talk about me like I'm not in the room."

"Right, you got me," Arthur said. "Now this big bar is called a trapeze, runs from one end of the bed to the other. Reach up here and grab hold of these little straps. See, you can pull yourself up and down, get your arms strong." He moved my hands into two loops. I could barely pull myself more than a couple of inches off the bed.

"Swing around like a monkey, you mean." But this monkey was a long way from swinging at all.

"Call it whatever you want, just so you do it. This thing I put over here in the corner is a stationary bike. I just have to attach the front wheel, and we're ready to go. That other stuff can wait 'til later."

"Maybe I don't want to. What if I refuse?"

"Well, there's three of us, your mom and me and Max, too, and we all want to see you ride the bike. Just five minutes, nice and slow."

"I'm afraid I'll fall." Before my time in hospital had sucked most of the life out of me, few things scared me. Now I felt like a baby, afraid to try anything new. Of course, not being able to see it made it worse.

"I'll be right beside you."

Five minutes was a long time. After the bike ride there were more pull-ups, then stretching until I felt like my arms and legs were coming apart. I lay back, completely spent.

"Great workout today," Arthur said. "I'm proud of you."

He picked up my right foot. What now? "What are you doing?"

"Measuring your foot."

"What for, ballet slippers?"

"Your new shoes, for when we go out for our walks."

I jerked my foot away. "Forget about that. Listen to me for once, will you? I do not take walks. Period. Absolutely not. Never. Got that? No walks."

As always, he laughed. "Yeah sure. Now, other

foot."

I was losing the battle. My resolve, once as solid as any concrete foundation in Warrensburg, was melting away like the last snow of winter. Now, new shoes. I needed new shoes like I needed a new motorcycle. But next week, just as sure as sunrise, Arthur would be there with new shoes, and he would lead me around the house, guiding me past obstacles. He even mentioned bringing along a friend, someone who could help arrange things, so I could get around by myself.

"You mean another therapist?"

"You say therapist like it's a dirty word."

"No," I said. "I didn't mean it that way. I'll work with whoever you want, just not outside."

"That's my girl."

But he wasn't fooling me, not now. Soon he would have me walking around inside the house, then through an open door out into the back yard. I might fuss a bit, but I'd do it, just like he said. And yes, I would be scared, but it would happen anyway.

Late that night, after all was quiet in the house, I lay in bed, repeating some of the stretching exercises Arthur had taught me. I wasn't even sure why I was doing it, except that Arthur had said I should, and, in spite of all my misgivings, I now trusted him. The only person I had ever trusted completely was my father, that, in part, because we seemed two halves of a whole. Whatever my father said, that was how it was, no questions asked.

As a pair, Dad and I had kept most of the world at arm's length, even excluding Mom. I had never before given much thought to the pain my mother must have felt, being shut out that way. Now, as I pulled my right knee up tight to my chest, held it there for a count of ten, I felt some of that pain of exclusion. It wasn't fair, none of it.

All this contemplation had started at dinner. As Arthur was packing up to leave, Mom came in, bringing with her the aroma of her famous pot roast, spicy, just a notch below a Leroy's cheeseburger. Her pot roast was always Dad's favorite. I remember him rubbing his hands together in anticipation whenever he smelled it. "Hot dang," he always said.

"You're staying for dinner," Mom said to Arthur. "And I won't take no for an answer."

"Mmm, that does smell fine," Arthur said.

"You can wash up in the bathroom just down the hall."

Then she came to sit beside me. "I thought we'd all have dinner in the dining room, just like we used to."

"No, mom, I can't feed myself. I'll make a big mess."

She wrapped her arms around my shoulders and pulled me close. "You'll do fine. It's all a part of the process, like Arthur says."

Great, now I was getting the gospel from both of them.

My first real sit down dinner in eight months. Mom sat beside me and carved my meat into edible chunks. Max pressed close against my leg, ready to gobble up anything I dropped.

"Best pot roast I've ever tasted," Arthur said.

The awkwardness that I dreaded never happened. I stabbed about on my plate with my fork. Sometimes I hit, sometimes I missed, and anything I dropped went straight into Max's waiting mouth. Never even once did

I get the feeling they were watching me, waiting for me to knock over my glass of milk or dump my plate into my lap. And even if I did, so what? Not like I would be the first person on the planet who spilled something.

Arthur must have got up to help clear the table, but Mom was on him before he got started. "You sit right down. I've been doing this for years," she said. "I know where everything goes. You two just sit here and chat."

As I listened to Mom working in the kitchen, I felt Arthur's massive hand on my shoulder.

"You're doing good, girl, real good."

"Daisy. That's my name."

"Okay, you're doing good, Daisy."

Mom was back in a moment. By smell alone I could envision the tray she was carrying—peach cobbler with ice cream and coffee, the cobbler all crisp and golden with the melted ice cream running down the sides.

"Would you look at that," Arthur said. "I might have to let my belt out a notch or two."

I laughed, and the sound of my own laughter surprised me. How long had it been?

The dessert was consumed in silence, just like always when Mom's peach cobbler turned up. Then it was over. I heard Arthur step away from the table. I turned toward his footsteps. "Hey, don't I at least get a hug or something?"

Chapter 9

I had to admit the new shoes that Arthur brought felt pretty good. Better still, they had nubby soles that allowed me to navigate across hardwood floors without slipping. Arthur was obviously pleased with his efforts. "See, they got little Velcro straps, so you don't even have to tie knots."

"What color are they?"

"Kinda pink."

"Pink shoes? You brought me pink shoes? That's for babies."

"They only had two colors. I thought the pink looked more cheerful."

New shoes. The last pair of new shoes I'd worn had been the pair of heels my mother had insisted on buying, back before Christmas of last year when she was trying to get me to dress more grown up lady-like. Well, for damned sure I would never be wearing anything with heels again.

With Arthur's help I made my way through the house with little difficulty. The initial fear was my main obstacle, but I got past that without much trouble. After all, I had walked through those same rooms in the dark hundreds of times.

Arthur let go of my arm. "Know where you are?" he asked.

"Living room. Sofa should be right over there." I

took small steps, located the edge of the sofa with my foot, then sat down. For the first time in many months I began to think about things I *could* do, rather than those things I could not.

The day before Arthur brought my new shoes, the therapist he had mentioned had paid a visit. The woman spoke with a rapid Hispanic accent, and I occasionally had to ask her to repeat herself. Like everybody else that sees me for the first time, I could feel her shock and disbelief, but, short of wearing a bag over my head, that was just something else she would have to accept.

The therapist, named Rosita, had a number of suggestions that she said might be helpful for the visually impaired.

"I'm not impaired. I'm blind." I waved my hand in front of my face. "Nothing, nothing at all." It still pissed me off when people talked as if my condition was partial instead of complete. I couldn't see a damned thing.

"Okay, then." If Rosita was daunted by the slight hostility in my voice she didn't let on. Maybe Arthur had warned her ahead of time that I might be a tough case. Perhaps other patients she'd seen had reacted in much the same way. It seemed unlikely that many individuals who had lost their sight would be happy about it.

Mom stood by while Rosita ran through her list of recommendations. "It is very important to put things back in the same place every time, Mrs. Sugarbush. That reduces the chance that Daisy might trip over them."

I found this advice amusing, even laughable.

"I don't understand," Rosita said. "What's funny?"

"Just that my mom has been after me forever to put things away after I finish with them. Now she gets the same lecture she always gave me."

Before long, I could manage the house. I didn't dare take the steps down into the basement, but upstairs I was good. It was a comfortable, familiar area, so I wouldn't have to call my mother every time I needed something. But safe and comfortable apparently did not fit into Arthur's plans. As soon as he mentioned going for a walk outside, I got off the sofa and headed for my bedroom. He made no attempt to help me along.

"I already told you, no walks outside."

I heard him pull the familiar chair alongside my bed. "Beautiful day out."

"I don't care. I can't see it anyway."

"But you can smell it, you can hear it, and you can feel it."

"If you think it's so great outside, go right ahead. Enjoy yourself. Be my guest. I'm staying right here."

He went all quiet on me again. Just one of his tricks, the silent treatment, sort of like the one Mom uses on me. If I didn't trust him so much, it would never work, but I did, and it would. Anybody else, they could play quiet games until hell froze over, but with Arthur it was different. Whatever he had to say next would be important. I would listen; I might not agree, but I would listen. Still, a walk outside? No way, no matter what he said.

He shifted in his seat, and the chair groaned for mercy. How the poor spindly thing hadn't collapsed beneath him before now was nothing short of miraculous.

"So, tell me, what makes you so special?" he

asked.

"I never said I was special. I'm burned, in case you haven't noticed." Where was this going? Of all the arguments he might have tried, this one threw me. What was he up to?

"Go ahead," he said. "I'm listening."

"What are you, totally stupid? Look at me." I waved my arms in the air.

"I'm looking. Have been for several weeks now. Listened to you babble on about how bad you got it. I ask you again, what makes you so special?"

What the hell kind of game was he playing? Why, I could go out on Halloween and scare kids half to death without even wearing a mask. If that didn't qualify me as special, I didn't know what would. "I don't have the slightest idea what you're talking about, except you're full of shit. That's for sure."

"Could be, could be." More silence. Then, "You ever lost anybody you cared about?"

"My dad. You know that already."

"It hurts?"

"Damn right it does." Son of a bitch. He played my emotions like he was plucking a banjo—confusion, anger, pain, all of them at once, and I couldn't stop him.

"What do you suppose, if you and me walked down the street together, knocked on doors and asked the people inside whether they'd lost somebody they really cared about?"

"This is bullshit."

"Most of them, Daisy, most of them have lost someone they cared about. And the ones that haven't, it's just a matter of time. And they hurt, too, every blessed one of them. That's life."

"Okay, then, Mr. Smartass, how many of them will look like me? How many of them look like some creature from outer space?"

"Not so many. But you spent a long time in that Burn Trauma Unit, then in rehab. How many of those people came out looking the same as they went in?"

"How the hell am I supposed to know? I'm blind, remember?"

"I'll tell you, then, damned few of them. The ones that survived were all different."

"Are you trying to make a point? I'm getting tired of all this blabber."

"Just this, everybody is special. If you are, so is everybody else. Mainly, you're special to people who care about you. The rest don't matter."

I lay back, defeated, deflated. He'd yanked away the crutch I had used for so long, about how I was exclusive, a "special' case. Just being one of many who'd all taken their own hits, carried their own scars, took some of the bite out of my own situation, but not enough to make it tolerable. I am and will always be, a freak. Nothing he can say will change that. Okay, so he'd scored a point, and whether I remained standing or fell, would be up to me. Son of a bitch. But I reminded myself, this was a battle, not the war. My goal remained the same. Before I packed it in, ran up a white flag, I had yet another wall to scale. All in good time, I thought, all in good time. "Okay," I said. "Where are you dragging me off to?"

"Nope, not like that. This is your call, right here and now. You tell me what you want."

I took a deep breath. "I want to go for a walk with you."

"That's my girl."

Of course, I couldn't see the expression on his face, not in the usual way, but I could feel it, and I knew that he looked as happy as if I'd just handed him a million bucks. "Hey, can Max come along?"

"Yeah, he got a leash?"

"He doesn't like it," I said. Indeed, Max always acted as if being tethered by a leash was a personal affront, like he was too stupid to find his own way.

"Doesn't matter. Time he started earning his keep around here. Max, old buddy, I've got a little job for you."

"Oh, no, I know what you're thinking. That will never work. He'll drag me all over the place."

"Then he'll just have to learn how to behave himself."

Now I knew the man was crazy for sure. Max had about enough of a chance of becoming a seeing-eye dog as I had of sprouting wings and flapping my way over to Norfolk.

"You'll probably need a sweater," Arthur said. "A little cool out."

"The blue one," I said. "It's in my closet."

He said nothing, and from the sounds in the room hadn't moved from where he stood.

"What?"

"Go get your own sweater. You know where it is. Come on, Max, we're going to find your leash."

As it turned out, I was wrong about Max. Arthur walked between us, holding the leash in his left hand while providing support for me with his right. The jingling of Max's dog tags located him right alongside Arthur.

"How far have we come?" I asked.

"Just over a block from your house. Do you need to stop?"

"No, I'm good." Even this short distance was farther along than I'd thought we would come. If I got completely wasted or started coughing, we would stop. Simple as that.

Only once did Max surge ahead, when I heard an unfamiliar voice call out, "Brenda, come back here."

"Everything's fine," Arthur said. "Max is as friendly as they come."

"I'm sorry. She just got away from me." Same unfamiliar voice.

"No problem. I'm Arthur. You met Max, and this is Daisy."

"I'm Abby Dalton, and this is Brenda. She just turned five. We moved into the Smith house just after the first of the year. I've met your mother, Daisy. She told me about your injuries."

"What happened to your face?" The little girl's voice was high-pitched, almost a squeak.

"I got burned."

"Does it hurt?"

"No, not any more."

"Can I touch your face?"

"No, honey, you can't," Abby said. "That's very impolite. Stop bothering Daisy."

"It's all right, really," I said.

"Can you bend down a little?" Brenda said. "I can't reach you."

"Sure." With Arthur's help I dropped to my knees.

Brenda ran her hands across my face. Her touch was soft, like a butterfly. "Wow. Thanks," she said.

"Really, I'm so sorry about this."

Abby's voice sounded close to panic, that mixture of fear and regret that I had heard so many times before. And I knew what lay beneath Abby's fears: if something this horrible could happen to someone else's daughter, it could happen to her own as well. That's what scared them the most, all of them. Right about now Abby Dalton wanted to scoop up her daughter, hold her and protect her from the bad things that might happen, all the while my burned face reminded her that she could not always be there.

No guarantees in this life, I thought, and there's some pretty bad shit around just waiting to happen. Still, I tried to reassure Abby. "No problem. She's probably never seen anyone like me." Try to make it sound like a numbers game. Faces like mine were one in a million. With luck, neither Abby nor her daughter would ever see another one. With luck.

We continued down the street, Max pacing at Arthur's side. His arm tightened around my shoulders. "You know, sometimes you just flat out amaze me."

"And you said I wasn't special."

"And I was so wrong, as wrong as I've ever been in my life."

****

My alarm clock was set for seven, but, as usual, Max was tugging at my blanket some time before that. This was turning into a real bummer, not being able to be sure of the time. Not that it made much difference; most of my days were pretty much alike anyway. Still it would be nice to have some idea of the schedule the rest of the world operated on, besides Max. I made a point to ask Rosita, if she ever came back, whether there was some sort of clock for the blind. Surely there had to be something.

I let Max out the back door, then headed for the kitchen. So far, the two food preparation tasks I'd mastered were making toast and a bowl of cold cereal. Today seemed like a good toast day. I'd learned there were other things one could put into a toaster besides slices of bread, frozen waffles, for instance, but my fingers were very sensitive to cold, so mostly I stuck with bread. While I waited for my toast, I searched the top shelf of the refrigerator for jam. I located the strawberry, my favorite, the old-fashioned way by unscrewing the lid, sticking my finger into the jar and tasting the contents. Maybe not the most sanitary method, and one of which Mom would surely disapprove, but this had saved me on a couple of occasions from slathering mayonnaise on my buttered toast. Even Max wouldn't eat it.

"You're up early," Mom said. "I'll make coffee."

"Max woke me up. He had to go out. What time is it?"

"Just after six. We have to get that dog on a better schedule."

She was correct in this, because Max was the order of the day. In subsequent sessions on his leash, Max had behaved nicely enough when Arthur held the other end, but with me he was uncontrollable, lunging about, tripping me up, in other words, more of a hazard than a helpmate. Maybe I didn't know the magic words.

According to Arthur, one of my old school chums, Annette Bentley, knew how to train dogs in assisting blind folks, and he thought Max might be a good candidate. I'd known Annette for many years. She was one of my few black friends, but then, there weren't many black kids in our school. I liked her because she didn't take shit from anybody. She was a good friend, but not somebody you wanted to mess with, so we got along just fine.

Annette volunteered at the Warrensburg Animal Care Facility half days on Monday, Wednesday and Friday, so on a Wednesday morning in July, Mom and I drove to the Facility with Max bouncing around in the back seat, unaware that his life was to change forever.

"Sure doesn't look like much," Mom said as she pulled off the road.

"They never had much of a budget to work with. Almost everybody here is a volunteer." I could easily visualize the sad, gray cinderblock building that was a final destination for so many homeless animals.

"We probably should leave Max in the car until we're sure they're ready for him," Mom said.

Max apparently did not agree with the plan and began yelping when we were just a few steps from the car. "I just hope he hasn't torn the back seat out before we get back," Mom said.

Two weeks before, she had traded in our truck on a new Buick Roadmaster just like Mrs. West's except ours was red, not that the color made much difference to me. I did appreciate the cushy ride, though.

We walked together to a weather-beaten door that I remembered well. I'd been through it many times before, and, if I wasn't shedding tears when I entered, for sure I was when I came out again. If I ever have a spare million or two, I'll set up an animal shelter where no dog, cat or anything else with four feet gets turned away. And they can stay there as long as they want and have all the treats they want.

"Ugh, sure smells like we're in the right place," Mom said.

I knew exactly what she meant, but to me the earthy aroma meant something different. Next to the inside of Dad's old truck, which smelled of grease, tools and worn leather, I loved the acrid fragrance of the animals best of all. I found myself even more sensitive now than before to the mixture of fear and hope that emanated from the cages that lined the walls behind the front desk.

There were sounds, too, equally familiar. Annette's voice, gravelly from years of smoking, boomed out at us. "Daisy, sweetheart." That's all I heard before I was wrapped in Annette's strong arms, almost lifted off the floor.

"Hi," was all I could manage in return, because Annette had effectively squeezed the breath out of me. Hugs still hurt a bit, but the good feeling inside made up for the discomfort outside.

"Oh, my goodness, girl, you're a mess." Annette laughed.

I could hear some of Arthur in the laugh, genuine, hearty and loving.

"Yeah," I said. "I guess I am."

"I hear you have a dog for us to train," Annette said.

"Max is out in the car," Mom said. "Arthur thought you might be able to train him to help Daisy around. He does just fine for Arthur, but he's a real handful for anybody else."

"That might be a problem. Usually we start them out as puppies," Annette said. "Older dogs can be a

189

challenge. I have a couple of really cute puppies in back if you'd rather try them. I've already begun their training, and they're both doing really well. Four, maybe six months, and I think they'll be great guide dogs."

"But Max is my dog," I said. "I want to work with him."

"Then Max it is."

After Mom fetched Max, Annette led us both back to a small fenced exercise yard. She stopped along the way to pick out a harness for Max. "First thing he has to learn is that when he's wearing this harness he's on duty, work time, no fooling around, no chasing cats or anything like that."

She had me kneel down alongside Max while she put on his harness, showed me the buckles, how it fit over his head and chest. Max might well have flunked the course at this first step if he'd fought and struggled as Mom and I both expected, but he seemed to sense that he had an important role to play now and behaved accordingly.

"I'm going to walk him across the yard now, see how he does," Annette said.

We waited anxiously. What if Max went on one of his crazy binges? But in a moment Annette was back at my side. I felt Max pressing against my leg.

"Amazing," Annette said. "I thought you said this dog hasn't been trained."

"He hasn't, so far as I know."

"Well, he takes to it like a pro, like he knows what to do without being told. Do you want to have a try with him?"

"Is that safe?" Mom asked. "I mean, he's smart,

but he gets these crazy spells."

"If he starts pulling you, just let go of the leash," Annette said. "He won't get far."

We walked across the yard together, Max matching my slow, tentative progress. Once he pressed against my leg, causing me to step aside. A few steps farther along he stopped. Must be near the fence. "Let's go back," I said. Max crossed in front of me, effectively turning me around, then led me back to where Mom and Annette waited.

"I wouldn't have believed it," Mom said.

"Pink shoes," Annette said. "Where on earth did you get pink shoes?"

"Arthur. They have special soles so I don't slip."

"That makes sense. You know when I noticed them? When Max nudged you aside, you were about to step in a little pile of dog poop. Is he a gentleman, or what?"

I knelt and wrapped my arms around his neck. "Good boy." He licked my face.

"He still has a lot to learn, how to cross streets, leading you around obstacles, stuff like that. I'm here Monday, Wednesday and Friday, so we'll get in some work on those days. In between you can work with him at home." Annette put her arm around my shoulders. "Well, now that we've got Max all squared away, we have to see about you."

"Me? What are you talking about?"

"Your new job. We expect to get some work out of you, just like Max."

"I didn't know anything about this. Did you know, Mom?"

"Arthur might have mentioned something about it.

I don't remember exactly."

"Liar. You did too know. This was all planned, wasn't it?"

"Maybe, just a little, but you need to get out of the house, and I can't think of a better place than right here."

"But I can't do anything. I can't see."

"We're not expecting you to perform surgery. You remember how scared all these poor things are when they get here? That's your job. Make them feel like somebody cares about them. Make them feel safe. And I know you can do that."

"Arthur," I said.

"Right. He says you've got a special ability to connect, and Lord knows, we can use somebody like that."

"How do you know him?" I asked.

"That's a long story, but I promise I'll tell you when we have more time. Right now I want to show you around, introduce you."

"Aren't you afraid I might scare somebody?"

Again, Annette's heavy arm around my shoulder. "Anybody gives us any trouble, I'll smash 'em, but that won't happen. This is a good group, and you'll fit right in."

"I'll pick you up about one," Mom said.

I felt myself squished between two hugs, one from my mother, one from Annette. In times past, before the big burn, I was never much of a hugger, not even with boys. Now they felt just fine.

Later that day I found myself sitting on a stool in the treatment room holding a small stray dog in my lap while the veterinarian, a woman with a soft voice whom

Annette had introduced as Corrine—"first name basis around here," Annette had said—stitched up a laceration in the dog's flank. The dog, which had been trembling uncontrollably until I cradled it, lay quietly as Corrine worked.

"This is so much better," Corrine said. "Otherwise we'd have to sedate him, and all that takes time and money. We'll have to get you some scrubs to wear, though. Got a little blood on your jeans."

"No problem. These jeans have seen a lot worse," I said.

By the time Mom returned to pick me up, I was in a nervous state that vacillated between exhaustion and exhilaration. Before I left, more hugs, this time one from Corrine. "You come back whenever you can," Corrine said. "We need you."

"Let's see if Max remembers his job," Annette said.

I knelt beside him and hooked the leash to his harness. He stopped to pee on the fake fire hydrant just outside the door, but otherwise led me straight to the car as if he'd been doing it for years.

"Amazing," Mom said.

So, once a week I went to the animal care facility. When I wasn't helping out in surgery, they let me wander around in the areas where they kept the cages. I could feel their wet doggy noses through the wire. Sometimes I'd take them out of their cages, just hold them. They never tried to run away, like, all they wanted was a kind word and a pat on the head. Works for me, too.

****

Thursday would begin with my morning workout

with Arthur. Now that I had a few more items on my calendar, time was passing faster. The summer had zipped by, and August, not my favorite month, was almost over. Late August was when Mom and I had to own up to the fact that it wasn't just the hot weather knocking my father down. It was something much worse. August was sort of the beginning of the end.

Mom put up a token resistance: "Between your workouts with Arthur and your job at the animal center I hardly get to see you anymore." But not so much as her words as her tone of voice gave her away. I could tell she was happy about me getting out of the house, even if I did have to depend on someone else once I was past the front door.

Fortunately Max was proving to be a quick study, and, on a couple of occasions, he and I had gone for short trips, just down to the corner and back. But knowing I could do it on my own was a big deal for me, Max, too. I was scared half to death the first time. I mean, what if Max saw a rabbit? What if a carload of kids stopped to laugh at me? All possible, and none a reality. Max was a real treasure, and if somebody didn't like my looks, too bad.

Arthur insisted we move our sessions to the local rehab center.

"How come? So they can all stare at me? Like, hey, here comes the freak."

"Don't you dare start that shit with me again. We been through that a dozen times before. Somebody don't like the way you look, fuck 'em."

"Oh, boy, you said the f-word. I'm gonna report you. 'Dear Sir, my therapist swears at me.' Say, who do I report you to anyway?"

"Bet you'd like to know, wouldn't you?"

"I'll ask Linda. She'll know."

He laughed, that big booming laugh that caused ripples in standing water and set Max to racing around the room. "She's heard a lot worse than that out of me. Anyway, I got to get some of this junk out of your room. With you wandering around now I don't want you tripping over any of it."

"Max takes care of me. He doesn't let me bump into stuff."

"God bless Max. Where'd you find him anyway?"

"More like he found me. He just followed me home one night, like someday I'd need him, even though I didn't know it yet."

"Funny how things work out like that."

Mom met us at the door. "Sweater today, honey. It cooled off last night. Besides, I heard you coughing again."

"The cough's here to stay. That's what the doctors said."

"I just don't want it to get any worse."

"Don't worry," Arthur said. "I'll keep her warm. About twenty minutes from now she'll be sweating up a storm."

"You pick on me, and I'll set my dog on you."

"Max? Me and him are best friends, right boy?"

Max yelped his approval. The dog was already excited about going out. As a rule, dogs, even guide dogs, weren't allowed in the therapy center, but Arthur had his own set of rules, Max included.

Mom was right, again. After two weeks of late August heat, even the slight northeast breeze felt chilly. I pulled my sweater around my shoulders.

The rehab center had that same stuffy smell that I associated with my old high school classroom after it had been closed up over the weekend. The thing lacking was noise, of any sort. The room was so quiet I could hear Max's paws padding on the floor. "Is there anybody else here?"

"Nope. We got the whole place to ourselves. We'll have us a good hard workout today."

"We? You mean me. All you do is stand around and give orders."

"Yeah, that's what all us therapists do, stand around and give orders."

"Not fair."

"You got that right. Life ain't fair."

"Great, another one of Arthur's famous epigrams."

"Epigrams? Where did you learn that?"

"I used to be able to read, you know. Besides, I'm remembering all this crap you pile on me. Someday I'm going to throw it right back at you."

"Man, you are feisty today. Just for that we'll start over here on the pulleys." He guided me over to a spot, then turned me around. "Back to the wall. Start with overheads."

This was one I hadn't done before. I grasped the handles he placed in my hands and began tugging the weights over my head in a throwing motion. "This hurts."

"It's supposed to. You keep complaining and I'll add more weight."

After a dozen reps he told me to stop, then turned me around facing the wall. "Curls now, build up those biceps."

I began tugging the handles upward from my waist

to my shoulders. "Don't see why I need biceps in the first place."

"Don't argue. Ten good ones, come on."

Finally I stopped, arms hanging limp at my sides. I don't think I could lift my hand if my life depended on it.

"You cheated," he said. "That was only eight."

"That was ten. I counted."

"Just for that, give me five more."

"I hate you." But I started up again.

"Max," he said, "all this hard work is making me thirsty."

"Beer break," I said.

"Not on your life, but there's a coke machine over there in the corner. Think I'll get me one while you finish up."

A moment later I felt the cold can as he pressed it into my hand.

"Here, let's sit down for a minute. I'm wore out," he said.

"Yeah, I guess all that standing around, yelling at me, that can make you tired."

Without the grinding of the exercise pulleys the room became quiet once again. "Weird, how there's nobody here," I said.

"Yeah, I don't think they've ever been real busy here. I know most of their staff is part-time."

So, we sat, sipping our cokes. I heard cars creeping along the side street that ran in front of the building, otherwise, silence.

"You know, one thing that bugs me. I don't know what you look like."

"Not much to see," he said. "I'm never gonna win

any beauty contests, if that's what you mean."

"I just want to know what you look like. Can I touch your face?"

He took the coke from my hand, then placed my hands on each side of his face. "Satisfied now?"

This was new territory, touching a face I had never seen, would never see. I ran my fingertips upward through the coarse stubble of beard. "You need a shave."

"If I'd known I was gonna be inspected I would have tidied up some."

"What's this?"

"My eye patch. Lost an eye years ago."

"Holy shit, you mean between the two of us we've only got one good eye?"

"And we're not gonna have that if you don't stop poking around so hard."

"Sorry. What's this?" I ran my fingers along two parallel ridges that traversed the right side of his face from just beneath his eye down to his jawbone.

"Keloids."

"Huh?"

"They're scars. When black people make scars they get big and ugly."

"I remember a kid in class had one on his arm where he'd been cut. Can't you have them taken off? I mean, if you want to."

"They just come back again, worse than before."

"How on earth did you get them?"

"That is another story for another day. Now, finish your coke. You got more work to do. Leg presses next."

"Oh, shit. I hate those."

At just past noon we got back to the house. The

breeze had dropped off, and the late August sun beat down on us. I had ditched my sweater, and I clung to Arthur's arm for support. "You nearly killed me today," I said. Arthur had relented only because my coughing got worse.

"No pain, no gain," he said.

"I'm gonna remember that one, along with all the others. Mark my words, you'll hear it again someday—from me."

As usual, he chuckled. "I pity anybody that tried to pick on you in school."

"Not many did. At least, not more than once."

Later I lay in my bed, Max snoring at my feet, my arms and legs so weak I could hardly lift them. We'd crossed a line today, Arthur and me. Oh, he'd touched me plenty of times, but today was the first time I had touched him, explored him. Keloids, long ones, across the entire side of his face. And a missing eye. And he wouldn't tell me what had happened to him.

Before, when I thought of him, I thought immediately of his megaphone laugh. I'd always thought that someone who laughed like that could never have known pain. Now I realized different. *Only* someone who had known pain could laugh like that. You had to pay your dues first, get the shit kicked out of you, then you could laugh the big laugh.

What was Arthur's pain? Would he ever tell me? Would he ever let me get that close? He always made a joke about maintaining a professional distance, as he called it, always stretching the phrase out, making it sound like some unwritten law of the universe. Then he'd laugh like a kid who'd just told a whopper and expected you to believe it anyway. Just so much bullshit, I realized now. It wasn't professional at all; it was personal.

Max whimpered at my feet. "Sorry, boy," I said. I hadn't even realized I'd been kicking him, or that I'd been coughing.

Chapter 10

Monday morning was Mom's regular grocery shopping day. I'd asked her about it once, why she didn't do laundry on Monday like everybody else, and she explained that was the very reason she shopped on Monday: the market wasn't so crowded because everyone else was home doing laundry.

Before she left she made her usual plea for me to come shopping with her, but that wasn't going to happen. I could just hear the other shopping moms as they pointed me out to their kids. "See, that's what happens when you play with matches." Nope, I wasn't up for being anybody's poster child for fire prevention week.

The new clock in my bedroom had just chimed one o'clock when I heard Mom enter through the kitchen door. I climbed out of bed and walked myself in, maintaining contact with the wall, although I scarcely needed to now that my ability to get around the house unaided was improving. This time as I entered the kitchen there was something new. I knew Mom's shopping habits so well that I could guess the contents of the bags before they were even emptied, but this new aroma....

"I got pizza for lunch," Mom said. "Thought you might like a change from sandwiches."

As changes go, this one was seismic. Mom had

always resisted fast foods or anything that wasn't prepared in her own kitchen. I'd thought the hamburgers she'd served up soon after my return from the hospital were a big deal, but pizza? Why, that wasn't even real American food to begin with.

"But you don't like pizza," I said.

"I'll give it a try. If I don't like it Max can have mine. And I got you something else. Hold out your hand."

The cold bottle, slick with condensation, fit into my palm like a gift from heaven. "Beer? Mom, you bought beer?"

"Don't tell anybody, you hear? I went by Sparky's, and Ralph told me what you'd like. Besides, it's time I stopped being so hard-assed about little things like beer."

"Hard-assed? Mom, you just swore." I laughed so loud I almost dropped the bottle.

"Just a little one," she said. "And that stays between us. Don't want the neighbors to know. Now, sit while I put this stuff in the fridge."

Beer and pizza, on Monday, no less. What next? Then I had a thought. "Mom, I dare you."

"What?"

"Have a beer with me. Like you said, if you don't like it, we'll give it to Max."

"The dog drinks beer?"

"Loves it."

****

The dream still came, but less frequently than before. It had started in the hospital, and for a long time there I didn't know what was dream and what was reality, both were equally horrible. It has come less often now, maybe a couple of times a week. Will it ever go away for good? I doubt it. I can still see it, hear it, even smell it, but worst of all I can still feel it. The pain is just as real in my dream as it was in the hospital.

I am being wheeled down to the hydrotherapy room. Even blind, I can see everything. The attendants all wear hoods that cover their faces. The corridor is almost dark, lit by candles stuck in the walls, casting wavering shadows as we pass. The floor is uneven, and the gurney bumps and lurches along. The walls are formed from cut stone, irregular, with gaps where cold damp breezes seep through. It smells of rotting flesh.

In my dream I am naked, secured to the gurney by cords that cuts into my burned flesh. I can see down the length of my body where what used to be skin is now something raw and disgusting.

The door where we stop is constructed of massive timbers secured by a single bar that requires two of the attendants to slide it aside. I know what lies beyond. I've been there before.

Once inside there will be no escape. I scream, but no sound comes forth.

When I wake up I keep telling myself it's just a dream, but I am lying. I am trying to reduce a horror to a minor inconvenience by saying "You can't hurt me. You're way too small." But the joke's on me. No amount of rationalization can diminish this monster. When it appears, it overwhelms.

Later when the storm had passed, for now, anyway, I sat on the side of my bed, afraid to even try to sleep. Strange, how you can feel darkness even without seeing it. I felt my way to my closet door and opened it. Inside I located the dress my mother had bought for me almost a year ago, still in its plastic cover. A church dress, Mom had called it, dressier than everyday wear, but not too flashy. It would have done nicely for most of the activities I would ever be involved in around Warrensburg. That was the idea.

But the dress, aside from wearing it briefly to show off for my mother, had never been worn. Had I even taken the sales tags off? I couldn't remember. It remained one of many things from the past that Mom and I did not discuss. For all I knew, she made secret trips to my closet herself, looking at the dress, wondering what might have been, but never would. Wearing it now would be a travesty. Besides, it wouldn't fit. The dress was cut to accommodate a full bosom, and my breasts had been seared right off in the blast. A surgeon had offered to reconstruct them if I wanted; I did not. E.T. with big boobs, what a joke.

I knelt and opened the box that contained the shoes, new one year ago, the soles as smooth and unscuffed as the day they'd come off the assembly line, never worn since. The only footwear I could handle now were the little pink slippers Arthur had brought. I ran my gnarled fingers over the smooth leather, and what began as a bitter laugh evolved into a sob. I went back to bed, pulled the sheet over my head.

****

On the last Saturday in September, according to Mom, Linda arrived and suggested we drive over to the park. Mom, of course, insisted on bundling me up fit for a polar expedition.

"It's cool out, Daisy. If you get too warm, you can take off your jacket."

There would be no winning this argument. Thank

God for Linda.

"Thanks for rescuing me," I said as she backed out our driveway. "I know you have lots of other things to do."

"Actually, you rescued me. Otherwise I'd have to spend the day cleaning the condo."

In spite of a beautiful fall afternoon, crisp air, leaves crunching underfoot, we had the whole place to ourselves, or so Linda said. "There's a picnic table about twenty yards up the hill. Think you can make it?"

"Lead on." I clung to one of Linda's hands, while she lugged a picnic cooler in the other.

"I've gotten so used to Max leading me around that I hardly ever go anywhere without him."

Halfway up the hill I had to stop because of my cough, a deep hacking that bent me double. My inhalers weren't helping at all by now so I didn't bother bringing them along.

"That sounds worse," Linda said. "Do you bring anything up?"

"No."

"Fever?"

"No, just the cough."

"Have you seen anybody, a doctor, I mean."

"Don't plan to."

"Maybe just a short course of antibiotics. Might make things better. It helps patients with chronic lung disease."

"I'm okay now." We continued up the hill where Linda helped me to a seat by the table.

"The sandwiches aren't much, just tuna salad. But I brought along a few beers to wash them down with."

"Oh, God bless you, woman." I clapped my

withered hands. Few things I know of can't be made better by a cold beer.

I'm getting pretty good at listening, not just the words people say, but how they say them. Yeah, mostly I listen to Mom and Arthur, but even they hit a false note from time to time. I might call them on it, I might not, but I hear it just the same. And of course, the poor folks who see me for the first time, anything they say is going to come out weird.

Anyway, Linda seemed to be holding back. I wanted her to feel like she could be completely open with me, because I needed to feel the same about her.

"So, what's up?" I asked.

She didn't respond right away, adding to the suspense. Finally. "I'm seeing someone."

"You mean, like a therapist?"

"No, silly, a guy."

"Oh my God, seriously?"

"I don't know yet. I hope so, but we've just gone out a few times. His name is Smitty. He's the senior resident on the Burn Trauma service. I'm sure you remember him."

"Oh, yeah, he's one of the good guys, in my book, at least. He was one of the few people who actually talked to me."

"He thinks you got a raw deal. He remembers how you begged them to stop all your treatments. We've talked about it a lot."

"Fat lot of good it did me."

"Actually, you became famous. Smitty says there was a big ethics conference about your case, and whether you had been denied your right to make choices about your care. Dr. Dawson was mad as hell about the whole thing."

"I never heard anything about that. Wonder if Mom knew about it."

"I doubt it. I wouldn't have known myself, except, Smitty told me about it afterward. From what he said, they've formed a new committee to study patient consent; it will report right to the hospital board of directors."

"You should be on that committee."

"I'd love to, but every time I open my mouth, I come closer to getting fired. Smitty said the discussion part of the meeting, when they weren't screaming at one another, was quite good. Apparently it all turned on whether you were capable of making choices."

"Capable? Hey, I might be blind and crippled, but I'm not stupid."

"But the main point was, with being so sick and having all those medications pumped into you, whether you could understand the consequences of what you were asking."

"That's ridiculous. Of course, I understood. I understood a hell of a lot better than God-almighty Dawson. Just stop all the crap and let me go on my merry way. That's all I wanted. Everybody would be better off, me in particular."

I hadn't been this pissed off in weeks. All that anger, that hatred, came bubbling up again. It felt good, strong. "The bastard," I said.

"Yeah, that's what Smitty calls him, only he calls him a goddam bastard. How about that beer?"

"Absolutely." Not many things could put out the fire in my gut as quickly as sucking on a cold beer.

For a moment Linda went all quiet on me. Was she

just enjoying a pleasant afternoon out of doors? No, she had something else in mind, I should have expected it.

"I don't know if I should ask this or not, no, forget about it. It's really none of my business."

"Come on, out with it, girl." Otherwise it would just sit there between us taking up all the oxygen until she brought it out in the open.

"Okay, you used to talk about when you got home, you planned to do yourself in. Do you still feel that way?"

"Yeah, no, maybe, I don't know. I was one hundred percent certain when I got home. My kidneys, so they told me, were already halfway gone, so all I had to do was nudge them over the edge. But then I ran off the rails. Mom ambushed me with her cinnamon buns and sugar cookies. Then Arthur with a Leroy's cheeseburger that I couldn't resist."

I made the whole thing sound trivial, I know, having the biggest decision you could ever make based on cookies and cinnamon buns, but I didn't really want to get into a deep ethical discussion of autonomy just now, especially after the episode I'd had with Mom. Enough was enough. Talking helped up to a point. After that it was just so many wasted words.

"I never heard of Leroy's," she said.

"Never heard of Leroy's? They only make the best cheeseburgers on the planet."

"I'll tell Smitty. He's a real cheeseburger freak. He could live off the things. Maybe we'll all go to Leroy's together, cheeseburgers all around."

"He'll love them, guaranteed," I said. "So, with all the food I was right back where I started. Maybe I was fooling myself all along. Maybe I wasn't as ready to go as I thought."

"What changed your mind?"

"For one thing, if I had gone through with it as planned, I would have died hating my own mother. She was partly responsible for what they did to me in the hospital. She could have stopped it all, and I begged her to. Of course, she'd just lost Dad, and even as burned and ugly as I was, maybe she thought I was better than nothing."

"And she loves you, don't forget about that."

But loving me still doesn't make things right about making somebody suffer the way I did. There are other things to consider, me, for one. Still, hating her was not the answer. She deserved better.

"This is how crazy people think, isn't it?" I said. "Back and forth, up and down, can't decide on anything."

"It's how people think when they get the crap kicked out of them," she said.

"So, the big answer to the big question is, I just don't know. Maybe it will come to me like a big bang of thunder, maybe not. Right now I have to pee."

"Me, too."

Linda found an outhouse, but it smelled kind of raw, so, since there was nobody else around, we did a quick squat right out there in the open. We both giggled until I started coughing again.

Afterward we strolled arm-in-arm along a level stretch of ground, shuffling our feet in the dried leaves.

"Almost to the pond," Linda said.

"Yeah, I can smell it."

"You can smell water?"

"Sure. Us blind folks have to get around some way,

so I can smell things better than I used to, hear better, too."

"So you don't really need me leading you around."

"Yes, I do. I can't trust Max in the park. If he saw a rabbit he just might take off after it and drag me with him. So today you're Max."

"I'm your guide dog."

"Right, and I have to say, you smell a lot nicer than he does."

Linda laughed. "That's the last time I bring you beer."

"It should be about here, on the right."

"What am I looking for?" Linda asked.

"A little flat grassy spot with bushes on each side."

"Oh, yeah, it's just ahead."

"When I was in eighth grade we snuck in here after school to drink some beer that one of the older kids had brought from home. We were being real quiet about it, like it was some major crime or something. When we got here we saw two kids screwing on a blanket in the same little grassy spot. First time I ever saw anybody really doing it."

"What happened?"

"We watched for a few minutes, then I started laughing, everybody did. I never saw anybody as pissed off as that guy. We all ran like hell."

"*Coitus interruptus*," Linda said. "That's the worst."

"And how would you know?"

"Let's say I've been caught myself, embarrassing as hell."

"That's funny. You know, I never thought of nurses doing it. Angels of mercy, that sort of thing, doesn't fit with the image."

"Oh yeah, have to do something to take your mind off work."

"Would you miss it if you couldn't ever do it again?"

Linda hesitated for a moment. "Yes, I would, and I can guess what you're thinking."

"No big deal," I said. "Anyway, nobody is gonna screw somebody that looks like E.T."

"E.T.?"

"You know, the movie, the Extraterrestrial. That's what the kids down the street call me."

"Little shits. If I ever hear that I'll warm somebody's ass for them."

"No, it's okay. I don't think they mean any harm. Sometimes they stop by the house, hang out. I sort of like having them around. One of them brought me a grape slurpee last week."

"Really?"

"Yeah, and besides, when I was their age I was probably worse."

Linda's laugh filled the quiet space. "I'll just bet you were."

After Linda had gone I sat in my room thinking. Just a year ago I would never even consider something like that...thinking. Back then there were too many options, all of them a hell of a lot more fun than sitting and thinking. But not many options now. Not like I can go ice skating or shopping for sexy lingerie. So, I sit and think.

This afternoon it was Arthur.

Back in the beginning, in one of our earlier discussions, when he asked me, *what do you want*, I simply shrugged, my trademark dismissive gesture. After all, my abilities were so limited that I could only do a few simple things. What difference did it make what I wanted?

But when he turned the question around, *okay, then, tell me what you don't want*. This was a query I could answer directly: "I don't want me," I'd said. I figured I'd scored a point. "I don't want to live in this body. Can't you understand that?"

In most cases that would have ended the conversation, probably the therapy session as well. God knows, I'd chased off other well-intentioned therapists with less, but not Arthur. He didn't respond right away. When he did, his voice was just above a whisper. "Yeah, I get it. Now, we got work to do."

It was the sort of thing my dad would say.

Not until late that night, hours after I'd gone to bed, did I catch his meaning. Had Arthur gone into some lengthy discourse about living with disability I'd have tuned him out immediately. I'd heard all that crap before, lots of times. People, always with the best of intentions, feel bound to offer some inspirational words, trying to make it all better, trying to fix it. But these were always people who had never been patients in the Burn Trauma Unit.

Arthur, instead, in just a few words, he'd made his point, as much in what he hadn't said as what he had. His message, I think, was about acceptance, like my father had said years before about how *you can't fix everything, you just do what you can do*. This was the choice he'd placed before me, acceptance, or not. In the meantime, while I was making up my mind, we would get back to work.

Sometimes it seems to me that there's a fundamental disconnect between the thinking side of things and the doing side. I mean, you can think and do nothing, or you can take action without much thought at all. For instance, my dad was all about doing stuff. I don't think he wasted a lot of time thinking about a job, he just did it. Thinking things through, like you do when you're up to your ears in choices, doesn't get very much done.

Arthur seems to understand that very well, just like my dad did. Like, "Okay, Daisy, you can think and figure all you want, make all the choices you want, but for now, get back to work."

****

"Have you thought about Thanksgiving?" Mom asked. For almost two weeks she had been dropping hints about how she'd like to have a big Thanksgiving dinner, invite Linda and Annette, and, of course, Arthur. When I mentioned that Linda had a new boyfriend, Mom said, "We'll invite him, too, of course."

I had been trying to come up with reasons for not doing it. Meal times were just a bit too close for comfort. I felt as if I was on display, particularly when Mom had to cut things into bite-sized portions for me. This is what you do for two-year-olds, right? And when I dropped something, as often happened, she had to fish the food from my lap, which is why soup was still not on our menu. Of course, if it landed on the floor, Max took care of it. Even worse was when I dribbled it down my front and had no idea I'd done it, so I sat there looking like the loser in a paint ball battle.

"Well?" Mom said.

"I'm thinking about it." I know this was her way of trying to reestablish some normalcy in our house. Holidays for us had always been a big deal, more than just dates on a calendar, they were special landmarks in time, times to look forward to, then to remember. Maybe because ours was such a small family she felt these times deserved our full attention. Just two of us now, three, counting Max, so it's hard to turn her down.

"I can guess why you're hesitating. Just remember, these people are your friends. They love you. And they're not going to love you any less if you spill some cranberry sauce. And that goes for me as well." She kissed me on the cheek.

Love, that word kept popping up in new ways, some that I really hadn't considered. The way Mom said it, love was supposed to smooth over everything, from poor knife-and-fork skills to the common cold. But love had its limits, too. For instance, I always wondered, how could anyone love a person that looked like an extraterrestrial? But that's exactly what had happened, at least in the film. The little kids loved E.T., saved the creature's life in spite of its appearance.

Not so fast. Where was the love when they were dunking me in the Hubbard tank while I screamed for them to stop? If that was love, then God help us all. I can do without it. This was the same circular thought pattern that I'd been rotating in for months, and never getting anywhere.

Arthur's arrival snapped me out of my mental whirlpool. I felt Max leap from my side, then Arthur's voice as the dog ran up to greet him.

"Hey, Max, how's the little lady today? She in a good mood, or should I go back to the car and get my body armor?"

"Before you go anywhere, I baked an apple pie this morning, and I want each of you to have a piece. Made fresh coffee, too," Mom said. I halfway expected her to issue an invitation to Thanksgiving dinner right then and there, but she held off. I guess she was waiting for a final response from me.

"Rhoda, you keep feeding me like this, and I'm gonna have to buy some larger pants."

"Nonsense, apple pie is good for you. Every mother knows that."

While I listened to their banter another word jumped out at me—mother—something else I would never be. I no longer had any place in the human reproductive cycle, not that I was ever very enthusiastic about it in the first place, but being shut out completely didn't sit too well.

The closest I came was my feelings for my four-legged friends at the animal shelter. I loved holding them, feeling them become calm under my touch. I guess they couldn't care less that I looked weird.

Still, the M-word reinforced my concept of myself as a being without gender. Neither male nor female, I was an *it*, and would remain so as long as I drew breath. Barren...I didn't like the sound of that word, but that's what I was and would be. Back before I got burned I'd rejected the whole idea of pregnancy and its aftermath, but now that the door is permanently closed for me I feel differently. Might not be so bad after all, and Mom would love grandchildren. But it wasn't going to happen, and accepting it or not wouldn't change it.

A bit later, as Arthur was putting me through my paces at the rehab center, my cough reappeared with a vengeance. I was hacking like a car backfiring.

"That's enough for today," he said. "We gotta do something about that cough."

"It's my cough, and I'll decide what to do about it." I'd already gone through that long discussion about my hacking with Linda, and wasn't about to repeat it now. "Let's go outside. It smells dusty in here."

We wound up in the parking lot outside Sparky's, Arthur sipping on a coke while I worked my way through a grape slurpee. He'd gone all quiet again. I knew this trick. He was waiting for me to spill my guts. But not this time. I was tired of thinking about myself, tired of talking about myself, tired of being myself. "Your turn," I said.

"Huh?"

"You know my story. Now I want to know yours."

****

Arthur, as I saw it, had some explaining to do. He owed me that. He had changed my life in so many ways, and in doing so he had incurred a responsibility to me. Time for him to come clean.

"Well?" I sucked on the straw, draining the last few drops of my slurpee. "And I'll know if you're lying to me, so don't even try it." I could say this with confidence knowing that he would not lie. He might hold back information, but what he told me would be true.

"You won't like some of the stuff you're gonna hear."

"I'll be the judge of that."

"Where do you want me to start?"

"I want to know who you are, where you're from, why you do what you do."

"Where I'm from is the easiest part. I was born in New Jersey, grew up in the projects."

"What are the projects? I don't know about projects."

"Take the worst section you know about in Warrensburg, then imagine it about ten times worse than it is. The projects were bad, really bad. Just one big dead end, nobody going anywhere except jail or the graveyard."

"You didn't say anything about your family."

"Nothing to tell. Never knew my father, and my mom had a habit. That's about it."

I slipped down into my seat, suddenly ashamed of how often I'd complained about my own mother. What if she'd been absent altogether, or, as Arthur said, had a habit? For a moment there, I felt small and bitchy.

"I had a little trouble then, spent some time in juvie—that's Juvenile Detention Center. When I got out I moved around some, New York mostly. Things got a little too hot for me there, so I took a bus ride to the west coast."

"What did you do that was so bad?"

"Small stuff, drugs, gangs, same things everybody else did. There was an armed robbery thing, a guy got shot. I didn't do it, but the cops grabbed everybody in sight, including me, so I spent a year in jail."

"Wow. Is this a big secret? Does anybody else know?"

"Linda knows most of it, so does Annette. Now you. But unless they told somebody else, you're the only ones that do."

"I don't think they told anybody. When I asked them about you they said you'd tell me what I needed

217

to know."

"You want something else to drink?"

"No, but I have to pee. Can you take me home? I don't like public toilets."

Mom was out when we got back to the house, so we continued our talk in my bedroom. Max took up his usual position at the foot of my bed while the chair I always thought too flimsy for him creaked beneath Arthur's bulk.

"Guess you didn't know you were working with a hardened criminal," Arthur said.

"You aren't finished yet. There's more. I know it."

"It don't get much better, if that's what you're expecting."

"I don't care. I want to hear it." But did I really? With every new lurid detail Arthur's pedestal eroded just a bit. The iconic status that I had bestowed upon him was shrinking. No, I didn't want to know, but I had to. I had to know all the things he'd told me came from a real person, from Arthur himself. Otherwise he might just as well be quoting from some book he'd read.

I had to know that, if I opened Arthur up, poked around inside him, this was what I'd find. He could tell me nothing meaningful about pain unless he had experienced it himself. I had to know. He had become such an important part of my life. *I had to know.*

Okay, to be honest about it, I wasn't looking for some cosmic discussion of pain, or his philosophy of life and how he arrived at it; my reasons were more personal. I had feelings for him, feelings I had no realistic expectation he would have for me. Yeah, Mom loved me, so did my friends, so they tell me, but what I'd begun to feel for Arthur was something else, something I'd best not even think about. So, I was going about it in a circular fashion, not straight on, like my dad taught me.

"I moved around LA for a couple of years. Got into trouble, got out of trouble. Took up with a woman, right sharp looking lady, part Chinese, part something else, I'm not sure what. Had her own place. Before she met me I'm not sure she'd even heard of crack cocaine, but I got her started. Within a month or two I had her turning tricks, bringing them right back to the apartment. When they'd finished I'd bust in, take whatever he had. One guy, I even took his shoes."

"You're making this up."

"Wish I was. You want me to stop?"

"No."

"How it turned out, she started losing her teeth. Crack does that. Skin got all wrinkled, sores on her face, got so ugly she couldn't give it away, much less sell it. She got crazier and crazier. I wasn't much better. I'd have moved out if I had any other place to go.

"One night I passed out on the kitchen floor. Can't even remember what I was drinking or what I was taking. Didn't matter much. When I woke up my face was all bloody. She'd cut me while I was asleep. That's how I got these scars. She cut me other places, too, but you ain't gonna hear about any of that.

"I had it coming, after what I did to her, but when I looked in the bathroom mirror, all that blood, what she'd done to my face, I wanted to kill her. I boiled some water in a teakettle. She was asleep, probably passed out herself. I put my knee on her neck so she couldn't scream, couldn't even move, then I poured that water on her face, scalded her."

"Did you kill her?"

"I don't know. I left. Never saw her again."

"I think I'm going to be sick."

Breath sounds, about the only noise left in the room. Max whimpered once, obviously concerned and probably confused as well, otherwise nothing. Those horrible trips down to the hydrotherapy room, they were only marginally worse than I felt right now. Those sessions, at least, had a beginning and an end. And back then I could scream. Now I had no scream. I had nothing left at all.

"What am I, then, your redemption project? Help the poor burned kid to make up for what you did to that woman?"

This was a new Arthur voice, one that reminded me of the plaintive sounds I heard down at the animal shelter, like trying to put into words something for which there were no words. "I'm not done yet," he said.

"I don't want to hear any more."

"But you're going to. When you go into the dark place you can't stop halfway. You have to go all the way to the bottom. And you can look at it any way you want, whatever suits you, but you're going to hear the rest of my story first, if I have to sit on you to make you listen."

I lay down, and Max crept alongside me, tucking himself into the curve of my body. I wrapped my arms around the dog, drawing him close. "Say your piece," I said to Arthur. "Then I want you to leave."

Arthur's response came out like a snort. "That's what the cops said...leave and don't come back. That's after they drove me to the emergency room, got me all stitched up. I got as far as Oklahoma before I ran out of money."

I heard him get up, walk across the room. He must have been standing by the window, but whether he was looking out or watching me, I couldn't tell.

"Oklahoma ain't much, at least the part I was in. Then again, I guess a big black dude with a face full of stitches can't expect people to jump for joy when he shows up, much less stop and give him a ride. You think people stare at you because of your face, you should have seen the looks I got, like I just stepped off the shuttle from Mars. People couldn't get away from me fast enough.

"I just started walking, middle of August, hot as hell. I turned off on a dirt road, walked until I couldn't walk any more. Not one damned tree in sight for shade, so I just sat there in the sun. Felt like my brains were frying inside my head, but it didn't matter. The way I figured, the world would probably be better off without me. Sure as hell nobody would miss me.

"I woke up, somebody was poking me with a stick. 'Get up, you'll die out here.' Little old woman looked a hundred years old, maybe more. Skin like leather. Looked a lot like yours, in fact. She had on some kind of robe, mostly rags, same color as the sand.

"I kicked at her. Go away, leave me the hell alone. End of the line for me. This was where I got off.

" 'Drink some water.' She held a jar up to my lips. 'There, not so fast. You'll get sick.'

"Sick? Hell, I was half-dead already. My tongue was so swelled up I could hardly swallow, but she kept after me. 'Little bit more. Good, now a little bit more.'

"I woke up next time in a wagon. No idea how I got there. I didn't climb in, and there's no way on earth that old woman could have lifted me up. She'd put a damp cloth over my forehead.

" 'We have to go kind of slow,' " she said. " 'Old Abraham is not as young as he used to be.'

"What's Abraham?"

" 'He's my mule, of course. Getting on in years now, but he's a fine mule.'

"Laying in a wagon pulled along by an old mule named Abraham, somewhere in Oklahoma with some old crone fussing over me. Thought I must be dead already. This must be the way they cart people off to hell. Every time I tried to raise up, see where I was, the inside of my head started doing cartwheels. The old woman would reach back, push me down again. 'You rest. We'll be there soon.' It didn't take too much to figure out where we were headed. All the shit I'd done, there was only one place people like me ended up. If things were hot now, they were going to get a lot hotter.

"By the time we stopped the sun was beginning to set. Voices calling out 'Sister Agatha.' She must have been the one driving the wagon. 'And who is this?'

" 'I finally found him. We have to get him inside.'

"They put me in a cool, dark room on a cot. Fed me some kind of soup, then some more water. 'You sleep now. You'll feel better tomorrow.' Sister Agatha again. I could swear I heard her say 'We've been waiting for you,' but that didn't make sense. I must have been out of my head.

"Just before daybreak, must have been. When I woke up I heard singing, chanting was more like it. I'd never heard the song before, but I'd never spent much time in church, so no wonder.

"Turns out I was in some kind of convent, about a

dozen nuns, all of them ancient, looked like they were as old as the red rocks that poked up out of the ground. I asked them the name of the place, but they'd just smile and shake their heads. All they had was a well, a little garden and a few goats. They got some supplies from town. That's what Sister Agatha was bringing back when she found me, like I was part of her shopping list.

"You still awake?"

"Yes," I said. I had my face buried in Max's fur.

"I'm almost done. I stayed there almost three years, did odd jobs around the place. Put a new roof on the chapel. I got into their routine, the morning sing-along, then again in the evening. It got to feel perfectly natural. Nobody had to call me, remind me it was time.

"Then early September, Sister Agatha said I was to go into town with her in the wagon. Same wagon, same old mule, same old woman as three years before, but somehow everything was different. I knew I'd never pass along this road again. She took me straight to the bus station, gave me forty dollars, and said 'It's time for you to go. You have other work to do.' I didn't even ask her what work she was talking about. I'd know when I got there. When I turned around to wave good-bye she was gone, wagon, mule, everything vanished, like she'd never been there in the first place. That was eight years ago. Now here I am."

'You expect me to believe that?" I asked.

"Don't make much difference now whether you do or not. You take care of yourself, hear me?"

As best I could tell, during all that time he hadn't moved from his spot by the window. Now I heard him walk to the door, and he was gone.

Chapter 11

Thursday morning brought a cold rain pushed along by a north wind. Pellets of rain mixed with sleet woke me in the night as the frigid mixture lashed against my bedroom windows. Sometime during the night Max had crept from his position at the foot of the bed and now lay tucked beside me. The warmth of the dog's body was better than any blanket.

In my eternal darkness I could only guess at the time. I hadn't yet heard Mom in the kitchen making coffee, something she always did at six a.m., so I huddled closer to Max and waited. From time to time the wind rose in intensity, as if there was something outside trying to huff and puff and blow the house down.

I had slept little, but it wasn't the noise of the storm outside that kept me awake; it was the storm inside my own head, my own heart. Over and over again I replayed Arthur's confession, but was that even the right word...*confession?*

It wasn't something he had tried to conceal. I had just never asked him before. He had divulged the information about himself freely when I'd requested it. His only caveat was that I hear all of the story. Now I had the information, but what could I do with it? *Be careful what you wish for.*

Coming from anyone else, I would have dismissed

the final act in his tale—the ancient nuns who had appeared out of thin air, saved his life, then vanished back into that same thin air—as pure fiction, and the idea they'd been looking for him, waiting for him to arrive sounded far more like myth than reality. But Arthur would not lie. That he was near death when Sister Agatha found him might have distorted his perception, but I was sure he'd given me a truthful rendition of the event, as he'd experienced it.

But what about those years before Oklahoma? What about the terrible things he'd done to that woman in California? Why had he turned up in my life? Or Linda's? Or Annette's? Or all the others he must have helped? Was this all just about atonement for stuff he'd done before? Perhaps the nuns in Oklahoma had set him on a spiritual path of redemption, a path of helping others, but that didn't clean the slate. If we could make up for bad actions by accumulating enough good ones—no, that didn't hold together either. Whatever drove Arthur to share his terrible story, whatever got him out of bed in the morning and sent him off to work with people like me was something else, something I hadn't smoked out yet.

Max began twitching in his sleep, apparently in the midst of whatever dogs dream about, so I slipped out of bed and found my pink shoes. Thank God for Velcro snaps. I was steady enough now that I could pace back and forth alongside my bed. My room was chilly, but if I went fumbling around trying to locate my robe I would probably wake Mom, so I continued my march, arms wrapped tightly around my chest.

There had to be an answer, a reason why Arthur had told me his fantastic tale. Back and forth, back and forth across my bedroom floor, I seemed to get farther away from an answer, instead of closer. When the realization finally hit me, it buckled my knees. I plopped back onto the bed. Max grumbled but did not move from his warm place. This was big, if I was on target in my thinking, Arthur had just dropped a big one on me.

Of course, why had it taken me so long to see what was so obvious? Or maybe being obvious was exactly what made everything seem so muddy. My breathing changed to a short panting rhythm like Max did on a hot day.

As I saw it now, he had restored my freedom to choose. More than that, he'd forced me to make a choice. For almost a year now almost every aspect of my life had been regulated by others. Even my choice to die had been subverted by others, mostly by Arthur himself, all with the best of intentions, of course, but now he had restored my free will, at least as far as he was concerned.

In laying bare his past he also gave me the option to accept him as a man or to reject him. I never had that choice with Arthur the therapist. He was far too persistent and determined, and I really had no way to get away from him. But now he had shown me Arthur the man himself, the good, the bad and the ugly, all of it. No argument, no rebuttal, just my choice, that was enough.

When I sent him packing, he simply left. I lay back and pulled Max close. I buried my face in his fur. So this was Arthur's gift to me, and perhaps his final gift, the freedom to choose. It was, I thought, one of the most courageous things I could have imagined, because it's a big deal, opening up, lowering the shield, more than just letting someone peek inside, giving them the option to choose or reject. I think this was the reason I built a wall around myself, partly to keep myself hidden, but also some fear that people would reject what they'd seen. Sure, it's one thing to say the people who love you matter and to hell with the others, but it really doesn't work out that way. It all counts, it all matters, and Arthur had just dropped the big one in my lap, like this was my final exam, and I had a bad feeling I'd flunked.

He must have known that there was a good chance that I would be bowled over by his story, that I could not accept the things he had done. But, hey, I come from a small town. I'd never even heard of anything as awful as he told me, much less met the person who had done it. And indeed, I found myself unable to separate the man from his actions. He would have known, as well, how painful rejection would be, and still he had put everything on the table, for me to choose.

"Max, what have I done?" I moaned into his fur.

****

Max stirred as breakfast noises came from the kitchen, followed by breakfast smells, first the welcome aroma of coffee, then bacon frying. Oddly enough, the fact that the Burn Trauma ward also smelled the same way had never put me off about bacon. Max either. I heard Mom's voice at my bedroom door. "Are you warm enough, sweetie?"

She didn't wait for an answer, and I felt a blanket draped over me and Max as well. "I'll call you as soon as breakfast is ready. I put your robe on the chair by your bed. I feel sorry for poor Arthur, having to be out and about in weather like this. If I had his number I'd call him, tell him to cancel today."

"Maybe he won't come, I mean, because of the weather." I felt my mother's weight as she sat beside me on the bed.

"Oh, I think it will take a lot more than bad weather to stop a man like Arthur. Your father used to be that way, remember? I always thought he got that from his Navy days. Rain or shine, he was up and out the door every morning, usually with you right behind him." Then she leapt up, and the bed shook. "Oops, if I'm not careful I'll burn the bacon."

After breakfast I curled up on the sofa, still wearing my cozy fleece bathrobe. Max had gotten soaked when Mom let him outside to pee and was now confined to the kitchen while he dried out.

The storm abated, the morning came and went, but no Arthur.

"I wish he'd call," Mom said. "Let us know he's okay."

But he wasn't okay, and it wasn't weather that was keeping him away.

****

News travels fast in small towns, and Warrensburg is no exception; bad news zips around at just under the speed of light. I was sitting in the kitchen working on a second cup of coffee when Mom answered the phone. The tone of her voice, almost shouting, got me up and out of my chair and over to where I could hear her side of the conversation.

"What? No, he couldn't have, not our Arthur. That's just not like him at all."

I wedged in close beside her trying to pick up the

other end of the conversation.

"Where is he now?" Mom asked.

I heard the caller say jail, but couldn't catch the rest of it.

"Thanks, we'll take care of it," Mom said.

Take care of what?

"Arthur got into a big fight at Kelly's Bar, and now he's in jail."

"Is he hurt?" I asked.

"I don't know anything about that yet, but we'll find out soon. First, we have to get him out of there, then you can tell me why he did such a crazy thing in the first place. I'm going to make a couple of calls."

She assembled a war party—I was included. "Annette is on her way over, and Linda will be here, but it will take her about thirty minutes. I'd better make more coffee."

Within the hour all four of us were gathered in our kitchen making ready to head off to the Warrensburg County Jail where Arthur was being held. Mom hadn't yet pressed me for an explanation for his behavior, but that would come up eventually for sure.

"We'll take my car," Mom said. "I have more room."

"Is there room for Max?" I asked, even though he was still a bit damp.

She didn't answer immediately, but finally said, "Oh, what the heck. Bring him along."

Sheriff Tate hadn't seen me since I got burned, so he was in for a big surprise. Somehow I figured having Max along might make it a little easier, and I needed that special support—no questions—that only my dog could provide.

After a short and very quiet ride Mom pulled up beside the jailhouse. I remembered it well, a squat red brick building with windows on the front, but nowhere else. Of course, I'd never seen the inside of it, and now never would. The tension inside the car was thick enough to be palpable. Everyone knew it would take something sizable to run Arthur into a ditch, and the questions it raised were serious. Linda, Annette and I knew enough about Arthur's past to worry—had he fallen back on his old habits? Or was this all my doing? Yeah, the finger pointed right back at me. As the saying goes, I had some explaining to do.

I had more information than the rest of them. Mom had already figured that out, most likely the others had as well. But I kept it to myself, because I still didn't understand enough to be comfortable with it. When I finally put a label on it, I wanted it to be of my own doing, and not someone else's interpretation.

"Okay, ladies, let's go get him," Mom said. This was not day-by-day Mom voice. This carried a note of authority. We were here to do something and wouldn't leave until we had accomplished it.

I fastened Max's harness before we got out of the car.

No sooner were we in the front door than a stern female voice said, "No dogs allowed."

"Max is a trained therapy dog," Mom said. "By law he can go anywhere we need him." Dang, this was Mom-in-charge, Mom who would not take no for an answer.

"It's okay. The dog can stay." I recognized Sheriff Tate's voice. "Been a long time, Rhoda," he said. "Sorry about Sam."

"I don't remember seeing you at the funeral," Mom said.

"I was on duty. Couldn't make it. Sorry."

"I understand. Anyway, why we're here, we came for Arthur."

"I don't know, he made quite a mess out of Kelly's. Made a mess out of Bill Kelly, too."

"If there are fines or damages, I'll pay them," Mom said.

I heard feet shuffling on the floor, like the sheriff couldn't make the connection between Arthur and this group of women.

"He's a close personal friend," Mom said. "He's been a great help to Daisy."

"He's in back."

Small town stuff all the way through, Mom knowing the sheriff from way back so he bends the rules a little. No harm done. I have to confess that, on a couple of occasions, he'd bent them for me, too. I guess he knew when I got home afterward I'd catch far worse than anything he might hand out.

I followed Mom who must have followed Sheriff Tate back to Arthur's cell. The smell got worse and worse the farther we walked, like somebody had vomited, peed and pooped all in the same place then walked away and left it. I guess you can get used to anything, but it would take a long time to be comfortable with this aroma. But then I'd gotten used to the smell of burned flesh, so I could probably handle this if I had to. Max was tugging at his leash, too excited to behave.

"Get up." Sheriff Tate spoke in a loud voice that left no room for negotiation. "There's a whole bunch of women out here to see you."

What came back in response was a low groan. "Oh, no." Like a prisoner whose executioners had just come for him. The words trailed out and just tapered off. This couldn't be Arthur, the man with the huge laugh, but it was. This was Arthur at the bottom of the pit. I'm sure that, when we showed up, his discomfort turned to pure agony. In other words, just when he thought he couldn't possibly feel any worse, he did.

"Are you hurt?" Linda asked

"No."

"Good, then get up, like the sheriff said. We're taking you home with us," Mom said.

"Let me be," Arthur said.

"Arthur, there are four of us here, five if you count Max, and we're taking you home now." I'd never heard Mom use this tone of voice with Arthur before.

"You sure you can handle him?" Sheriff Tate asked.

"Absolutely."

The squeak of metal on rusty metal as Sheriff Tate opened the cell door, then feet shuffling across the floor as Arthur came out into the hall. Linda took one of his hands, and I found the other. Mom led the entourage. We retrieved his car keys from the woman at the front desk.

"Linda will drive over to your apartment and pick up some dry clothes for you," Mom said. "You're coming home with us."

The drive back was almost intolerable, and would have been if Max hadn't broken the ice with Arthur. Only the dog acted normally, jumping around Arthur as if he hadn't seen him in years, happy dog talk.

Otherwise, silence. This was all my doing. I knew it. Everyone else knew it. Arthur was as solid as a rock. Only a major catastrophe could cause him to fall back on old habits, and that catastrophe was me.

Now, just as when he had fallen in with the old nuns, if that story was true, he was under the direction of a small group of women. With Mom as supreme commander, we assumed control of his life, paying no heed to his protests. Linda brought back from his apartment, not only dry clothes, but a small bag packed with his toiletries along with a couple of his Dickens novels. Mom, in the meantime, plied him with hot coffee and apple pie, her version of chicken soup.

"I'll put you in Sam's room for a couple of days," Mom said in a matter-of-fact voice, like a schoolteacher addressing a tardy pupil.

"Huh? No way. I can't stay here."

"You're not leaving until we say you're ready."

Four women and a dog. He didn't stand a chance.

"Okay," he said. "But it ain't permanent. I got stuff to do."

"We know, but not yet." Mom's voice softened. "I expect you could use a shower and a nap after all you've been through. I'll call you when supper is ready."

I waited on the sidelines with Linda and Annette. Some very large issues lay between us, mostly between Arthur and me, and until those bridges were crossed, there wasn't much to say.

****

During the two days Arthur was with us, the key word was awkward. I stayed in my bedroom, rolled up into my little ball, facing the wall. I didn't like it. The thing is, I didn't want to live like this any longer. Shutting everything out was not the answer.

Poor Arthur, if I felt awkward, he must have felt just plain awful. But Mom wouldn't relent. He was our prisoner until Tuesday. Of course, he could just walk away if he chose. Arthur could walk right through walls if he chose. But he let himself be kept indoors for those two long, long days.

Mom wasn't blind, not like me, but to her everlasting credit, not once did she try to force the issue. She was tender and loving with Arthur just as she was tender and loving with her own daughter. She asked no questions, offered no advice. Only once did she say to me, "Give it time, sweetheart. It will all work out." What would work out? What did my mother realize that I did not?

On Tuesday, Arthur got his conditional release. The conditions were that he stay out of trouble and return for dinner on Thanksgiving Day. I cut him off at the door, and grabbed for whatever I could reach, which happened to be his right arm. I squeezed as hard as I could. "You're coming back, right?"

"Do you want me back?"

"If you don't show up, I'll come and get you, and I'll bring Max."

"Then I'll be here." A kind of collective sigh emerged, allowing everything to settle down. I felt like a heavy weight had been lifted off my shoulders.

There it was, right in front of me. Yes, I was right about what he had done about my freedom of choice, but something more basic was going on. This wasn't just some mental exercise, choosing between two alternatives; it went beyond acceptance or rejection. I wanted him back with me. I wanted him back like crazy. I couldn't imagine life without him. For me, looking into the future was not an issue. As I saw it, there was no real future for me, but whatever time there was, I wanted Arthur to be a part of it.

So far, we'd kept it all professional, like on a patient/therapist basis between us. But what if things moved closer? What if real feeling, even love became a part of the equation? The thought, now that I'd considered it, left me shaking, even more scared than the day I was discharged from the hospital.

Love was scary because I considered myself unlovable. Oh, Mom loved me, of course. She had to. It was an automatic thing, part of the Mom-code. And my friends, Linda and Annette, they loved me, too, but in a different way. And I shouldn't forget Max. Weird how I could count all my pals on the fingers of one hand, with one of those fingers missing.

But how could a man have those special feelings for me? I could hardly be classified as a woman. My chassis was all messed up, and no auto body shop on the planet could ever fix it up. I was an *it*; I was E.T. What if I make a move in his direction, and he pats me on the head and says, "Sorry, Daisy, I like you just fine as a patient, but that's all. Besides, you shouldn't be getting romantic ideas in your head, not the way you look. The only way anything like that is going to happen for you is if a family of zombies moves in down the street. Maybe one of them would take a shine to you."

So there's the catch, one of the permanent rules of life: *There's Always A Catch.* A fantasy such as the one buzzing around inside my head required two people, two hearts spinning in the same orbit, and that didn't seem possible.

The best thing, it seemed, was just to forget about it. Romantic stuff wasn't in the cards, not for me. Arthur and I would never be on the same wavelength. Even if he'd said the magic three little words I'd have laughed right in his face. "In a pig's eye," I'd have said. "Now go try your BS on somebody else."

So how could I complain if he turned right around and said something similar to me? The fear of rejection hung around like a bad smell. Like I said, there's always a catch.

Poor Max got the worst of it. When I don't sleep well, he doesn't either, not with me pulling on him all night. "Max, what the hell am I gonna do now?" I asked.

****

Dead set as I was against what I was sure would be an awkward event at best, an outright disaster at worst, I finally gave in to Mom's wishes for a big Thanksgiving dinner, with guests. She deserved this much, since we'd blown off that last Turkey Day after Dad died. I took care of Christmas all by myself by getting torched, so she had earned a shot at normalcy, even if it turned out weird, something that seemed possible if not probable.

For me the holiday marked a turning point, an anniversary of the fall of the house of Sugarbush, not something I really wanted to commemorate. But clearly it held a different significance for my mother, who clung to the hope of maintaining the diminished family unit, in spite of the destruction that had fallen on our poor heads.

The guest list would include Arthur, of course, Linda and her beau, Smitty, and Annette. Mom invited Mrs. West, too, which made perfect sense considering their long term friendship. I only wondered why she never had before. Besides, this meant we'd be sharing one of her world-famous pecan pies.

The dining room table, passed down from Mom's mother, and unused for the past year, would seat eight comfortably. I would have preferred taking my meal into the bedroom where my clumsy efforts at feeding myself would go unseen by anyone but Max. With Max on hand I never had to worry about messing up the floor. The dog was a four-legged vacuum cleaner, without all the noise. But Mom insisted that I join the grownups.

"This is different, Daisy. It's all about sharing a meal with friends, sharing good feelings, sharing love."

When she put it like that, what was I going to say? Bah, humbug?

"You need some new clothes," Mom said. "That stuff you wear might do for a trip to the gym, but I want you to look nice for dinner."

"It's going to take a lot more than new clothes to make me look good."

"Nonsense, new clothes, and that's final."

"If you're thinking about me going shopping, forget about it. No way. Just remember what happened last time." It slipped out, like a little joke, but not funny at all. It brought back memories of the time when, after years of trying, Mom had finally coaxed me into a real dress, then a trip to the beauty parlor. A complete transformation, that's what she'd done, but it was all gone in an instant, burned off in the blast.

"I'm sorry Mom. I should never have said that."
Will somebody kick me, please?

Instead of a kick, I got a Mom hug. "We do what we can, Daisy, we do what we can."

"Yeah, Dad used to say that."

****

The neatest thing about Thanksgiving, the thing that brought back memories of happier times, was the aroma that floated out of Mom's kitchen, that wonderful cloud of spices, pies, even the vegetables smelled great. Because the holiday kitchen was Mom's domain. From that position she was, and would remain, the leader of the band.

I had heard her bustling about in the wee hours, doing all those mysterious things that ultimately came together as a feast any family could relish. I suppose Mrs. West was working away in her own kitchen, assembling one of her magical pies. All a part of why Thanksgiving was always printed out in red letters on our calendar.

It was small compensation, but Mom never badgered me anymore about learning to cook. That was never going to happen.

Back in the good days, by Mom's rules, Dad and I, Max, too, were banished from the kitchen on holidays. I remember Dad trying to sneak in, filch a sliver of pumpkin pie, Mom chasing him out, a large spoon raised above her head threatening to whack him if he tried again. I was expelled, for a different reason; I was a disaster in the kitchen.

"Make sure you marry a man who can cook," Mom had said.

Now my blindness rendered me incapable of

anything more complicated than making toast.

In spite of me insisting that new clothes would be a waste of money, the new outfit my mother had brought me was quite comfortable. I now wore a soft cotton T-shirt, and over that a long-sleeved top, also soft cotton. "What color is it?" I had asked when I tried them on.

"Yellow."

"Yellow? Mom, I'll look like some half-dead bird in yellow. I'll look like the turkey." Come to think of it, that comparison wasn't far off the mark, seeing as how the bird and I had both been roasted.

"Oh, for heaven's sake. It's only a pale yellow, and there's a blue trim around the collar and the cuffs. You look very nice, and you most definitely do not look like a turkey, so let's hear no more about that."

"Gobble, gobble."

"Daisy, stop it."

****

Arthur arrived first, and I met him at the door. I knew it was Arthur, because every time he came around, Max would go into his stupid dog dance, running around, yipping like his tail was on fire. I was more than a little nervous, didn't know quite what to expect. What I did know was that I wanted to see him in the worst possible way. Maybe Max's ridiculous act wasn't so silly after all. If I could pull it off without bumping into walls, I might have tried it myself.

"Well, well, look at you all dressed up," he said. It was almost the strong, confident Arthur voice that I knew so well, almost, but not quite. We still had things to discuss, and until that conversation took place our situation would remain a bit delicate.

"I brought you some flowers," he said. "Daffodils,

almost the same color as your outfit."

"Daffodils, in November?"

"The florist lady said they're always in bloom somewhere."

"Thanks, but I told you before, I can't see them."

"And I told you before, you're not looking hard enough."

"Arthur, welcome," Mom said loudly.

I guessed they were hugging because Mom said something about how good it felt for "an old lady to get squeezed by a big strong man."

But no hug for me, not yet.

"Smells like heaven in here," Arthur said.

"Hope it turns out good," Mom said, like there was ever any doubt. "Now, you two just have a seat on the sofa while I find a vase for these lovely flowers. I'll put them right in the center of the table where everyone can enjoy them."

Annette arrived a few minutes later with Mrs. West close behind. Hugs all around. This time I got one, too. It would have looked strange if they'd left me out, but, since I was the one who'd thrown a monkey wrench into Arthur's life, I'd have understood if they had.

Linda showed up alone. "Smitty's junior resident fell of his bike, broke his leg, so he had to stay and work."

"Oh, poor guy," Mom said. "I'll give you lots of goodies to take back to him. *And what is this I see?*"

"Oh, wow." Annette's voice was shrill.

"What?" I had no idea what they were talking about.

"A ring. Our Linda is engaged," Annette said.

I guessed there was a lot more hugging going on,

and when my turn came Linda squeezed the breath right out of me. Yeah, the hugs still hurt a little, but the good feeling so far outweighed the bad that I didn't care. I would take all the hugs I could get.

We fell onto the sofa, Linda and Annette with me in the middle. Lots of giggles and exclamations about all the sparkle, which I couldn't see. I was glad they'd included me, but this new development made me feel more isolated than ever. This sort of normal relationship developing into love and marriage was off limits, something else I would never experience. So here's where I give myself a little pep talk, "Be happy for your friend, and stop feeling sorry about things you can't change." Okay, I get the message.

Mom, apparently sensing Arthur's exclusion, as well as her own, said, "Come on into the kitchen with me and Althea. They'll just sit there and whisper and giggle. I could use some adult company myself."

I wound up squeezed between my two friends. Linda had her arm clasped tightly around my shoulders. "In a way, you brought us together," she said. "Back in the bad days, when you were in the BTU, I used to cry on Smitty's shoulder sometimes, a lot of times, actually. So, you got us started."

"I'm glad something good came of all that," I said.

"Lots of good things," Annette said. "Now I have a first rate assistant at the animal care facility. You should see the way she can calm the poor little things down when they're scared and hurt. Amazing."

They chatted back and forth. I joined in occasionally, but mostly I listened. With my friends so close, it was almost as if I was just one of the girls, so how much did appearance really matter? The people who really counted would accept me as I was, just as I accepted them. The others, to hell with them.

****

I was managing well enough with dinner, until I hit the cranberry sauce. I knew it was risky, but I love cranberry sauce. You simply can't have Thanksgiving dinner without cranberry sauce. Tasty and very slippery, right off my spoon and into my lap. "Mom, can I have a straw?"

I laughed, everybody laughed. I must have looked even more a fright than usual with red streaks down my front. There are so very few people on the planet who I'd want to see me like this, and it happened they were all in the same room, sitting at the same table. So, no big deal. The big deal came when Mom made her announcement.

"I have something to say. Since it's a holiday for giving thanks, I want each of you to know how very, very thankful I am for the joy you've brought to our house. It's been a hard year, and I don't know how we'd have made it without such wonderful friends." She named them each in turn, me included. "If any of you have anything to add, please, feel free."

They did exactly that, first Annette, then Linda, and even Mrs. West joined in. Hers was mostly about her friendship with Mom and our little family. She even came up with a few funny anecdotes about Mom's school days. Funny, how I never thought of my mom as a kid, like, to me she'd always been a full grown adult.

Nobody said anything about joining hands; it just happened. Arthur was sitting next to me, and I liked holding hands with him, like a first date in junior high, except now it really meant something.

Then, finally Arthur's turn came. He cleared his throat softly. "Rhoda, I want to thank you for this wonderful dinner. It's the best ever. And it's even better, because the people who mean the most to me in this world are gathered around this table." He gave my hand a gentle squeeze. "Right now I feel like the luckiest man alive."

For a moment, just silence. Damn, but I wish I could see. Then Mom said "Amen," then everybody else said it, too.

All of their short speeches came out as individual affirmations of love and friendship. I listened intently, knowing that shortly the bottle would point in my direction, my turn to speak up. But I blew it, big time. As much as I wanted to join in the love fest, I could not. The emotional transformation I'd begun by acknowledging to myself my feelings for Arthur was yet a small, fragile thing. Acceptance was one thing, but gratitude seemed a step too far. How could I be thankful? How could anyone in my condition be thankful?

I opened my mouth, but what began as a word turned into a moan. I pushed myself away from the table, tipping my chair over in the process. On hands and knees, I crawled toward my bedroom, and ran straight into the sofa. Only then was I able to pull myself up and continue on my way. I felt Max beside me, nudging me in the direction I wanted to go. That dog is tuned into a separate wavelength that I will never understand.

I heard my mother's voice behind me. "Daisy, wait, please, what's wrong?"

Then, Arthur: "Let her go. She'll be okay. I'll talk

to her."

By the time the creaking floorboards announced Arthur's entry into my room, I had curled back into my fetal posture, facing the wall. I heard the same poor chair protest beneath his weight.

"Too much for you, huh?" he said.

"I'm sorry. Maybe you should just go."

"Maybe I should, but I won't. That gratitude thing, that's a hard one."

"You didn't seem to have any trouble with it."

"I had over ten years to think about it. You only had a couple of minutes," he said.

"You've all been so good to me. Then I just run out of the room like an idiot."

"You weren't ready. After all you've been through, being thankful is the last big step. It's big, really big, but you'll get there."

"I guess Mom and the others are pretty pissed at me."

"Not a bit. They understand, it takes time and a lot of work. That reminds me, your mom said you've been sitting around on your fat ass all week. Ain't done a lick of work. Well, that's about to change. Tomorrow we start back again, and I'm gonna make you beg for mercy."

"I'll set my dog on you." But nothing would make me happier than working with Arthur, and if it hurt a little bit I wouldn't mind at all.

"I've already cleared it with Max. He's on my side now. Tomorrow."

After Arthur was gone, Max jumped onto my bed, and I hugged him so hard he whimpered.

Chapter 12

Wednesday morning the following week, I smelled apple pie baking. Mom didn't just whip up her specialty dish in the middle of the week for nothing, so, I had to ask, "Mom, what's up?"

She came and sat beside me at the table. "Someone is coming to visit us later this morning."

"Okay, who?" If they rated an apple pie, they must be at least a little special.

"Dr. Dawson, your surgeon from the hospital."

"What?" I almost fell off my chair. How could she? This was the worst kind of betrayal, the two of them, my mother and that horrible surgeon causing me more pain than anyone should have to bear. "Why did you do that? I don't ever, ever, ever want to see that man again. Look what he did to me. You two can talk all you want, but I'm not seeing him, no way."

"Daisy, you'll have to do what you think is best. No one can force you to do anything."

"You got that right. How did this come up in the first place? I mean, he's like, king of the surgeons. What's he coming way out here to dinky little Warrensburg for?" There had to be some hidden agenda, something she wasn't telling me.

"He's been very troubled by all you went through, and how you've been since you got out of the hospital."

"And how do you know that?" I asked.

"I've talked with him several times since you got home. Daisy, he's not like you think. He always made time for me when you were in the hospital, and he wanted me to call him after you were discharged, to tell him how you were doing."

"He could have asked me. I'd have given him an earful."

"I know you would have, but it's just not that way. He felt awful about how things went for you. So did I. I was hurting, and, believe it or not, he was hurting, just like we were."

"Hurting? You don't know anything about hurting. You two should have come to visit me in the hydrotherapy room. You could listen to me scream. That's what real hurting sounds like."

She was taking deep breaths. Yeah, I'm sure she felt pretty rotten just now, but this should not have come up at all. We hadn't talked about the hospital since that day by Dad's grave. That was as close as we would likely ever come to closure, and bringing Dr. Dawson back into the picture now didn't change things. If anything, him visiting would only make things worse, as I saw it. I went through six months of hell in that hospital and came out looking like a potato chip. Nothing Dr. Dawson could say or do would make that right.

"I hope you'll at least talk to him. It would mean a lot to him and to me."

"I'll go into my room and lock the door." Yeah, I was being childish, but I was pissed off and scared in a way even my own mother would never understand.

"If that's what you want to do, okay. It's your choice. But if you change your mind, could you please wear that cute yellow outfit you wore for Thanksgiving? I finally got the cranberry stains out, and it looks nice again."

"I want Arthur here."

"He's coming. I've already called him."

"So you and Dr. Dawson cooked up this little caper all by yourselves, and you did it without even asking me. Mom, can't you see, this is what keeps driving me crazy, people making decisions about me without including me. I have feelings, too, remember, and I'm not quite as stupid as everybody seems to think."

"Daisy, if I'd asked you before, what would you have said?"

"No, of course."

"That's why I never brought it up. And just so you know, he asked to come out. I didn't invite him."

What a great way to start the day. The guy who tortured me for so long is coming for a visit, and he's getting apple pie. I always thought of Arthur as a master trickster, but Mom has her own secret weapons, apple pies, sugar cookies and cinnamon buns.

Arthur arrived, and the three of us sat in an awkward silence, waiting. Mom was sitting by me on the sofa when the doorbell rang, and she jumped up like she'd been stung. "That must be Dr. Dawson."

"Rhoda, good to see you," His voice was softer than I remembered from the hospital, and it didn't help one bit that he and Mom were on a first name basis. But why not? He spent more time with her than he ever spent with me. Maybe he won't even recognize me, like, you can't tell one burned freak from another. *Bitchy, Daisy, very bitchy.*

"I thought we'd talk over coffee in the dining

room," Mom said. "I've made an apple pie."

I got up slowly, and Arthur led me into the dining room. We stood there for a moment, him with his big arm around my shoulders.

"Hello, Daisy, it's good to see you again."

"Oh, Dr. Dawson, I don't believe you've met Arthur." Mom jumped in when I didn't answer. We'll see how the great doctor likes the silent treatment.

"Don't recall seeing you around the hospital," Dr. Dawson said.

"I don't work in the hospital." Arthur's voice was like a low sonic boom that loomed over me like a protective shield.

Dr. Dawson didn't sound intimidated in the least. Gone was the commanding voice. He sounded like a regular human being. When we sat down he came around and took the chair next to me. I'd hoped to keep the table between us, but that wasn't to be. He put his hand on my shoulder.

"I'm glad to see you again, Daisy." His voice was as gentle as Arthur's had been menacing. "Maybe we can talk a bit, if you don't mind."

"What do you want to talk about?" I asked. Gentle voice or not, he wasn't getting a pass, not from me.

"It's been a very hard year for you, so much has changed. I just wanted to see how you're doing."

"How does it look like I'm doing? How would you feel if you looked like me?"

I heard a couple of deep breaths. Yeah, I had scored a hit.

"I can't answer that. All the burn victims we see, when they leave the hospital, I wonder what their lives will be like, but I never know, not really."

"You did this to me. I never wanted this."

"Daisy, that's a terrible thing to say. Dr. Dawson saved your life," Mom said.

She was right. I was being a little shit, but I had enough bad memories of that awful treatment to last three lifetimes, and they weren't going away easily.

"No, you're right," Dr. Dawson said. "I made a decision, and I accept full responsibility for it."

"But we all wanted her to live," Mom said.

"Yes, I know, but the final decision was mine and mine alone."

I thought I might be sick. Of all the scenarios I'd run through my mind, this one hadn't come up at all. The great Dr. Dawson, unsure and almost penitent. My brain froze, and I sat there clueless about what I ought to say next.

The ensuing silence got to Mom; she had firm rules about always treating guests with courtesy and hospitality. "Coffee," she said. "I think we could all use a cup of coffee. Arthur, would you help me in the kitchen?"

"Rhoda bakes a great apple pie," Arthur said. "Best I've ever tasted."

Dr. Dawson must have dug right into his pie. "Outstanding," he said between mouthfuls. "I think we should invite you to some of our committee meetings. People would be a lot more cordial if they could eat like this."

And it was true, as if the tension in the room was pushed aside by apple pie and coffee. After all that had gone on before, all I went through, a pie and coffee hardly seemed like a fair exchange, but that's how it turned out.

"I have one question," I said. "If you had it to do all over again, my treatment, I mean, would you do it different?" What I wanted him to answer was whether or not he would honor my wishes to stop the treatments.

I heard his fork drop on his plate. Then nothing, silence. If anybody at the table was breathing I couldn't hear it. He got up from the table, took a few steps.

"You're not going to like my answer, Daisy. The truth is, I don't know. I've thought about this hundreds of times, and I still don't have a better answer."

"That doesn't make sense," I said. "I don't believe you."

More silence. Four adults and one dog and not a peep from any of us, like we were frozen in time.

"Sometimes it doesn't make sense to me either, but it's a very hard thing to stand by and watch someone die when you can do something to prevent it."

Then he's quiet again. For a guy who was never short of words in the hospital, he seemed to be having a hard time. When he spoke it came out like a whisper. "Life is a precious thing, Daisy, and often as not, it doesn't turn out the way we wanted. Yours certainly didn't. But you're here now with family and friends, people who love you, and that means something.

"Every moment we draw breath, it's special, it's a gift. That's how I feel about it. Maybe it doesn't make sense, but it's the best I can do."

He took his seat beside me.

This was killing me. I could handle a yes or no answer, and I could hate him for either one, but not this, not thinking about him agonizing over the same question I'd been chewing on for so long.

"How about you?" he asked. "What would you

want me to do?"

I had that coming. All through my stay in the hospital, for weeks after I came home, I was positive. I knew exactly what I wanted. Now I was a ninny. I changed my mind a dozen times a day. "I don't know either."

Now it was my turn for a deep breath. Somewhere, somehow something had been resolved. I wasn't exactly sure how or what, but the troubled waters had settled down a bit. I extended my hand until I found Dr. Dawson's. "I guess we just do the best we can, huh?"

"That's about it," he said in a whisper. He cradled my gnarled remnant of a hand in his own. "That's all we can do."

"I never thanked you for saving my life," I said.

"Any time," he said. "Any time."

I knew what he meant. No, it wasn't about going through all that horrible pain and agony all over again. I think it was about an understanding, like we're all in this mess together, and we don't have an instruction manual, not one that covers the really big questions, anyway. So sometimes we get it right, sometimes we don't. Just so long as we do our best.

See, I'm learning a few things. I know now that I don't have a monopoly on suffering. Sooner or later everybody gets a kick in the ass. Arthur has taught me that much, at least we each have our own little private hell. Mine wasn't so little, but everybody has one. I'll bet that Lizzie Beeson with her perfect life has one, too.

Arthur slid his chair back from the table. "Anybody for more coffee?"

****

What a day, one of those crazy upside-down days

where everything has changed and nothing is different. And then it was over, and he was gone, and I was only slightly less confused than I was before, but that was okay. Confusion, I figure, is just another piece of the big picture, so live with it.

Mom gave me a big squeeze. "I love you, and I'm so very, very proud of you."

"Thanks, Mom, and thanks for fixing this up,and thanks for sticking with me. I know it hasn't been easy." Easy? How about almost impossible? I guess love has a lot more staying power than I thought.

"Any time, sweetheart, any time," she said just like Dr. Dawson, and I think she meant the same thing.

About that time I started coughing. "Fresh air," I said. "Need to go out for a minute."

"Do you want your jacket or your nice fleece robe?" Mom asked.

"Fleece robe, for sure."

I was all bundled up and headed for the back porch swing with Arthur. If you asked me at that moment if there was anywhere I'd rather be, I'd have said no, and nobody I'd rather be with.

"Don't you kids stay out too late," Mom said. "Dinner is at six, and you're staying, Arthur." Kids? Arthur? A big stretch, but if that's how she saw it, okay by me.

I was thankful for my cozy robe. Of course, what could you expect in late November? We sat together in the swing on the back porch. The way it creaked and groaned I wasn't at all sure it would hold his weight, but he didn't seem worried in the least.

"You're really something," he said. "The way you handled that. You let someone get close to you, someone you had every reason to hate, but you opened up. I don't know any other way to put it, but that takes balls."

I laughed. "You know, back when I used to work with Dad, sometimes I wished for a nice set of balls, and maybe a penis, just so I could be one of the guys."

He laughed so hard the boards that the swing was attached to groaned like they were going to part company with the ceiling. "I hope you never told your mother about that."

"Dr. Dawson surprised me," I said. "He was so different today than he was in the hospital. I used to think he was the world's biggest sonofabitch, but, like I say, he surprised me. Maybe I was wrong about him."

"Well, for damn sure, you surprised him, surprised everybody, me included."

"That's a first. I didn't think anything ever surprised you."

"Oh, yeah, life's just full of surprises. Keeps it interesting."

The swing held up, but not without protesting all the while. Between Arthur's big body and my fleece robe I was warm as could be. But the meeting with Dr. Dawson still bugged me. I'd expected an explosion, and all I got was a fizzle. For almost a year I'd dreamed of tearing into him, punishing him for torturing me, maybe dunking him in the Hubbard tank and pulling his skin off, not all of it, just enough so he'd know how it felt; but when the chance finally came I turned into a wimp, because neither he nor I could answer the big question.

"So weird that, after all that's happened this year, all my big decisions about ending it all, the best I can come up with is 'I don't know.' I must be a complete fool."

"If you are, you're in good company, because Dr. Dawson said the same thing." Arthur shifted just a bit, and the swing protested.

"That's even weirder," I said. "Think about it, like, the biggest event of your life, if you could do it all over again, what would you do? I was so sure about what I wanted, and now I'm not, just like that. It doesn't make sense. Maybe the fire cooked my brain along with everything else."

"No, that's not the answer," he said.

"I hope not, but it's scary, at least for me,how life can shift around, one minute something is rock solid, the next minute it isn't. Not fair."

"There's another way of looking at it," he said. "This freedom of choice thing you've been stewing over for the past year, what if it doesn't make any difference? What if you can choose and choose and choose all you want, and whatever is gonna happen, happens anyway?"

"That's awful. What a rotten thing to say. If you're right then things just happen, one after the other, all random. And that doesn't make any sense at all. There has to be some purpose behind things."

"Could be, though, if things aren't like you say, random."

"Oh, no, don't you dare." I knew where he was going with that, and I didn't want to hear it. Maybe choosing didn't change things. Maybe everything was all set out ahead of time, or maybe the only sure thing was the sun rising every day and the rest of it was up for grabs. A few months ago this sort of information would have been critically important to me. Now I don't have to know. I don't want to know. I can live without knowing. I can do that because nobody really has an answer. I know some people think they do, philosophers and scientists and poets and such, but they don't.

"Let's talk about something else," I said. I had to take a few deep breaths before I could get into what had been sitting between us since just before Thanksgiving. The sharp edges had worn off by now—time can do that—but it still needed exposure, out in the open air, before it could properly be put to rest. I was sure Arthur needed it as well. After all, his response had been outright violence, getting himself thrown in jail.

"That day, after you told me your story, I didn't respond very well. I wasn't thinking straight. I'm sorry," I said. "I never dreamed you'd get into a big fight like that. You could have been seriously injured."

"Been my own fault if I did. Besides, that story was a lot to swallow all at once."

"Yeah." More deep breaths. "But I asked you to tell me, and you did. It must have been really hard for you. And I believed it, every word of it. I want you to know."

Now it was his turn for the deep breathing bit. "I didn't know, not for sure. Maybe you thought I was the world's biggest liar, telling a tale like that, but I wanted you to hear it, all of it."

"Why? I mean, I know I asked you, but you could have just blown it off with one of your corny jokes." Yeah, why, that was the big question, wasn't it? And it must have been a big one for Arthur, because it was a long time before he answered. We were getting into a gray zone, out beyond the margins of his usual therapeutic boundaries, and we both knew it. He'd been leading up to something all along, but what? Maybe the question bugging me was bugging him too?

"The reason I went a little crazy after I left that day, and the reason I had to tell you everything, was that it matters what you think about me. It matters a lot. I left here afraid that I'd blown it big time, that maybe I wouldn't ever see you again. That's what I couldn't handle."

I didn't know what to say, and when I finally did it caught in my throat and wouldn't go any further. Perfect. I pressed up against him. "I'm scared." Scared and, dare I even think it, happy?

"You should be. So am I."

At least we were scared together.

****

Dinner was meatloaf, mashed potatoes and green beans, all stuff I can manage pretty well. Only problem with the beans is, Max doesn't like them, so if I drop one it stays there. But I was extra careful.

And we had an after-dinner treat. For the first time in a long, long time, Mom went back to her piano, and what a treat it was. Even on a crummy old upright that probably hadn't been tuned since the great flood, even without practicing for years, her talent was something special, even to a musical clod like me.

But hidden in the joy of the music was a note of sadness, and it crawled around in my gut like a bad case of heartburn. What if life had taken my mother through the Julliard school and on to the great concert halls of Europe, instead of plunking her down in a modest little house in Warrensburg, Virginia, with a brat for a daughter?

What if, what if, what if? Life needs a reset button. What if the Universe, or the Big Guy upstairs, or whoever is pulling the strings sent down an angel for just one visit, and the angel says something like, "Okay, you can pick one time in your life that you want to change, and you can make a different choice, or you can leave it just the same, and you have five seconds to decide." Good luck with that. Maybe I wouldn't have lit that stupid match, but then I would never have met Arthur. Nope, better leave it as it is.

I'm beginning to think Arthur was right. All our big choices don't amount to much. In fact, it's a big joke. Stuff happens, and we do what we can.

In the meantime Mom was making beautiful music.

"Dang, she can play," Arthur said.

"Dang right."

****

Back to the rehab center the next day, but Arthur's heart didn't seem to be in it. There was none of his usual goading, and that took some of the fun out of it. We knocked off early.

"Coke?" he asked.

"For sure."

"I never knew your mom could play the piano like that."

"She's really good, when she wants to be. She had a scholarship offer at the Julliard, but didn't go through with it."

"What stopped her?"

"Me. I guess I wasn't planned, and she couldn't do the music thing and take care of me, too."

"So she packed it in."

"Yeah."

"Must be hereditary."

"What do you mean by that?"

"Like giving up when you think that you'll never reach your full potential."

"Don't you dare start with me. I think I've done pretty damned good recently."

"You have, you certainly have. That's just something to think about, what I said."

"Yeah, I'll file it away with all the other crap you've given me to think about."

He got up, walked part way across the room. He made the floor squeak here just like at our house. Arthur will never sneak up on anybody. When he came back he only sat for a moment before he was up and pacing again.

"Will you please sit down? You're making me nervous."

So he sat. He twisted. He fidgeted, and Arthur never fidgeted quietly; he couldn't. That much mass moving about, even a little bit, always makes noise.

"Enough. What's up with you?"

"You never got married, did you?" he asked.

"I was almost engaged once, but it fell through. Dad got sick, then I got burned. Just as well. So, no, I never got married. You?"

"Nothing official." Another quiet spell. "You ever think about it?" he asked.

"Oh, sure, I dream about it every night, walking down the aisle in a long white dress, organ music, flowers. Then the groom lifts the veil off my face, takes one look and faints dead away. What is this, your idea of a joke?"

"You ever think about it without all the hoopla, just

something quiet?"

"Stop screwing around, will you?" I shoved him, but it was like shoving a house, nothing moved.

"Do you?"

"*Nothing like that is ever going to happen, not for me*," I said.

He took my hand, held it in both of his, cradled it soft, like a baby chick. "Why not?" he asked, his voice still in that rumbling whisper.

"Why not what?"

"Get married."

"Are you absolutely nuts? Look at me. Who in their right mind would marry something like me?"

"I would, and I'm looking straight at you, and believe me, I'm no prize when it comes to good looks."

"Go away, leave me alone."

"You ran me off once before, remember? This time I'm not leaving without an answer."

"Please, don't do this. Now you're scaring me."

"Scares me, too."

"Look, I can't do anything. The fire ruined me down there. Nothing left." I never gave much thought to the damage the fire had done to my womanhood, since it barely left me human it didn't seem to make much difference. But he would be better off marrying a stuffed animal, so he might as well know that right here and now.

"Yes, you can do something, the most important thing, you can love me." That low, rumbling voice, I could scarcely believe what I was hearing.

"So, you think that's all there is to marriage, do you?"

"It's not all, but it's enough, more than enough."

"Oh God, oh God, oh God. I'm in love with a crazy man, and I'm scared to death."

A lot of deep breathing now, we'd both stepped across a void, or maybe into one; either way the prospect was frightening, because there would be no going back to the way things were before, not for Arthur, not for me. We'd both made a declaration of sorts, and there was only one direction…forward.

I came close to panic. I wanted to jerk away from him, run like hell, but I left my hand, that small deformed thing cradled lightly between his two massive paws. I took a few deep breaths, coughed a couple of times. I was dizzy, and had I been standing, surely I would have fallen. The words that came forth did so as if of their own accord, with no thought of my own. "You really are crazy, but okay."

"Can I take that as a yes?"

"Yeah, and I meant it about the crazy part, too."

That got me a big Arthur laugh that rattled the windows in the rehab center.

I had a laugh of my own. "You just proposed to me in a dirty old rehab center. You got class, real style."

"Gimme a break, will you? I been thinking about this for weeks, but every time I get ready to ask you, something comes up, or I chicken out."

"Chicken? You?" I leaned against him, and, for heaven's sake, he was trembling, and when a big guy like him trembles, everything around him trembles as well. I squeezed his hand. "It's okay. I still think you're crazy, but it's okay."

He draped one huge arm across my shoulders and drew me close. "I think I can breathe now."

"Good, then you can tell me you love me."

"I do, I love you."

"I love you, too." There, we'd both said it. We'd put words to the feeling that had been whirling around us for quite a while. It felt good to finally give it a name. "I can't cook, you know."

That got me another booming Arthur laugh, and this time I joined him.

So we sat while the light faded. I couldn't see it, and I didn't care. I saw other things, more important things. Love must really be blind, I thought. If not blind, then crazy, or both.

"What do you think your mom will say?"

"We'll find out, won't we? She already considers you part of the family."

"We're not exactly a matched pair," he said.

"There is no match for somebody like me. I just have to accept that. You have to accept it, as well. In a way I know it's harder for you, because you can see me, see how people react to me."

"You still don't get it. That doesn't make any difference, none at all. Besides, I think we're matched in spirit, and that's what counts."

Me? Daisy Sugarbush, spiritual? What next?

So, when we got back home we broke the news to Mom.

She squealed like a teenager. "Oh, oh, oh, this is the best. This is the very best." She jumped from one of us to the other, a hug here, then a hug there, then starting all over again.

Max joined right in, running around and barking like crazy.

"When?" she asked.

"We haven't discussed that yet," I said.

"It's the end of November already. If you're planning a December wedding, we need to get started." She spoke in rapid bursts, like she was out of breath.

I wasn't too sure about this. December was an anniversary month. A lot of bad things had fallen on us in December of last year. But I don't know, maybe doing something good this year will cancel some of those out.

So, December it will be. Arthur managed to stay out of this discussion altogether. A wise move.

****

Details, details, details. They piled up so fast, and Mom and I disagreed on all of them. Again, Arthur, the coward, laid low.

One other thing I remembered from working with Dad, he never rushed anything. Whatever he started took its own time; he never pushed it through. "That's when you mess up, when you hurry," he always said. Now, everything was rushed. I never had time to stop and think. Maybe Mom knew, if I had time to think I'd probably cancel the whole thing. She was right.

I wanted a quiet event, no fuss. There was no way I could handle a big deal, not the way Mom was thinking. But she won that one. We would be married in her church, the First Baptist of Warrensburg, the second Sunday in December. The traditional seating arrangement of dividing the house into friends of the bride and friends of the groom was totally impractical. That was the first point on which both Mom and I agreed. But for the life of me I couldn't figure out why she was so frantic over the arrangements for a small ceremony. Since there would be so few people present, what difference could it make?

I only found out later, she cheated, big time. Instead of a modest gathering, she had something completely different in mind, and she secretly enlisted Linda's aid in distributing invitations to all the staff in the Burn Trauma Unit. She wrote a short personal note to Dr. Dawson, a special invitation. She made several trips to Sparky's where she left a stack of invitations for Ralph to distribute to my friends. In the weeks leading up to the wedding she seldom went anywhere without a sheaf of invitations in her purse, and it was always empty when she returned home.

Through all of this I remained clueless. How would I know? I'd never been part of wedding plans before. And I guess she knew that if I caught wind of what she was planning I'd have pitched a fit. Of course, Arthur probably suspected, but he kept her secret.

Then there was the matter of a dress for me. "My regular clothes will do just fine, Mom."

"Out of the question," she said. "You'll wear a dress, a white dress like a proper bride."

"But I'm not a *proper bride*. Look at me. A white dress will make me look even more ridiculous than I already do. And if you think we're going shopping, you're crazy."

"It's all taken care of. One of my friends from church is a dressmaker. She'll come right here to the house to get you fitted out. Don't worry. It will be a simple dress, nothing fancy."

"But why throw away good money on something I'll wear for an hour at most?"

"It's a special occasion that only happens once in your life." There was that little catch in her voice, something she almost said but caught herself just in time. I caught myself, too, just before I asked about her own wedding dress. If she'd wanted me to know about that she would have told me, so I guess that discussion would have to wait until later.

"Poor Arthur," I said, although he'd managed to make himself scarce during all the fuss.

"Don't worry. I'm taking care of him, too."

"Poor Arthur," I said again.

A scorekeeper would have Mom far ahead in the tally. More and more I found myself in a grin-and-bear-it position, coasting along with the current was a lot easier. It would take a damned fool to reverse course and paddle upstream. But there was more to come.

For instance, there was the matter of rings. Mom had already taken Arthur shopping for a gold band for himself. The only problem had been finding one large enough to slip over his very large fingers. I posed a different problem. Size wasn't the issue; the problem was deformity. Scarring had reduced the fingers of my left hand to something resembling claws. Getting a band on my ring finger would require a surgical procedure.

"Why not just put it on a gold chain? I'll hang it around her neck," Arthur said. "Means the same thing, right?"

"Bless you," Mom said. "That's a great idea."

"One more thing," Mom said. "Someone has to give the bride away."

I was a step ahead on this one. "Max."

"Don't be ridiculous. You can't have a dog give you away."

But I dug in my heels. "Max is my best friend. He's been there for me through this whole thing. I want

Max."

"Let's think about it," Mom said. "We can talk more tomorrow."

"Max," I said. "Or I swear, we'll elope."

"Then at least give him a bath."

****

As if in marking an end to the mother-daughter conflict, or a truce, at least, that second Sunday in December dawned clear and bright, or so I was told. The town of Warrensburg was, in its own way, already in a festive mood with the Christmas holiday less than two weeks away, so peace and harmony prevailed over discord, for the most part.

I stood in the middle of the living room in my new white gown while Mom fussed about, making last minute adjustments.

"What's that?" My fingers probed the base of my neck.

"Pearls," Mom said. "They look perfect on you."

"I've never worn pearls in my life."

"They were your grandmother's. I wore them at my wedding, and I'm sure your father would want you to wear them at yours."

"I wish he was here, but I wouldn't want him to see me like this."

"I wish he was here, too, dear." Mom kissed me on the cheek. "And if he was, you'd still be his daughter, and he'd still love you, no matter what."

"Where's Arthur?"

"He'll meet us at the church. You know very well that the groom can't see the bride before the ceremony."

"Yeah, one look at me and he'll run away."

Mom grabbed me by the shoulders. "Daisy, stop it. Enough. We've been over this a hundred times. Arthur loves you, just the way you are. So do I. So do your friends. Anybody that says otherwise can go to hell."

"*Mom, you swore, again, and on my wedding day at that.*"

"I'm sorry. No more of this ugly talk, okay?"

A few more adjustments. "There, we're ready. I'll get your coat."

"I have to get something, too." I had my white baseball cap stashed in my closet. I wore one all the time now. "Arthur got it for me. How do you like it?"

"Oh, no, you can't."

"Yes, I can, and I will. My wedding, my hat, my choice."

"But, a baseball cap."

"Arthur says it looks cool."

"I'm going to hurt that man."

****

Mom pulled up to the side entrance of the church. She didn't tell me until later, but she'd driven past the main parking lot—packed, with some overflow parked along the street. "Well, we're here. Shall we go in?"

"What if he doesn't show up?" I said.

"Who?"

"Arthur, of course. What if he's changed his mind?"

"He's here. I promise."

"Go look. I'm not getting out of this car until you check."

She was back in a moment. "He's here, and he's waiting for you."

Mom led Max and me down a corridor that opened

onto several classrooms.

"Where are we?" I asked.

"If you had come to church with me more often you'd know. Careful of the carpet. It has a few holes."

A little farther along Mom stopped. I could hear a low buzzing sound like a lot of people speaking softly, a *lot of people*. But this couldn't be. Panic began creeping in, but what could I do now? Running away is not an option when you're blind. And then I had to pee. Oh, God, why hadn't I gone before we left the house?

"Daisy, this is Charlie Brewer, one of your old friends from school."

"Hey, Daisy. Great hat." Charlie, as I remember, is tall as Arthur but rail thin, and probably hasn't changed much since the last time I saw him. He bent down and hugged me.

"Charlie, what are you doing here?"

"Charlie is one of the ushers," Mom said.

"Ushers? I didn't know we were going to have ushers."

"Oh, yeah, couldn't handle a crowd this size without ushers," Charlie said.

"*Crowd? Mom?*" Too late. One breath at a time, one step at a time, otherwise I might faint dead away and wet myself in the process.

"Everything is just fine, sweetheart, just fine. I love you so much. I'm going down to take my seat. When the music starts, Charlie will give you the signal, and you can get Max going."

"Uh, Charlie, maybe you could lead the way?"

"Sure, that okay with you Ms. S.?"

"Absolutely, but go slow, and just you make sure she doesn't try to sneak out the back door."

"All ready?" Charley asked.

"Just a second. Are there really that many people?"

"Packed. Not an empty seat in the house."

"Oh, my God. Who are they? I couldn't possibly know all of them, or even most of them."

"They're your friends, and they're all here for you."

"But I don't have many friends, hardly any."

"More than you know, Daisy, more than you know." Charlie's voice sounded funny, like he was about to choke up. "We should get started."

As scary as it was for me, it was probably just as scary for poor Arthur. For all his bulk and bluster he didn't like crowds any more than I did, especially when they were all looking at him.

As we walked along the buzzing noise increased. Either there were a lot of bees in the church or a lot of people. Max was enjoying himself, prancing along like he was the center of attention. Easy enough for him. He wasn't getting married. And he didn't look like a freak.

The service went off smoothly enough considering that the bride was handed off to the groom by a dog, and the groom himself acted as his own best man.

"Who better?" Arthur had asked. Who better indeed?

We exchanged vows in whispers that only we could hear. I had trouble getting the ring on Arthur's large finger, and he had to assist me. My own band hung from a gold chain that Arthur slipped over my head. Then we hugged.

We'd done it. What had seemed impossible had just happened.

When we turned and faced the crowd the applause

erupted as if someone had just scored a winning touchdown. I didn't know you could applaud in church, but it was like they couldn't help themselves. Arthur would probably say something momentous, something remarkable had just happened, and the folks had to acknowledge the fact, that intimate statement about what it means to be human. But then, Arthur is better at words than I am.

A rush of crisp, winter air came in as the church doors opened, just beyond that, bright sunlight. We must have been quite a sight as we stepped out into that Sunday afternoon: a tall black man with an eye patch, a scorched girl wearing a white dress and a baseball cap, both led by a spotted dog named Max. Yeah, quite a sight.

There was a reception in a hall called the recreation center in back of the church. I always thought that was a funny name for a church building, and Mom said she'd never seen it so full of people before. After a few hugs I grabbed Mom's arm. "Please, please, please, I have to pee. And you might have to help me with the dress."

It was only a brief respite. I had to get back to Arthur. He didn't know hardly any of these people. But I needn't have worried. Before I even reached his side I heard his booming laughter...everything was okay.

So many people, so many hugs, Linda, Smitty, Annette, Dr. Dawson, most of the staff from the Burn Trauma Unit, the rehab staff, Ralph and the Sparky's gang, and at least half the town of Warrensburg.

"Mom, how on earth did you do this?"

"It's a very special day, and I had lots of help."

And it was special. All the times I'd been told

about how people who really loved you would still love you no matter how you looked, I finally understood it to be true. Of all the things Mom ever taught me, this was right at the top of the list.

Chapter 13

Monday morning, December eleventh, 1994, I awoke as a married woman. Sunday's festivities left me completely drained, and I crashed around nine p.m. on my wedding night, alone in my own bed. No, this wasn't the regular newlywed behavior, but this particular newlywed had spent much of the year in a Burn Trauma Unit, so the usual stuff was off the table. I slept in my own room, and Arthur slept in the guest bedroom.

We'd agreed on this arrangement earlier during another of those chilly evenings when we'd sat together bundled up on the back porch. There hadn't been enough time to sort out all the nuts and bolts of married life, but this one had troubled me the most.

"Are you sure this will be enough for you?" I'd asked him several times. "I mean, I can't do anything, you know." He was only thirty-six years old and had taken no vows of celibacy, so far as I knew.

"You mean, is a marriage without sex enough for me? Yeah, just so long as there's plenty of love, that's the main thing. And, as I see it, we got more than enough of that." He gave me an extra squeeze for emphasis. We'd already had a similar conversation with a similar outcome, but hearing it again was reassuring.

"Like I said before, you're crazy."

He laughed. "Then so are you."

"Perfect, finally, something we have in common."

****

The time between Arthur's proposal of marriage in the romantic rehab center to our trip down the church aisle had been brief, so much so that the whole thing might have appeared on the impulsive side, sort of like jumping off a cliff and discovering halfway down that you'd forgotten to let the cat out. I figure a lot of weddings occur in a hurry. If people stopped to consider all the possibilities, all the things that might not go as planned, there would be far fewer weddings.

But we did it anyway. Did we leave a lot of loose ends lying around? You bet. Still, our own vows were not so impetuous as they seemed.

Usually, it seems, in a fit of passion, an act is undertaken that will have lifelong consequences, and you have to ask whether this state of mind is the one you want to be in when you make choices for the long haul. My own wedding lacked that heat of physical passion. I had no doubt about it being a union of love, but the consummation that usually drives the process forward was a non-starter, physically impossible. Still, we had taken the leap, formed a union between two souls so mismatched as to have appeared from different planets. Since the chance of either of us finding our exact opposite was remote, this didn't seem like such a bad idea.

As always, the devil lay in the details, and we had yet to discuss a number of them, such as who would sleep where and when. Arthur left himself an escape route by keeping his own apartment. He moved most of his stuff into our guest bedroom, but I never knew when he would be there. I knew he had other patients besides me, but who, what, when and where were questions I hadn't asked.

One thing, as a new bride I finally got to know my husband's last name. "Hemingway? For real?"

"Don't make such a big deal out of it. I never had much to say about it."

"So, officially, I'm Daisy Hemingway. I think I like that better than Sugarbush. I won't even tell you some of the nasty little variations they made up on that name when I was in school. So now I'm a Hemingway."

"Don't wear it out."

"How come you never told me before?" I asked.

"I never thought much of it. I don't even know for sure that's my real name. Mom just had that put on the birth certificate. Could have been any one of the men that were in and out back then."

"Hemingway."

"Give it a rest, or I'll change it."

For the time being, everything was on a trial basis as we tried to figure out what fit and what didn't. Through all this breaking in period, Mom was a shining star. She was so patient. She didn't question, she didn't probe, she offered no advice. She could have made a difficult time even more difficult, but she didn't. There must have been dozens of times while I was floundering, flopping and falling flat on my face, but she let me find my own way. How else would I ever learn?

But triangular family units can be difficult—I learned that years ago—particularly when two points of that triangle are newlyweds. Mom must have known this, because midway through the second week she called for a meeting in the kitchen on Wednesday afternoon, complete with an apple pie, which made it an official gathering. She, Arthur and I sat round the table while Max sprawled in front of the sofa.

"I'm planning a short road trip," Mom said. "I don't have any place in mind, but I really should get out of here so you two can have some privacy."

"Yeah, we'll probably be having wild, crazy sex all over the house," I said.

"If that's what you want," Mom said. "I'll be back just before Christmas. I haven't been away since your father and I took that trip to Savannah in 1989. I recall that someone had a big party while we were away."

I could feel her give me that look, not unkind, just recognition of another family adventure that we'd survived.

"Sorry, sorry," I said. "I'll never do that again." Things had gotten a little out of hand with my party, fifty kids instead of a dozen, and a few household repairs were needed afterward, all of which I did myself.

"I do want to hire a housekeeper to help out, someone who can cook and clean and do the shopping. She can also help you with personal stuff, bathing, things like that."

"Sort of like a mother," I said.

"Sort of."

"If I tried to cook I'd probably burn the house down, and I've started all the fires I ever want to start," I said. "But won't a housekeeper be expensive?"

"That's the other thing we need to discuss. Before he died, your father arranged for his lawyer to sell his three rental properties. It took almost a year, but he got a good deal, and they brought in a lot of money. He set up a trust fund for you, to become active on your twenty-first birthday, or on your wedding day. Since you're a married woman now, that money is all yours to do with as you please. When I get back we can meet with the attorney, so you'll know how much is in the fund, and how you access it."

I laughed, couldn't help it, and it wasn't a happy laugh. But I swallowed what I was going to say, because even I was getting a little sick of my moaning about things I couldn't have, things I couldn't change. "I should have known he would look out for us," I said.

So now I was burned and rich, big deal. There was a time when having a lot of money would have been an exciting proposition. Now it meant little to me. The things people usually do with money, travel, new cars, new clothes, were not on my radar screen now and never would be. Maybe Arthur would have some ideas, I certainly didn't.

Mom left on a Thursday morning. "I'll call you every day," she said. The concern in her voice came through like a whine, something Max might do when he wants to go out. I know she was torn between wanting to stay and help out and wanting to get out of the way so Arthur and I could figure things out for ourselves.

"Don't worry, Mom, we'll be fine. You go and enjoy yourself."

Would she? I could only hope. Her whole world for almost two years had been filled with caring for sickness, death and dying. For her to embark on a happy ramble was a lot to ask. But if not this trip, maybe on those to follow. Arthur and I had our own brave new world to face.

The new housekeeper was a young black girl named Irene. Mid-twenties, a big girl, not as big as Arthur, but a lot bigger than me. She lived right in Warrensburg and had her own car. I think we both were trying so hard at first to make a good impression that the situation was awkward. She was trying to be helpful, and I was trying to become more independent. But good intentions won out. I was making an extra effort to be nice to her, because when you're blind and almost helpless it doesn't pay to have too many people pissed off at you. And the most critical issue evolved on its own, Max liked her.

Bathing and dressing myself were requirements I placed on myself. "If you'll just check me out, make sure I haven't put things on inside-out..." I said to Irene.

The next item on my agenda was going out, without Arthur's support. He'd become part of my dependency issue, since I relied so heavily on his presence to fend off any unpleasantness I might encounter out in the world.

"Do you know where Sparky's is?" I asked her.

"Sure, just up the street."

"I want to go, but I'll need your help at first. I've been there a thousand times, but that was back when I could see. Things are different now, and I have to warn you, I have some old friends at Sparky's, but most people have never seen anything quite like me. So be prepared for some weird reactions. I can't see them, but you can."

"Won't bother me. I know your friends will be glad to see you, and nobody is gonna mess with us, not with me and Max around."

"That's good enough for me," I said.

I talked a pretty good game, but that first trip I was scared stiff. I'd lived no more than two blocks away from Sparky's my whole life, now the trip seemed like it would require a herculean effort to complete, and who knew what would happen when we got there?

I grabbed my jacket from the closet, along with a new ski hat Arthur had given me. "Cold out?" I asked.

"Not bad," she said. "You should be fine like that."

I trussed Max up in his working harness and clipped on his leash, all the while the few fingers I had left were shaking like crazy. At this rate I'd be sweating before we even left the house.

Then we were off. It might not seem like such a big deal, walking out my own back door, but not too long before this would have been on the impossible list. Then left foot, right foot, left foot, and so on.

"Sorry to keep latching onto you," I said. "I'm still not very steady."

"You're doing fine," she said, a confident voice like this was something she did every day.

This girl was beginning to sound like Arthur.

"Your dog is really good," she said. "Must have taken a long time to train him like that."

I had to laugh. "Mostly he figured it out himself."

More tentative steps. Two blocks had become such a long, long way, but between Max and Irene there was no stopping. We crossed a street, then, "We're here. I'll get the door."

I tried to hold back. This would be the first public place, besides the church, that I'd entered in a long time,

"Daisy, sweetheart." Ralph's voice boomed out at

me. In a moment he'd lifted me off the floor. "Damn, but it's good to see you. I thought you'd forgotten about me."

"Not likely," I said. "This is Irene, and you already know Max."

"I got a grape slurpee over here with your name on it," Ralph said. "Come on around behind the counter so you can sit down. Anything for you, Irene?"

It couldn't get much better than this. Ralph chatted away like I'd just been off on summer vacation instead of stuck in a hospital for six months. He seemed to hit it off with Irene, too, another plus.

"I hope I'm not scaring off your customers," I said.

He and Irene both laughed, Max barked. "You worry about the damndest things," he said. "I ought to call Janey, let her know you're here. She'd love to see you."

Not very much, not in the grand scheme of things, just a two-block walk to one of my old haunts, but it had seemed like a mountain at first. Then it became just another trip to Sparky's. Maybe I could do this, maybe, maybe, maybe.

A walk every day, weather permitting, that was my new routine. I figured that, unless I went out and talked with the neighbors, I was going to be spending a lot of time alone. I would have preferred it that way before, but things change. Irene seemed to enjoy getting out, and Max loved it. He led the parade, the big show off.

Most of the neighbors seemed glad to see me. A few shuffled along like they couldn't wait to get away. Fine by me, screw 'em.

Some of them seemed a bit unsure when I introduced Irene, nothing hostile, just a moment's hesitation while they sized up the situation. I'd gotten better at catching onto the nuances, since sometimes that was all I had to go on. Maybe a moment of fear? I'd sensed that occasionally when Arthur was with me, someone figuring that this big guy could do some real damage if he wanted to, then the change as his big smile won them over.

My goal was to reach the point where I could go for short walks with Max, just me and my dog. That's about all the independence I could handle.

I'd never lived any place but Warrensburg, and thought I knew it pretty good, but I was learning new things about it every time we went out. Before I lost my sight, the area where I lived was always the same, even the people. I never gave it a second thought. Over the years there'd been only a few new neighbors, just a progression through the families that had been there all along, new ones were born in, old ones checked out. When I walked past the Gardner's house, there were still Gardners there, always had been and would be.

New priorities now, new smells, how does it sound, is the ground smooth and level or is it tricky and treacherous? I pay attention more, because I have to. Won't Mom be surprised when she comes home and finds me wandering around the neighborhood? I know she worries about how dependent I am, and how she won't be around to fend for me forever, so maybe she'll feel just a little less anxious now. Maybe she'll even join us on our walks.

Arthur—I called him Mr. Hemingway until it pissed him off—has been there for me. Every evening he clears away the dinner dishes, and we spend time on the sofa. He watches TV, I listen. He's hooked on a new show called *The X Files*. It sounds weird, and I don't get it.

Cuddling is about as close to intimacy as we'll probably get, and that's just fine with me. I hope it works for him. I guess we behave more like an old married couple than like newlyweds, you know, like when the first flames of passion have run their course, and you have to get down to the business of living together. It was something I wanted to ask Mom about when we were settled in. It seemed that my list of things to discuss with her grew longer every day. The change seemed a bit funny; it wasn't too long ago that her advice set my teeth on edge, now I needed it in more ways than I could count.

She had been away for four days—it seemed much longer—when Arthur and I came up with the same idea simultaneously. We were sitting at the kitchen table having coffee after dinner wondering about a Christmas present for her.

"A piano," he said.

"Yeah, I've been thinking the same thing. But I have no idea where to get one, or how to get it in the house."

"I know somebody," he said. "But a nice little baby grand will be costly. I don't have much put away."

"We can buy it with what Dad left for me. It will be the perfect present. She would never buy one for herself."

"Our first big decision together. This calls for a celebration," Arthur said. "Two cold ones coming up."

I went to bed that night happier than I'd been in a long time.

The new addition to our home arrived Friday

afternoon. My job, as I saw it, was to stay out of the way. There were two other male voices besides Arthur, ending up in a lot of huffing and puffing and a little swearing. Irene and I were waiting at the kitchen table. "Better clear out," she said. "The guys are coming."

We hid out in my bedroom. "Why did we have to leave?" I asked.

"Big guys like that, they'll drink beer and fart and laugh about it. You don't need to hear that stuff. I don't either."

But then, drinking beer and farting and laughing didn't sound too bad.

Eventually they got the new piano in and the old one out, and Arthur came to release us. "It's safe now. Come out and see what we've done."

"Gosh, it's beautiful," Irene said when we walked into the parlor. "It's a miracle that you got it inside."

I trailed my hand across the polished wood and walked around the piano. "It's huge. I thought you said a baby grand."

"That's what it is. No way we'd ever fit a grand piano in here. We'd have to take out a wall."

"Mom's gonna love it," I said.

"You bet. The guy comes by to tune it tomorrow. Then all we need is somebody to play it."

****

The one constant in this time of change was my stupid cough. The dry barking occurred so frequently that I paid it no mind at all. It was like the sound of traffic in the street, a bit annoying but of no consequence. What did get my attention was those times when my cough wound up and gave me a double dose. Those times were so fierce that I had to sit down until the storm had passed.

Once I had a particularly bad bout during one of my walks with Irene. With no place to sit except the sidewalk I clung to her while I raised a fearsome racket. The lady whose house we were in front of, and whose name I never knew, came out to see if she could help.

"Thank you, but I'll be fine in a minute." Fortunately, that proved to be the case, and we resumed our walk. But the experience must have been unsettling for Irene, and she was reluctant to usher me around the neighborhood again.

My coughing jags reminded me of how fragile my world was still. Surely it wouldn't have to get much worse before it required some intervention, and I was determined as ever I would never again darken the door of a hospital.

"Not even for a tune-up?" Arthur asked. "Just a few days?"

"No tune-ups, no time," I said. What did he think I was, a piano? Besides, when they got you in the hospital they could do whatever they wanted, and all the yelling and screaming in the world wouldn't change a thing.

Chapter 14

A few days before Christmas, Mom called from Washington, GA.

"What in the world are you doing there?" I asked.

"I wanted to see some of the old mansions that date back to the Civil War. They say that General Sherman spared the town because he had a girlfriend here. I have no idea whether that's true or not, but I thought I'd have a look, since he burned everything else."

"Are you visiting anybody?" She'd never shown interest in the Civil War before. Where had this come from?

"I tried to find one of Sam's cousins who's supposed to be here, but couldn't locate him. I've never met any of his family, so it would have been nice to know one of them at least."

My mother wandering around the countryside with no plans other than what caught her fancy that day? Hardly seemed like her, but then maybe she still had to work off a year's worth of stress and sorrow. If travel eased that pain, so much the better.

"I'll be home Friday afternoon, and we can start working on our Christmas dinner. I can't wait to see you."

It was a rather brief conversation, considering that we'd been in almost constant contact for the past year, and this was our first separation, even for a few days.

Maybe she was giving me room to make the big adjustment, and not asking a thousand questions about how I was doing was her way of saying she trusted me to make a go of it. I wish I felt as confident myself.

****

Irene fashioned a big red bow for the piano. This would be our big surprise for Mom. Sometimes loss of my vision was more hurtful than others, and this was one of those times. How I would love to see the look on Mom's face when she saw the piano. Yeah, I can compensate for blindness to some extent by listening harder, but I don't get the whole picture; I just know it. No question, seeing the piano would make her very happy, but somewhere in there she must have the nagging thought of what might have been. What if she'd gone to the Julliard? Could she, as some had predicted, have become a famous musician? Would the new piano seem like a consolation prize, a reminder of what she missed out on?

According to Arthur, life is full of such bittersweet events, and most of our happy moments come with strings. Pure, uncompromised joy is, as my new husband says, as rare as finding diamonds in your breakfast cereal. That said, you can focus either on the joyful part, or on the part you wish were different. It's a choice, isn't it? I'm not there yet. So much of my life seems to me more bitter than sweet, but I'm trying, trying very hard, for myself and everyone around me.

Mom arrived a little after one o'clock. Arthur went out to help with her bags, and I went out to greet her just to show her that I could. That got me a big hug, a tentative one. I know she was still afraid of hurting me, so I hugged her back even more forcefully. "You don't have to be so careful with me, Mom. I won't break."

"Wonderful," she said, "and you're up and about all by yourself."

"Usually I go with Irene, but I can do short trips myself."

"And you all managed without me?" she asked.

"Irene has been great," I said, "but nobody bakes an apple pie like yours."

We went in the side door so she wouldn't see the piano right away.

Then she did. "Oh, oh, oh." She sounded a little like Max when he's about to get a treat.

"It's so beautiful." Everybody got a hug. Max, too, I think.

"Merry Christmas," I said.

"The best ever," Mom said. "The very best."

I didn't remind her that she'd said the same thing before last Christmas, before the big burn, but I think she remembered.

She didn't even unpack before she attacked the kitchen. I think Irene tried to help out, but realized that this would be a solo performance. The kitchen was Mom's special domain, always had been, always would be. Eventually she'd expended whatever pent up energy she had, and we all settled in for a cup of coffee.

"Irene, will you be having Christmas dinner with your family?"

Irene didn't answer immediately. "No, it's just me now."

Mom didn't ask for specifics. She went straight for the remedy. "Then, you'll have to have Christmas dinner with us."

And so it went. After a brief flurry of shopping,

Mom did herself proud, a feast that left us all gasping for air. This time she gave me a soup spoon for my cranberry sauce, and that worked out much better. I'd hoped Irene would feel comfortable with us, eating with a new family, and she fit right in. She told funny stories, about how, on one of our walks I tripped over Max when he stopped to pee on a mailbox. "I thought he was trained not to do that," she'd said. I'd never thought about it before, but how could you berate a dog for taking a whizz?

Her life history, which we hadn't counted on, but got anyway, was a good look at growing up in Warrensburg as a black person. The big civil rights movement was long gone by then, but little things still hung around, like store managers watching her as if they expected her to swipe something.

"Sometimes I would make like I'd stuck some merchandise in my bra, but they never asked to check," she said. She topped her story off with a big Arthur laugh, the one that came from down deep, that take-it-or-leave-it laugh. When I heard that laugh, no matter who it came from, that person was okay by me. And Max usually agreed, which made it unanimous.

Afterward Mom let Irene help with the cleanup. Arthur, Max and I retreated to the sofa and did a fine job of being invisible. That is, until Mom asked him to take out the trash. Then our evening routine underwent a serious upgrade, a piano recital. Mom played nonstop for almost an hour. All classical works that I loved but could no more identify than I could fly around the block. Still, Arthur and I both agreed that the new piano was our best investment ever. Mom's skill turned the new instrument into a virtual orchestra.

"I'm rusty," she said at the end, and the elation in her voice came through loud and clear.

"If that's rusty, I can only imagine how good you sound when you're in top form," Arthur said.

"I'll get better," she said. And she did.

Later that night, when all was quiet, I lay in my bed thinking about food, yeah, that's right, food. No, I wasn't hungry, just considering food in, like, an existential way. Months back, food had been a major part in my plan for making an early exit; no food, especially no liquid, no Daisy. That was easy enough when all I had to contend with was hospital chow, mystery meat and rubber vegetables. Institutional food lacked one key ingredient; nobody cared. I know, they had hundreds to cook for besides me, but that little extra, knowing it was prepared by someone who'd put heart and soul into it, somebody like my mother, that was the trick.

Food prepared in Mom's kitchen was more than just sustenance, especially on the big family holidays, Thanksgiving and Christmas. Sharing food was like an affirmation, it was like edible love. Our little family had taken some big hits during the past year, and having some tangible reminder that we were still in the game made all the difference. Mom understood this far better than I did, but I was beginning to catch on. Right about now I could sure do with one of her sugar cookies.

We left off ringing in the New Year to folks who could stay awake until midnight. By ten o'clock we were all snoozing, except for Max who had to go out to pee. But we didn't call it a night before we took one last glance at 1994. The low points in the year past outnumbered the high spots, but those good times were the ones we clung to, and had to give voice to.

Unlike Thanksgiving, I was a full participant in this exchange. I probably spoke more than anyone else, because I had to catch up. I was thankful now for people, Mom, Arthur, Irene, and my friends. They had all become so precious to me. And something very special, I was so happy that I got to hear my mother play the piano again. Angels are supposed to play some pretty tunes, but no way could they outdo my mom, and I told her so.

She hugged me so hard I was afraid she would break bones, and this one did hurt just a bit, but so what? I'm a tough kid.

****

And what would 1995 bring us? Rotten weather for starters. The pavement was so slippery much of the time that walking outside was out of the question. Arthur had Rosita come back to help me along inside the house. She taught me how to navigate with a cane so that I didn't have to rely on Max or creep along the walls. I also have a clock with raised dials that I can read, along with a sound system in my room to break up the interminable silence.

Arthur came and went, as I expected him to do. He had other patients, of course. I only knew of myself, Linda and Annette, but there had to be many others, and I was not about to deny them the benefits of his care. I regarded him as a force of nature, something to be shared, like sunshine and rain, and I would make no attempt to contain or confine him.

The bright spot in an otherwise dreary new year came in the form of Linda's wedding announcement. They'd set the date for the third week of May. The invitation that came to the house included a handwritten note asking me to attend. I discussed it with my mother.

"It wouldn't work, Mom. I'd love to go, but I would be a distraction. It's her special day, and she shouldn't have to share it with a freak."

Mom took my hands, but didn't speak for a long time. I think she learned this trick from Arthur. "It's your decision, dear. Whatever you decide, I'll support you. No more second-guessing, not from me. And you don't have to decide right away. Perhaps you should give it some time."

Mothers are sneaky. They know when to take you head on, and they know when to circle around and get you from a different angle, but they always get you. And that's how she changed my mind; she let me do it all by myself. Maybe it would work out after all. So maybe, come that special week in May we would all pile into the Sugarbush wagon and take off for Richmond and Linda's wedding. I would wear a big scarf that covered my head and most of my face. Add on some dark glasses and nobody would know.

****

The new evening routine at our house seemed to suit everybody just fine, Mom at her piano, Arthur and I on the sofa, Max curled up at our feet. And, I must say, my husband's big arm wrapped around my shoulders felt pretty damned good.

Over time, as her musical reputation spread, Mom collected an audience. We had to rearrange the living room furniture to make way for extra chairs. The sofa went up against the far wall, and Arthur bought a nice set of folding wooden chairs, comfortable enough for an hour or so, but not so comfy as to make anyone want to linger too late through the evening.

Thursday night became official concert night. At first it was just Mrs. West and a couple of her friends, then those friends brought friends until we had a house full of music lovers. Irene still helped with the big cleaning extravaganza on Wednesday, so Mom could devote herself to baking. Good food and music, a great combination. But the baking was my favorite part. I could almost eat the aroma.

I got to meet and mingle with our guests, something I hadn't foreseen at all. After a while, I was just one of the folks, just Daisy. They didn't treat me special. I could almost hear Arthur laughing in the background saying, "I told you so."

So February and March could howl and dump on us, and I didn't care a bit. Arthur still insisted on two trips a week to the Rehab Center, just to get me out of the house.

"Are you getting lazy on me?" he asked after I'd punked out before we even got started.

"I just don't feel up to it today," I said. My exercise tolerance had been on the decline for a couple of weeks at least.

"You're coughing more."

"Maybe you're right, maybe I'm just getting lazy." I wish. I couldn't help but recognize in myself some of the same denial I'd used when Dad was dwindling in front of me.

When we got home I went straight to bed. Moving at all took such a lot of effort. But I didn't bounce back after resting; I didn't bounce back at all. Mom hovered, Arthur exhorted, and Max whined, but I just couldn't get it together. After the short trip from my bedroom to the kitchen I had to sit and rest.

April came in with a warm spell, and Arthur suggested that, instead of an indoor workout that we go for a walk. Working harder, that seemed to be his remedy for most ills, and it sounded like a great idea, except that I couldn't. By the time we'd walked from the house to the sidewalk my legs were turning to rubber. And then Mr. Cough kicked in, something I really didn't need. Back to bed for Daisy.

The cough didn't let up at night either, which meant that my poor mother was right back where she'd been when Dad was so sick, sitting at my bedside almost 'round the clock. Not so much trouble with pain now, but the cough made up the difference.

"At least let Dr. Beacham take a look. That's all I'm asking." Mom had that desperate tone in her voice, and I couldn't very well say no, even though the likelihood that our family doctor could help much seemed remote. We compromised by Mom persuading him to come for a home visit.

Dr. Beacham hadn't seen me since the big burn. There was the usual gasp, followed by "Oh, no." Nineteen years ago he had brought me into this world, and seeing me now I guess he wished he hadn't bothered.

He listened to my heart and lungs. "Guess I sound like Dad, huh?" I said.

"No, worse. Yours don't sound like lungs at all, more like plastic wrap being crumpled up. Your mom says you're coughing more."

"The pulmonary specialist at the hospital said I got a lot of internal burn damage in the fire, and there wasn't much he could do about it. He gave me a couple of inhalers, but they never did much good."

"I wish I had better news, but there's not much I can do either. It might be worth a trip back to Norfolk, let the pulmonary fellow have another look."

"No, he was pretty clear. It's bad and only going to get worse."

"I do want to draw a couple of blood samples. I'll have the results back by the end of the week."

Friday afternoon he was back. Mom hadn't called him, he just showed up. I could hear the two of them whispering outside my door. Mom made a gagging noise, so I assumed the news was bad, but I knew that already. She sat on the side of my bed, and Dr. Beacham pulled a chair alongside.

"Daisy, I'm afraid your blood work doesn't look good. Do you want me to tell you what I've found?"

"Of course." For sure, part of the discussion outside my door was whether or not to give me the bad news. The fact that I was being allowed to decide for myself was a big step forward for Mom. She had dug in her heels about Dad, no discussion about cancer, nothing about dying, just a big game of pretend right up to the end. That was wrong, and she knew better than to try it with me, not now.

"You are severely anemic, and your kidney function tests are, well, they're awful." Doc Beacham's voice was low, like he didn't want to say it any more than I wanted to hear it. "In fact, you are in renal failure. You can't go on like this, and the only thing medicine can offer is dialysis. I believe you had a short course while you were in the hospital but if we don't do something quick I'm afraid there's no hope."

I rolled over and faced the wall, my old posture,

where I shut the world out. Well, I'd finally gotten my wish, my kidneys were about to give up the ghost, and they would take me along with them. Be careful what you wish for. My life as a married woman was going to be damned brief.

The rotten thing was the timing. For the last couple of months life had become less onerous. A few times there, I actually enjoyed myself, going for walks with Max, working in the animal shelter, and, of course, best of all, being married to Arthur, as unusual as it was. Still, it was all about love, and that's pretty good stuff no matter what you look like.

It seemed like fate had lurked in the bushes, waiting for just the right moment to knock me on my ass.

"Daisy, we should talk about what you want to do," Mom said. "We need to let Dr. Beacham know so he can make arrangements."

"No arrangements to make, Mom. Thanks for coming out, Dr. Beacham."

"If you change your mind, let me know," he said.

So, the big fight that I expected never happened. I was surprised that Mom didn't make more of a fuss. I'm guessing that our experience with Dad when he was nearing death must have changed her way of thinking. This was a big deal, that she would honor my wishes without trying to change them, a big deal for both of us.

I never asked Dad about how it was, dying, I mean. We were too busy back then, pretending that he didn't have cancer and that he would live forever.

In a way renal failure, even though I had wished for it, now coming just two months before Linda's wedding, confirmed my feelings about the perverse nature of the universe, daring you to nurse even a slight ray of hope then smashing you when you do. On the other hand, who was I to decide when or where life's big events were written on the big cosmic calendar? The soldier statue in the town square, I'm sure he had other hopes and plans that day that didn't include getting killed in battle, but that's what he got.

Sometimes, like now, I think Arthur was right about choices, about how you can choose all you want to, but what happens still happens, and I'm okay with that. I might wish things were different, but I can accept what happens, even if it's not exactly what I had in mind.

"Arthur will be home soon. Do you want to tell him yourself, or shall we tell him together?"

"I'll tell him." *I'll tell him, but he already knows.* He'd have to be a fool not to know what's going on, and my husband is no fool. Even as we exchanged our wedding vows we both knew the final bell would ring, and probably sooner than later. I think maybe this is why Mom was in such a rush to get me married off, like, she knew time was short. So much to do, and so little time…ain't that always the way.

Arthur sat beside me on my bed, and afterward, when I'd said my piece, "I guessed as much," was all he said. He held me, and that meant more than words.

"We didn't have much time," I said.

"No, but what we had was special, and I'm grateful for it." Arthur's typical booming voice was reduced to a whisper. Having understood the situation ahead of time didn't make things any easier, for either of us.

"Don't let them take me back to the hospital," I said. "Please, I couldn't stand that." I feared that possibility more than dying. That terrible image of the time Dad was in the hospital, Linda and I had walked through the Intensive Care Unit, seen all the poor souls tethered to their respirators, inflate, deflate, inflate, deflate, it could go on forever. Compared to that, death would be a welcome event.

"I promise," he said. A little later he asked, "Why are you laughing?"

"I wasn't aware that I was. It just seems funny that I finally get my wish, but not when I wanted it. The Big Guy upstairs should check out whoever does his scheduling. He's months behind, at least."

"Maybe you weren't finished back then when you were determined to bail out. Maybe there was more for you to do," Arthur said.

"What's that supposed to mean?"

"Just think back on these past few months, all the amazing things you've done, things that you would have missed if you'd checked out earlier like you wanted."

He was right; I had to admit it. Some of the stuff I wouldn't have missed for anything. So, I withdraw my complaint, never mind.

The progression of renal failure was much more abrupt than I'd anticipated. It seemed that one day I was up and about, then in no time flat, I could barely get out of bed. My appetite dwindled to nothing. Not even one of Mom's cinnamon buns could tempt me.

By the end of the following week it was plain enough, I would never leave my bed again. Mom called Linda and Annette. The four of them gathered in my room. Arthur sat at the end of my bed, holding my feet. Max huddled next to me. The room was surprisingly quiet. Except for some audible sniffles, I would have thought perhaps my hearing was going, too. I didn't know how much longer I'd be able to talk, so I guessed I'd best say what I wanted to say while I still could.

I thanked Linda and Annette for being the best friends ever.

"Mom, you always worried that you hadn't taught me the things I'd need to know when I got married and started a family of my own, but you taught me something better. You taught me about love. I'll never be a Mom, myself, but what you've given me is the next best thing.

"And will you please take care of Max for me?"

"Of course, we'll take care of each other, Arthur, too."

It wasn't much, but my energy reserves were close to zero.

Arthur and I had already had our little private talk, so there was nothing else to say there. Mostly we'd just held each other. That said pretty much all there was to say. We'd had so little time together, but what we had was magical. I wanted more of it, but that wasn't in the cards. Was it enough for him? I can only pray that it was.

As for Dad, the next time we got together I could only hope that I looked better than I did now. Maybe I could have back that nice new hairdo that the ladies at the beauty parlor had fixed for me. After all, it was practically brand new. I only used it for a few hours.

"Tell Ralph goodbye for me," I said. Another good pal I didn't want to leave out.

"You can tell him yourself. He's been here in the hallway, waiting for you."

"I brought you a grape slurpee," he said. "But it's sort of melted."

God bless Ralph and whoever came up with the idea of grape slurpees.

I must have drifted away for a bit. Then I heard "I love you," coming from several voices, like a little chorus, some of them in the room, some from somewhere else. And a piano making some seriously beautiful music. No, that couldn't be. Mom was right beside me.

And the weirdest thing, my bedroom smelled different. At first, I didn't recognize it, then it came through loud and clear...Thanksgiving, my bedroom smelled like Thanksgiving, that wonderful aroma that floated out of Mom's kitchen. Was this Heaven? If it is, I'm surprised I made the cut. Like, St. Peter must have lowered the bar to squeeze me in.

So, Heaven, if that's where I'm headed, smells like Thanksgiving. This is so weird, no, this is perfect, just as it should be. Thanksgiving, yeah.

Max whimpered, and I drew him close to me. Dogs know when things are about to happen. "It's okay, boy." Please, God, let there be dogs in heaven.

I'm floating now, no pain, no cough. And there's a body in the bed...mine. It's where I used to live, in that pathetic burned out husk. But I don't hate it any more, because if everybody else can love it, maybe I can love it, too.

I see other people, no, honest to God, even without eyes, I see them, real shapes, real faces, people I recognize. They know me, I can tell. They hold out their arms to me. And somewhere in that gathering, although I don't see him yet, is my father.

Mom's mouth opens, her hands cover her face, a wailing noise. She starts to fall, but Arthur catches her, just like he caught me so many times. So, things must be over here. I'm still drifting, not going anywhere, because I'm already there. The circle of my life seems complete now, and, instead of moaning over things that I missed out on, I can see how lucky I've been to have the experiences I've had. Sounds weird, I know, from someone who spent the last year of her life looking like a potato chip, but that's the way it is. And I wouldn't trade it for anything, not now.

Max crawls up and licks my face, my old face, I have a new one now.

That's about it. The lights in my room are growing dim, but others are getting brighter. The other stuff I see, I'm not telling. You'll have to wait and see that for yourself, in your own time. And Mom was right, you can see eternity, even blind, you can see it. It's pretty neat, really. And most important of all, don't be afraid.

A word about the author...

Mike Owens is from a small North Carolina town, nearby Winston-Salem being the closest identifiable landmark. He claims to bleed Tar Heel Blue, having received both his undergraduate and medical degrees from the University of North Carolina. He topped off the educational effort with an MFA degree from Old Dominion University, Norfolk, Virginia.

During his years of medical practice he worked extensively with hospice programs, and his writing themes frequently involve the often-contentious interaction of medical science and medical ethics.

He lives in Norfolk, Virginia, with his wife, Marilyn, and the ghost of their dog, Molly.

http://www.mikeowens42.com

Thank you for purchasing
this publication of The Wild Rose Press, Inc.

If you enjoyed the story, we would appreciate your
letting others know by leaving a review.

For other wonderful stories,
please visit our on-line bookstore at
www.thewildrosepress.com.

For questions or more information
contact us at
info@thewildrosepress.com.

The Wild Rose Press, Inc.
www.thewildrosepress.com

Stay current with The Wild Rose Press, Inc.

Like us on Facebook

https://www.facebook.com/TheWildRosePress

And Follow us on Twitter
https://twitter.com/WildRosePress